A
Cantata
of Love

JACKI DELECKI

First Print Edition
ISBN: 978-09863264-9-3

Published by Doe Bay Publishing, Seattle, Washington.
Cover Design by The Killion Group, Inc.
Interior Formatting by Author E.M.S.

Published in the United States of America.

To my brother.

Thank you for being my biggest supporter and fan.
You are sorely missed.

ACKNOWLEDGMENTS

Thank you to my astonishing team of experts. I couldn't do it without them, and I wouldn't have half as much fun. Thank you to Karuna, my plot partner, Kim Cannon, my amazing editor. And great thanks to my friend, the talented musician and composer, Greg Bartholomew, who shared his expertise in developing the musical code. And to my support team who keep me writing. Maria Connor, and Jen Rice. And to my lovely family who never stop believing in me.

PROLOGUE

1803

In the seaside town of Berck, France

Gabrielle De Valmont brushed back Lord Kendal's blond curls and applied the wet cloth to his burning brow. His long, golden waves and eyelashes accentuated his fiery red cheekbones. In their days of hard travel from Paris, the earl's gunshot wound had festered into a nasty infection.

At this moment, he rested. For days, when the fever spiked, he thrashed about, calling out about sending a code book to a woman named Henrietta.

Desperate to soothe him, Gabrielle discovered that he would calm with the French songs of her childhood.

They couldn't hide much longer without being discovered by Napoleon's or Fouché's henchmen. When the earl's condition had worsened to the point where he could no longer travel, Gabrielle had brought them, under cover of darkness, to her former *mémé's* tiny village of Berck, south of Calais.

For eight long days and nights, she had cared for the feverish earl. Their presence in the tiny town couldn't be kept secret much longer. They must leave Berck, and France, soon. But how could they flee with the French soldiers on high alert, inspecting every boat crossing the English Channel?

Monsieur Denby, Lord Kendal's valet, had assured her that he had a plan to divert their attention.

Exhausted and despondent, she beseeched the Blessed Virgin for their safe escape and the earl's recovery.

She also prayed that the earl would forgive her and Mother Therese for their deception. She had to believe that Lord Kendal would never abandon her to her terrible fate.

CHAPTER ONE

Michael Harcourt, the Earl of Kendal, woke to a soft voice and the delectable smell of a woman. She smelled like wildflowers. And her voice was soothing and sweet. Last night must have been one hell of a night of dissipation since he remembered nothing. But he had dreamed of his French mother crooning to him.

What was wrong with him? He had been in bed with a French woman, and he'd thought of his mother. His head ached as if horses had trampled over him. He tried to remember her name— Yvette? Or was it Mimi? He cracked open one lid. Big blue eyes the color of cornflowers stared down at him, and a lush, pink lower lip pouted. How could he have forgotten this angel's name? Yvette. Definitely Yvette. "Yvette? Or maybe Mimi?"

He needed her again to refresh his memory. He raised his arms to pull her against him. He grabbed for her, but his arms felt weak. Thank God the rest of his body wasn't that tired. She yelped when he wrapped his arms around her and pulled her on top of him. "Yvette, darling. Don't fight me. I need you."

Yvette gasped and tightened against him. He rubbed himself against her slender body. Not his usual type, he noted. Clearly not an opera dancer by the slender frame. What had he drunk last night that he couldn't remember this delectable handful?

"Let go of me," she hissed.

He whispered against her soft, tender neck, kissing her ear. "Were you this feisty last night?"

"Let me go, you brute." She shouted in his ear, causing his

head to feel as if it were cracking wide open. She jumped back, tripping on the bedclothes and knocking the water canister from the side table. The loud crash reverberated in his head.

Women didn't fight him. He was a generous lover. Was he overlooking something from last night?

Michael looked at the disheveled, bewitching woman glaring at him. Hair the color of honey sparkled in the morning sunlight, but her bright eyes were now dark and stormy.

Damn, damn. She looked far too innocent and way too marriageable. What had he gotten himself into?

He rearranged the bedding to hide the obvious, then lifted himself to the head of the bed.

The mademoiselle didn't look so much offended as just plain pissing mad. Her eyes had narrowed, and she glowered at him—the look of a woman who might impale him with the fireplace poker. He had gotten into a lot of scrapes, but this wasn't how he imagined finding a wife.

The door to his bedroom swung open, knocking against the wall. The pain behind his eyes pounding like a son of a…

Denby, his valet, stormed into the room, swearing under his breath. "What the hell? Are you alright, Mademoiselle Gabrielle?"

She gestured with her hands and spoke in rapid French to Denby. Had she just called him, the Earl of Kendal, a "stupid horse's ass"?

Denby took the irate woman's arm. "I'll clean up the mess. Now that he's awake, you should prepare yourself to leave. We've a long journey ahead of us."

With no word of farewell, the Mademoiselle Gabrielle huffed and left the room.

Denby chuckled. "Barely awake and already causing problems." He bent to pick up the water container. "It is good to see you back, my lord. You scared the hell out of me. If it weren't for Mademoiselle Gabby's nursing, I'm not sure…"

"I've been sick?" He did feel a bit weak after his tussle with the delectable young woman.

"You developed a fever right after we escaped from Paris."

The memory of fleeing Paris and Fouché's men brought him totally awake. "My last memory is leaving Paris dressed as a nun."

Denby handed him a glass that had survived the mademoiselle's spirited response. "You developed a fever from your gunshot wound, and we had to hide out here. This is where Mademoiselle Gabby's nanny is from and the people helped us."

Gabby. He didn't have any recollection of Gabby when they left Paris. "How long have I been out? And who is Gabby?"

"I'm glad you're ready to travel. I've got a bad feeling if we don't get out of here soon, all of Fouché's and Napoleon's men are going to descend."

He only remembered Denby, and the boy, Pierre, fleeing for their lives dressed as nuns. He had stolen the code book from Le Chiffre, and everyone in Paris seemed to be after him. He wondered if Henrietta had received the book.

"Any news from England? Do we know if Henrietta received the package?"

"I haven't been able to make any contact. We've been in hiding. I've arranged for a boat from Calais. They've been waiting for a signal that you're able to travel. We go tonight with the tide. I want to get us out of France. I can't breathe here."

"Did you shake the villain who was posted at my house in Paris too?"

"Yes, but we can't stay here any longer. I'll change the bandages and get you some breakfast. You'll rest up before we make the trip. We have to go by horseback, and I hope it won't open your wound."

He suddenly was assailed with the ignominy of the location of his wound. He had been shot in the arse by an unknown assailant while fleeing after he had stolen the code book. The code book, literally, was a pain in his arse.

He sure hoped to hell it gave England a tactical advantage against the power-hungry Napoleon.

CHAPTER TWO

Gabrielle couldn't catch her breath. Her lungs had stopped momentarily. The insufferable ass had thought she was "Yvette" or maybe "Mimi." What a giant oafish pig's tail. After all she had done for the infuriating man, fighting to bring down his fever, singing to him in French, forcing fluids and willow bark down his throat—and that's how she had been repaid? He had the audacity to grab Mademoiselle Gabrielle, daughter of the Marquis De Valmont as if she were a common tavern wench

Denby, who had assisted her throughout this arduous journey, entered the small dining area. "Mademoiselle Gabrielle, I'm sorry for Lord Kendal's behavior. I'm sure he'll apologize once he can appreciate all you've done for him. He's confused and disoriented."

Gabby snorted. She refrained from replying that for an ill man, he'd felt pretty healthy when he rubbed against her. If her brother ever learned about Lord Kendal's outrageous behavior, he'd kill the English earl. Her brother was a hothead and took exception to any insult to her honor.

"Please, I know you've been spared exposure to men's baser ways, but Lord Kendal, if he were himself, would never offend you."

Gabby raised her eyebrows. "I have a feeling Lord Kendal causes trouble wherever he goes."

A grin spread across Denby's coarse features.

"Although my brother's had me hidden in a convent for the last years, I am not as innocent as you believe," she said, jutting her chin proudly. "Before Napoleon's interest in me, I enjoyed all the pleasures of Paris life."

"And I hope you'll be able to enjoy good society again in London. You need to rest. I'll take care of his lordship. You'll see that Lord Kendal will treat you with all the respect and decorum you deserve. He does know how to behave like the gentleman that he is."

Gabby didn't try to hide her skepticism. Hopefully it would not be long before she was reunited with her brother and free of Lord Kendal. The tiniest twinge of regret tweaked her heart, but she ignored it. She would never admit to missing the way his dimples crinkled or the way his green eyes playfully schemed, or the pleasurable sensation of his hard body pressed against her. *Never.*

CHAPTER THREE

Safely back in England and now facing a long carriage ride from Dover to London, Michael bit down on his lip, squeezed his hands into fists, and crossed and uncrossed his legs, trying to hide from Mademoiselle Gabby the agonizing ache in his arse. No small feat since they sat face-to-face and his tender arse took the impact from every bump.

After his boorish behavior, Gabby offered none of her tender, solicitous care. He gazed at her lush, pink lips, recalling her sweet, lilting voice and the French songs she had sung. He gazed down at her tiny hands, now gloved, recalling how she had soothed and comforted him during the burning fever. He had overheard her tell Denby that any man who behaved like he had was well enough to take care of himself.

"May I say again, mademoiselle, how truly sorry I am for my shocking behavior. We still have a long journey. Could you please try to find warmth in your heart to forgive me?" He flashed his full-dimple smile, which his sister, Henrietta, had declared capable of charming any woman over the age of twelve. Obviously not the French Gabby. "In my invalid state I was confused and mistook you for someone else."

Gabby stared out the window, behaving as if she hadn't heard him. He was usually quite adept with women, but for some reason he couldn't make this right.

Gabby never took her gaze away from the window. "You thought I was Yvette or possibly Mimi. You couldn't remember."

Michael felt the tops of his ears burning. The chit, for someone he had believed to be a child, sure had a woman's way of making him suffer.

"With your permission, shall we change the subject?" Michael asked.

"Of course." She turned back to look at him.

"When did you and Mother Therese plan to inform me that I was not bringing a child out of France, but a young woman? I didn't think nuns could be devious."

"Mother Therese is not devious."

Oh, he liked the way her pert breasts puffed up in indignation. "And I thought the nuns had no sense of humor. The joke is on me."

"Joke on you? Never. Mother Therese wasn't playing any jokes. She didn't laugh when you fell on your backside and spilled brandy in your shoes. She was desperate to ensure my escape from the long reach of Napoleon. She was more concerned that you might not be the man for job."

He wanted to defend himself, but he didn't deserve the credit. She had been the one to rescue him from the deadly infection. "I'm most grateful for your care and hope I can repay you when we're in London."

She shook her head, causing one errant curl to fall across her puckered forehead. "It is of no consequence. In England, I'll be living with my brother, and he will take care of me."

"Tell me why Napoleon is after you. I can't believe the First Consul has time for chasing down young women."

"Oh, you're mistaken, monsieur. Napoleon always needs to replenish his coffers and fortify his position of power. My father was a marquis before…the Terror." Her voice quivered.

No wonder Mother Therese was protective of Gabby. She was an orphan.

He reached across the carriage and took her small hands between his own. "I'm very sorry. Both your parents?" He wouldn't make her recount the horrific circumstances of their death.

Her body shuddered and she nodded her head, obviously fighting to bring herself under control. He squeezed her hands. He missed his own parents very much, but they hadn't been murdered by an out-of-control, angry mob.

"All I have left is my brother. He has protected me and will now keep me out of the clutches of Napoleon."

This young woman wasn't much older than the English debutantes whose biggest concerns were their coiffures, gowns, and gossip. But, unlike the flighty debutantes, Mademoiselle Gabby had survived her parents' deaths, the Reign of Terror, and now Napoleon. She bore her suffering with an understated grace he would have expected of a much older woman.

"What plans does Napoleon have for you?" he asked.

Color rushed into her perfect porcelain skin. "He plans to wed me to his younger brother, Jerome."

"Of all the damn, bloody…" The idea of this young, gentle woman who had tended to his care forced into marriage outraged him.

Gabby' eyes widened in surprise by his use of blasphemy.

"Excuse my choice of language."

Michael couldn't understand his extreme reaction since arranged marriages for advantage were the norm in their aristocratic world. Marriages were contracts between dynasties. His parents had been an exception. They had married for love, and their example influenced his own beliefs. He'd never force his sister to wed for economic reasons. His estate was more than adequate without forcing Henrietta into a loveless marriage, but he knew this was not so for others.

"He'd like to fuse my family bloodlines, and my wealth, with his family."

"How far-reaching and far-sighted of Napoleon. And what is his brother like?"

"Jerome is immature, three years younger than I." Her perky chest puffed up again in the most distracting way. "Still a boy. Not even a man."

"And what do you know of men, living in a convent?"

Michael teased, glad for her willingness to speak with him.

"I spent time in Paris, before my brother became aware of Napoleon's interest in me. It was only when my brother heard the rumors that he hid me in a convent. Lucien then escaped to England and had planned to return to rescue me. His letters had stopped by the time Monsieur Denby stumbled into Notre Dame. Mother Therese believed it was a miracle to discover Monsieur Denby, and that we must seize the blessed opportunity to make my escape out of France."

"But why wouldn't Mother Therese explain the situation to me? Why disguise you as a boy?"

"She planned for me to remain a boy to throw the men off the scent until I was safely in the care of my brother. And she said the English have rules about women travelling with men, and if the truth came out I might be forced to marry you to protect my good name. But when you fell ill, I had to reveal myself to my *mémé's* family to ensure your care."

"Yes, and I am very grateful for their willingness to assist me. But your brother may not like the idea that we have travelled together unchaperoned. It is not done in England."

She pushed a curl away from her face. "My brother will not worry about such trivial matters, recognizing the danger we have faced. I think the English are very uptight about 'proper' behavior. And I can't imagine why anyone would think marrying you would salvage my good name. You being a..."

"My being a what?" He didn't like how the conversation had swerved back to the uncomfortable topic. Blast it. He had been delirious with a fever when he groped her.

Gabby raised perfectly arched brows that framed her large eyes, more aquamarine today in the bright sunlight.

"The English aren't uptight," he said stiffly. "There are standards of behavior to protect young woman against the advances of spurious fellows."

"Like being accosted and mistaken for 'Yvette' or 'Mimi'?" Gabby's eyes sparkled, and she compressed her lips together, trying not to laugh.

"Now, Gabby—I mean, Mademoiselle Gabby—I was delirious. I've tried to apologize." And how did he start calling her Gabby?

"Oh, I understand. But, I think it's best if we don't share your mistake with my brother. French men are quite possessive of their sisters, and my brother is more protective than most since he has had responsibility for me since our parents' deaths."

Michael's stomach started to roll, and it wasn't because of the bumpy road. He might have to marry this young woman. If anyone had manhandled Henrietta like he had done to Gabby, he'd demand amends. But he would never make Henrietta marry the man.

"I'm prepared to do whatever is necessary to appease your brother. I meant you no dishonor, and I understand he might demand that we wed. Marriage to you would be an honor." He watched Gabby, trying to gauge her reaction.

"My lord, I do believe your color has gone pale. Rest easy. I've no desire to force you into a marriage that neither of us desires. Why would I escape one man's clutches to be thrown to another misalliance?"

He shifted his weight on the seat, trying to find a comfortable position. "I hope that you can appreciate the difference between a marriage to me and Napoleon's brother."

Her eyes narrowed and her plucky chin thrust forward. "Both would mean I had no choice, and then my escape would be worth nothing. To be forced to marry another…" She didn't finish the sentence, but whatever she'd intended to say wasn't complimentary.

Gabby shook her head again. He had the strongest desire to release the pale ringlets that were twisted into a knot on the crown of her head.

"Rest assured, I will not tell my brother about your conduct, since my brother is a hothead and an amazing duelist. You wouldn't survive."

Michael sighed a breath of relief. Not that he would shirk his responsibility. "I'm a fair shot myself. But I would not add to your worries and stress."

Gabby leaned back against the carriage seat. "Thank you, my lord." Her dainty hands were clasped tightly in her lap.

"I'm very glad that you will be reunited with your brother. Do you have his location in London?"

"No, but he is now the Marquis De Valmont. I'm sure it will be simple to locate him."

Michael winced and was ready to swear when the carriage wheel hit the latest rut.

Gabby pursed her lips and asked quietly, "The journey is still difficult for you?"

"A bit uncomfortable, but nothing I can't tolerate. But as you know, this injury is in a most inconvenient location."

And the chit giggled, just as she had done when he had fallen from the settee in Paris. Her lilting laugh did something to his insides. She was a delightful surprise of innocent sensuality and gentle compassion. How had he missed that she was a woman, an enchanting woman with enchanting curves? Had she worn some sort of bandage to hide her rounded, sweet breasts?

Her eyes narrowed, causing a pucker to form between her arched brows. Had he given away his lustful imaginings?

He cleared his throat. "Back to your arrival in London. It can never be known to anyone that we travelled without a maid. Once we get to a big enough town, I will hire one."

"The English are so bourgeois."

"Remember that if it were found out, your brother might be forced to fight me in a duel or force you to marry me."

Gabby turned her face and looked out the window. "How long before we get to the next town?"

CHAPTER FOUR

Gabby rested her head against the carriage window, trying to find a comfortable position for the long journey.

Lord Kendal had slept most of the trip. He was still weak and in pain, but healing from the infection. The young maid they had hired from the last inn also slept. Gabby had time to closely inspect Lord Kendal's face—his blond hair the color of winter wheat, his dimples present even while his face was in repose. His round cheeks and dimples gave him a boyish, mischievous look. When awake, his bright-green eyes gleamed with amusement, as if he were privy to a secret joke.

He was unlike any man of her acquaintance in France. French men postured and made their importance known. The earl seemed not to have need to put on an airs of acquired insouciance or ennui.

The earl stirred briefly when they struck a large hole in the road. A flaxen curl hung over one eye which he'd carelessly brush away when he regaled her with stories of his childhood. Lord Kendal was a careless man who could easily trample over a woman's heart. Not hers. She was French and fully immune to silly, quirky smiles and dramatic bursts of hilarity.

He opened his eyes; Gabby immediately dropped hers. She didn't want to be caught staring at the attractive man she had soothed with French lullabies just days before, and spinning a silly girl's romantic stories of love and devotion.

"Are we close?" He stretched his arms over his head, pulling the fabric across his broad shoulders.

She shrugged. "Since I've never visited London, I do not know."

"It feels so long since I left. I've missed home." Then, catching himself like a guilty child caught in an act of mischief, he gave her a rueful smile. "I'm sorry, that was thoughtless of me."

She clenched her interlocked fingers together. "I understand." She understood that she'd never be able to return home. The estate had been destroyed, their belongings taken. If not for Lucien, she might be a pauper with no prospects.

Lord Kendal reached across and took her hand. "My sister, Henrietta, is going to love you. And until we can contact your brother, you'll stay with us."

"You often called your sister's name when you were delirious with the fever."

His hand tightened around her fingers. "Did I say anything else?"

She was surprised he didn't ask her about the code book. He never spoke about why he'd been fleeing Fouché or how he'd been wounded. Living in revolutionary France these past years, she had learned not to ask questions when the answers could come back to harm you.

She stared into his shining eyes. His cherubic face, filled with youthful openness, was not one of a deceptive agent on a secret mission.

"You called me your ma'am," she teased.

"I thought you were my mother when you sang the French lullabies. She had a wonderful voice, but nothing in comparison to your sweet soprano."

"I didn't know your mother was French."

"My father would say he fell under her Gallic charm and never recovered. Theirs was a love match—unheard of. And my grandfather, the earl, was not pleased."

"How wonderful to be able to marry for love."

"You don't think your brother will allow you to marry whomever you want?"

She didn't' know. The Terror had changed her brother. The violence had changed all of France. The idea of marrying for love and a future wasn't anything she had given herself time to ponder. She had spent her time surviving and waiting to escape France. But she wouldn't feel safe until she was with her brother.

"I don't know. Not anything I need to think about now." She nodded her head toward the maid who snored loudly, her head against the side of the carriage. "Tell me more about your French mother."

Apparently displeased by her diversion away from the topic of marriage, Lord Kendal's dimples disappeared with his glaring frown. "My mother made everyone laugh. My father would always say that I was too much like my mother when I played tricks, but I knew it was an admirable trait to be like my mother. What was your mother like?" he asked.

"My mother was married very young to my father, the marquis. He wasn't a very affectionate or approachable man, and I've always wondered what my mother's life was like. I always believed Lucien and I brought joy to her loveless marriage. She protected Lucien and me from the misery of her marriage. We never were exposed to my father's temper."

Lord Kendal's bright eyes faded as he searched her face. She didn't want his pity, but she wanted him to understand that she wasn't naïve after witnessing her mother's suffering. She knew what her life would be if she were forced to marry Jerome Bonaparte.

"Do you have any other family?"

"Yes, I have a younger brother, Edward, who is a cricket fiend. Do you play?"

"Cricket?" She couldn't imagine a French woman playing cricket. "No, only piano."

"He'll be very disappointed. And he won't be impressed by your skills as a pianist. Why do I have a feeling you're very accomplished?"

She shrugged her shoulders. How to explain that music kept

her sane during the long, lonely years? "Music helped me during the dark times in my country. Do you play?"

"I play a little, but my interest has always been more on the mathematical side of music."

"Mathematical?" Gabby's voice edged close to shrill.

"I didn't mean to offend your artist's soul. But you must understand, I'm a linguist. I study patterns." He leaned across the aisle, his lips curving upward into a knowing smirk. "But I always appreciate passion."

Gabby didn't return his grin. "How old is your brother?"

He sat back against the squabs. "He's eleven." She heard the rueful amusement in his voice. "Then there's my Uncle Charles. He is a bit unusual." He paused, as if calculating how much to divulge. "He is a brilliant scholar, quotes ancient Greek, but doesn't remember what day it is."

"And he also lives with you?"

"Yes, he never married. We're a jolly household. You'll find it's a perfect refuge to recover from our long journey."

Gabby leaned back against the seat and closed her eyes. She tried to imagine a jolly household—what a foreign concept. After the Revolution, the idea of happiness was fleeting. She'd like to make her household with her brother jolly, as her mother would've wished.

Lord Kendal sat up and peeked out the window once again. "We are getting close. It will be great to be home and eat Mrs. Brompton's biscuits."

He crossed his arms over his chest. His rascally grin softened the lines of fatigue framing his eyes.

He was a most remarkable man. He seemed to enjoy every moment of life—something she had lost.

They arrived at a classic symmetrical house with massive white columns flanking the entry. The sun shone on the house, dappling the red brick and the long windows. Lord Kendal's face was also illuminated, beaming with simple pleasure. And Gabby couldn't help smiling back, despite her fluttering nervousness.

By the way he easily jumped out of the carriage, Lord Kendal certainly didn't look like a man who had been hovering at death's door. She took satisfaction that he was better and that she had helped him. There was now no debt between them.

He linked his fingers with hers in his excitement. His gesture was surprising and his warmth reassuring as she prepared to face the English strangers.

The door opened before they reached the top step. A youthful, muscular butler smiled. "Welcome home, my lord."

Lord Kendal stopped suddenly. "Who in blazes are you? Where's Brompton? And how do you know to welcome me home?"

"Sir, Brompton now resides at Rathbourne House. The likeness between you and Master Edward is remarkable."

Lord Kendal pulled Gabby along and rushed into the house. "Hen, I'm home."

His voice echoed in the large marble foyer with high ceilings. "Hen, I'm home."

"Sir, Lady Rathbourne doesn't reside at Kendal house." The butler spoke hesitantly.

Lord Kendal dropped Gabby's hand to open the door of the first room off the entryway. "I don't even know a Lady Rathbourne so why would I care where she resides. Hen?"

"My deepest apologies, sir. I thought you were aware of your sister's marriage. Your sister is now Lady Rathbourne."

Lord Kendal jerked around. "My sister is married? When? And why wasn't I informed?"

The butler appeared flummoxed by the question. "Sir, I—"

Lord Kendal ran his hand through his thick locks. "Did you say Rathbourne? My sister married Lord Cordelier Rathbourne?"

"Yes, my lord."

"How can that be? I haven't been gone long enough."

The butler stood frozen. "Yes, my lord."

Gabby interrupted. "I assume you are the new butler?"

"Yes, my lady. I was an under-butler for Lord Rathbourne until Lady Rathbourne moved her household. Brompton chose me as your butler, sir. He felt I would be appropriate for a single man's residence."

"Her household? I don't understand. It's my household. And what of my uncle? He needs the Bromptons. And I need the Bromptons."

The servant grew more uncomfortable imparting information about Lord Kendal's family. "Your uncle and Master Edward now reside at Rathbourne House, as do the Bromptons."

Lord Kendal's hurt was etched on his guileless face. The poor man was in shock.

Gabby understood his pain and disappointment. She knew what it was like to have your safe world disappear in a moment without warning.

The discomfort on the young servant's face was almost as painful as that reflected in Lord Kendal's aggrieved expression.

"What is your name?" Gabby asked.

"Averill, my lady."

"Averill, Lord Kendal and I need luncheon, and Lord Kendal is in need of a strong libation. Can you lead us to the drawing room?"

She took Lord Kendal's arm and led him down the hall.

Averill walked ahead to show her the way. He opened the door. "Sir, which room would you like my lady to occupy?"

"What?"

"Sir, which room for my lady?"

Gabby felt Lord Kendal's arm tighten. "You cannot stay here in the residence of a single man. It isn't done. I must take you right now to my sister."

Gabby stopped in the middle of the hallway. "I refuse to get into that carriage until I've had sustenance and time to refresh myself. You'll have to hold on to your principles a little longer."

CHAPTER FIVE

The long hours on the bumpy roads had done nothing to improve the pain in his arse or his disposition. Michael shifted his position on the carriage seat on their ride to Rathbourne House. How could Hen marry during his brief months away? He felt lost that his sister had married someone he knew only as the Head of Intelligence.

He and Hen shared more than the bond of brother and sister. They both were linguists who had evolved by wartime needs into code breakers. They had developed an unusually close relationship by working together deciphering codes. He had great respect for his sister, watching her expand and grow confident in her abilities.

When they finally arrived at Rathbourne House, Michael rose to assist Gabby out of the carriage.

The young country woman he had hired to be Gabby's maid stood behind them with her mouth gaping at the size and grandeur of the towering, turreted Jacobean grey mansion.

Gabby squeezed his arm while they climbed the steps. "Remember, you must wait and talk to your sister before you say or do anything against your new brother-in-law. He is now part of the family, and you wouldn't want your sister to be torn between her love for you and her new husband."

Gentle Gabby was a bossy little package. A lot like Hen, she was soothing his hurt feelings, trying to get him to behave in a gentlemanly manner. She'd be outraged to know he was enjoying her next to him, her soft curves pressed against him.

"You really need to wait until you talk to your sister."

Michael quickened his pace up the last few steps. "But why would Hen marry in haste? He must have taken undue advantage. I may have to challenge him to a duel to defend our family honor." Nothing else made sense of whatever had prompted Hen to marry in such a rush. The old geezer must have seduced or compromised Henrietta.

Exasperated, Gabby pulled on his arm, stopping him from knocking on the door. "Tell me how killing your brother-in-law would help your sister?"

"To relieve her of a man..." He stopped, thinking better of what he might say to this innocent. Men with no morals could seduce a young woman and force her into marriage. It made no sense that sensible Henrietta would fall for such a ruse. "Rathbourne must have been in need of Henrietta's money. It is the only reasonable explanation."

Gabby shook her head, her delightful curls restrained under her bonnet, bouncing with the rapid movement while she said something under her breath in French.

They both startled when the door opened, revealing Brompton. "Master Michael, home at last! Lady Henrietta will be relieved, as will Master Edward, Uncle Charles, and my wife. They have all been worried about you."

Deep happiness swept through Michael with the family retainer's handshake. "Brompton, you're a sight for sore eyes. I'm pleased to see you in good health. And how is Mrs. Brompton?"

"My wife is as nimble and interfering as ever." Brompton spoke in a loud voice, enabling Bromie, moving briskly down the hallway, to hear his teasing comment.

The sight of the cheerful woman, in her familiar brown dress, her hair severely pulled back at her neck, who had acted as a mother to all of the Harcourts was a reassuring note in the disconcerting homecoming.

"Master Michael?" Bromie's voice was incredulous and welcoming.

All was going to be right.

"My boy, how wonderful it is to see you." The stout woman swept him into her arms, not standing on formality like her husband. She smelled of cinnamon and lemon and everything constant from his childhood.

Bromie released him and nodded at Gabby.

"Bromie and Brompton, this is Mademoiselle Gabrielle De Valmont, who will be staying with my sister until she can move to her brother's home."

Brompton bowed his head. "My lady, welcome to Rathbourne House."

Bromie raised her eyebrows at Michael before she smiled at Gabby. "Welcome, mademoiselle. I'd better rouse Lady Henrietta from her nap. She'll be upset that she wasn't here to greet you."

"Hen is sleeping in the middle of the day?"

Bromie patted him on the cheek, her calloused hand rough against his skin. "Your sister is right as rain. You'll see soon enough. But you look like you've lost weight. You've missed Cook's good old English cooking?"

Michael squeezed Bromie's hand. "I have missed everyone and everything."

Bromie grabbed at her heart. "Lady Hen is going to be pleased to see you, and Edward is going to be over the top by your arrival. I've got to tell Cook to get started on your homecoming dinner. This is a very special day."

"I will announce your arrival to Lord Rathbourne, Master Michael," Brompton said. "Mademoiselle, may I show you to the drawing room where you can wait to meet Lady Henrietta?"

"Dang it, Brompton. I don't want to be treated as a guest. Where are Uncle Charles and Edward?"

"Uncle Charles is also napping. And Edward is with his tutor."

Michael tried to hide his disappointment. He'd expected more of a ruckus when he got home.

Gabby took his arm and then gave him an encouraging nod.

Her gentle touch of support, when she was in an unfamiliar home in an unfamiliar country with no anticipation of seeing family, chastened him. He looked down into her smiling face. "I'll join you in the drawing room once I've seen my brother-in-law. Henrietta is going to love meeting you. And after you've rested tonight, I'll take you tomorrow to your brother."

"It will be good not to travel any further today." Gabby sighed.

"Right this way, mademoiselle." Brompton gestured toward the grandiose spiral stairs.

Gabby, her posture erect, ascended the stairs, showing no hint of the grueling journey. She had the same plucky attitude as Henrietta.

He never imagined his homecoming like this—disorienting and anticlimactic. He waited in the foyer, a stranger in a strange house.

After a few minutes, Brompton came down the stairs.

"Right this way, Master Michael." Brompton shook his balding head, and his punctilious voice filled with emotion. "I'm sorry to miss Lady Hen's face when she sees you."

Michael increased his stride, refusing to walk behind the old retainer, who was more family than servant.

"How long has Hen been married?"

"Two months."

"But I've only been gone four months. Why couldn't she wait until I got home? And why would she marry an old geezer?"

Brompton gave a most quizzical look before he opened the door and ushered Michael into a room adorned with masculine decor. "I'm sorry for the interruption, but Lord Kendal has just arrived."

Lord Rathbourne, seated behind a massive, mahogany desk, rose. "Your sister will be so relieved."

Another man, a blond gentleman, with his back toward the door whipped around to look at Michael.

His brother-in-law wasn't at all what Michael had expected.

He was a large, muscular fellow with an arrogant, patrician face—a fit man in his prime, not old.

Michael muttered under his breath. "Not an old geezer at all."

The other gentleman chuckled. "Well, I should say not, since Cord and I are of the same age."

Hell, had he said that aloud? "I was expecting a much older, I mean…" He should just shut his mouth. "More mature, like Sir Ramsey."

The blond gentleman looked familiar. His sandy hair hung over one eye, and his cravat was a bit mussed, like he had been tugging on it. Like a man who was more comfortable in a tavern brawl than a drawing room. The gentleman bowed his head slightly toward Michael. "Ashworth, at your service."

Michael nodded to Ashworth. He and his chums at Oxford held Ashworth and his friends in awe for being top of the treetop rakes. Now all the pieces clicked together. His brother-in-law hadn't acquired his title until his brother died. Known as "Beaumont," he had an unsavory reputation. Although Michael couldn't recall the details, Rathbourne was not deemed as good society. Then Beaumont had disappeared into France.

Bloody anger rushed through Michael's body, readying him for battle. He was going to massacre the bastard and move Henrietta back to Kendal House.

Rathbourne inspected Michael's face. Michael hoped that Rathbourne was savvy enough to realize the danger he was in. "If you'll excuse us, Ash. I'd like a few words with my brother-in-law before Henrietta gets up from her nap." The words were spoken quietly but held a challenge.

"Why is Hen napping?" Michael demanded.

Ashworth shared a conspiratorial raised eyebrow with Rathbourne before exiting the room. He closed the door quietly behind him.

Rathbourne walked toward the side table and poured himself a brandy. Michael watched his broad shoulders tighten beneath his black coat. He kept his back to Michael. "Brandy?"

"I want to know what you've done to my sister. She would

never marry without consulting me. I've been racking my brain to try to remember what I've heard about you besides your promotion to director. Your dissipated reputation as Beaumont precedes you. My sister would never marry a man like you."

Michael couldn't contain his outrage. His sister was smart and sensible and would never act rashly. How had everything spun out of control while he was in France? Nothing was right. And despite Gabby's warning flashing through his heated brain, he wanted to skewer someone.

Rathbourne swiftly turned, his dark eyes narrowed into slits, his glass held tightly in his hand. "You have the nerve to take me to task. Do you know what your little escapade in France did to your sister? If I hadn't promised Henrietta, I'd thrash you."

Michael stepped closer, clenching his fists hard. Now this felt better. He'd like to work out his agitation in the usual gentleman's method by pounding this pompous ass into the ground. "You are welcome to try. Hen never needs to find out."

The other man's eyebrows slashed together, a tick evident in his clenched jaw. Rathbourne wasn't as controlled as he pretended, which gave Michael great satisfaction. He might be recovering from his injury, but he was still capable of delivering some damaging blows.

Both men stared at each other, the hostile tension mounting.

The ticking of the clock was the only sound in the room until the shattering thunder of the door banging open.

"Michael! Thank God. You're home." Henrietta, her eyes tearing, rushed to him. She flung herself into his arms and squeezed him tightly.

He lifted his sister and spun her around.

She giggled like a young girl.

"Put her down," Rathbourne demanded in an imperious tone.

Ignoring Rathbourne, Michael spun her around again as he had done when they were children.

Rathbourne stepped closer. "Put her down before you make her sick."

Henrietta laughed again. "I feel fine."

Michael placed her feet back on the ground and took a step back to scrutinize her more closely. "You do look a bit pale. Why were you napping?"

Hen smiled shyly, her green eyes, identical to his own, sparkling. "I'm not ill. Where have you been? Why didn't you come straight home?"

"After I was shot, I developed a fever and went into a coma."

Her hands fluttered at her chest, and she stepped backward as if she might fall.

"You insufferable ass." Rathbourne's face contorted in anger. He pulled Hen next to him. "Why would you shock your sister that way?"

"My sister doesn't shock easily. Tell him, Hen."

Hen patted her husband's chest. "Cord thinks I'm some sort of fragile flower."

Michael snorted.

Hen did a small curtsy. "Thank you. It is so good to have you home. Isn't it, Cord?"

Rathbourne's tense face relaxed when he looked down at Hen. "Of course. Now you don't have to spend any more time worrying about him. I'll take care of him."

Michael bristled at Rathbourne's challenging tone. "Why did you marry hastily?"

Hen stepped away from her husband and linked arms with Michael. "I know it comes as a big shock. Let's go to the drawing room before Uncle Charles and Edward join us. I'll explain everything."

Rathbourne's jaw twitched again, and by the way his eyes constricted, he was anticipating retribution. Michael smiled faintly at his brother-in-law's annoyance.

"Yes, I want to hear why you married without my knowledge or permission."

"You must be joking." Rathbourne disengaged Hen's arm and placed it on top of his.

Michael planted his feet apart and drew his shoulders back, tight, to confront Rathbourne. "I am responsible for my sister's safety and future. It was my prerogative as head of my house to make the decision." Although he knew he never would have prohibited Hen from marrying the man of her choice. "How do I know you didn't marry her for her dowry? A man with your reputation…"

Hen gasped. "Michael!"

"If you weren't Henrietta's brother, I'd beat you to a pulp. In fact, I'm still considering it."

"Don't hold yourself back." Michael stepped closer.

"You both can stop this ridiculous male blustering right now." Hen's eyes darted back and forth. "My decision to marry Cord wasn't dependent on either of you. It was mine alone."

Michael immediately felt contrite. Hen wasn't quick to anger.

Rathbourne wrapped his arms around Hen and kissed her on the top of the head. "Sweetheart, I'm sorry. You're absolutely correct." Hen circled her arms around his waist, pressing close to her new husband.

Michael heard her say under her breath, "You promised not to bully my brother."

"You don't need to protect me, Hen. I can stand up for myself."

Rathbourne raised his eyebrow in a supercilious manner that Michael detested immediately. "Like you did in France?"

"Oh, my God. I've forgotten Gabby. She's waiting in the drawing room," Michael said.

"Gabby? Who is Gabby?" Hen asked.

"The lady who nursed me when my fever almost got the best of me."

"A lady who allows you to call her Gabby?" Hen smiled.

"You brought an unknown French woman to our home?" Rathbourne demanded.

Michael stiffened at the disdainful tone. "I took her to Kendal House, but had to bring her here since my entire family had been moved here without my knowledge."

Hen took his arm again. "Oh, Michael. I'm sorry I couldn't notify you."

"You don't need to apologize to him," her husband said. "It was your brother who decided to steal a code book and get shot."

"I didn't decide to get shot. And my plan was sound—decipher the code and return the book in the morning."

"This is old history. No need to discuss, Cord." Hen's voice was forceful; she was not in the least intimidated by Rathbourne's menacing manner.

"I need to go to Gabby. Brompton put her in the drawing room, and she is going to wonder where I am."

"You're worried about her?" His sister looked up at him.

"We've been travelling all day. I planned that she would stay with you at Kendal House, but you weren't at home. Neither was Uncle Charles or Edward or the Bromptons." He tried to not sound petulant but could hear it in his own voice. He was dog-tired and was having difficulty with all the unexpected changes. "Where was I to go? A lady in a single man's residence? I needed to protect her reputation."

Rathbourne rolled his eyes upward. "How circumspect of you."

"But, Michael, why didn't you return the lady to her family?" Hen's eyes were bright with curiosity.

"She fled France to be reunited with her brother, but she doesn't know where he resides. I thought it best that she rest after our grueling trip. We've been dodging both Napoleon and Fouché's men. All of this on top of Gabby's long hours caring for me when I was ill. I need to get back to her."

"What is this lady's name?" Rathbourne demanded. "And where did you meet this woman?"

"We can discuss this later. I need to check on Gabby."

Rathbourne grabbed Michael's arm. "You brought an unknown French woman into my home, possibly endangering your sister and your uncle's work."

"Our home, Cord," Hen said.

Michael wanted to blister Rathbourne until he got a glimpse of Hen's drawn face. "Gabby is a young woman escaping

Napoleon and his intention to marry her off to his brother. She is not a threat to anyone."

"I'll be the judge of the threat. What is her name? And how did you meet her?"

Hen protested. "Michael is a good judge of character. He wouldn't risk our safety by bringing a French spy into our home."

Michael cleared his throat. "Mademoiselle Gabrielle De Valmont. Her brother is the Marquis De Valmont."

Hen swayed back into Rathbourne's arms, her face devoid of all color. "My heavens."

Michael reached for his sister, but Rathbourne had already wrapped his arms around her and was leading her to a wingback chair in front of the fireplace. "Sit down. I'll ring for Mrs. Brompton." He knelt in front of her and caressed her hands.

Hen went willingly to the chair. This passivity wasn't like his hearty sister. Hen had never swooned or fainted in her life. He bent over his sister. "What is it, Hen?"

Hen shook her head. "Oh, Michael, her brother, he was a French spy. He was killed in front of my eyes. It was horrible."

Rathbourne's jaw jutted forward and the tick was clearly prominent. "You've only been back in England a few hours and you're already creating chaos. And stressing your sister."

"That isn't fair, Cord. Michael didn't know. How could he?"

"Oh, Hen. Gabby is going to be devastated. Her parents were killed in the Revolution. All she had was her brother. I must go to her, but how will I tell her? She has been anticipating her reunion with him."

"Henrietta is not going to meet this woman." Rathbourne glared at Michael.

Michael glared back. "I don't believe for a minute Gabby is a threat. When you meet her, Hen, you'll see she is a warm and caring young woman."

Rathbourne rose slowly from his knees, his body and voice rigid. "I will interview her and decide what is to be done."

Michael's muscles locked into defiance. "You will not do

any such thing. She is my responsibility, and I will not have her treated discourteously."

"My God, save me from such absurdity. Your Gabby's brother was a French spy, and I will not allow your sister or your uncle to be in the vicinity of this woman until I've decided."

Hen rose, her color restored to two bright red spots on her cheeks. "Have you two finished? This is my home, and I will have a say in whom I shall meet."

"Henrietta, please be sensible." Rathbourne took Hen's hand. "You don't believe in coincidences any more than I do. What are the chances that your brother just happened to bring home Valmont's sister?"

"I am being sensible. Have you forgotten that she saved my brother's life? And the poor woman is going to learn her brother is dead. I can only imagine how terrible the blow will be." Hen wrapped her arm around her husband's waist. "Darling, you would never want me or Gwyneth to be treated in such a harsh manner. She can stay in the east wing, away from the library and the family rooms."

Rathbourne smoothed a wisp of hair along the side of Hen's cheek. "You're right. Let her rest tonight."

He turned and spoke to Michael. "You will not share the news of her brother with her. We will make arrangements for her."

Hen gave him a pleading look. "A very sound plan. Don't you agree?"

Michael didn't want his sister to have to play peacemaker, but Rathbourne tested the patience of a saint and Michael was no saint.

"She has to be exhausted, and to deliver crushing news after her journey will make it more difficult for her," Hen added.

"Fine. But if she is not to stay here after tonight, where will she stay?" Michael asked.

Rathbourne placed his arm around Hen's shoulder, tucking her to his side. He kissed her on the top of her head. "I don't want you to be upset. Why don't you go and have tea with her while I speak with your brother and Ash. We will come up with a plan for Mademoiselle de Valmont."

"You won't bully my brother."

"For heaven's sake, Hen, I don't need to hide behind your skirts." Michael frowned at his sister.

Rathbourne raised his supercilious eyebrow again. "It won't take long for Ash and I to decide, then Kendal can join you in the drawing room with Edward and Uncle Charles."

CHAPTER SIX

When the door opened, Gabby startled and sat more upright on the settee. A petite woman in an unadorned green morning dress entered the drawing room. Her auburn hair was pulled back into a simple knot at her neck. At first glance, Gabby thought this tiny woman was a servant, but the winged arc of her eyebrows, the straight nose, and the luminescent green eyes resembled a familiar face.

Gabby stood and tried to smooth the wrinkles out of the ill-fitting dress she had been wearing for over a day. She patted down her wayward curls that hadn't been tended to.

"*Bonjour,* Mademoiselle De Valmont." The lady curtsied, her French accent as impeccable as her brother's. "Welcome to Rathbourne House. I'm Lady Rathbourne."

Gabby curtsied and spoke in English. She wanted Lady Rathbourne to know she spoke English as fluently as the lady spoke French. "Thank you for your hospitality. I apologize for the inconvenience of my visit. Lord Kendal had originally planned for me to rest at Kendal House to break up my journey."

"Michael explained how demanding your trip has been. You must be weary." As Lady Rathbourne smiled, the resemblance to her brother was even more apparent. She had the same round dimples in each cheek and the same shining eyes that tilted up in the corners. "Please be seated. Let me ring for tea before the gentlemen descend and nothing will be left for us to eat. You soon will have the opportunity to meet all the Harcourt men."

"Thank you, my lady." Gabby reseated herself on the damask settee and folded her hands in her lap.

"I owe you an incredible debt. You saved my brother's life. He just told me of his wound and his fever."

"You owe me nothing. Lord Kendal and Denby risked their lives enabling me to escape France."

"Yes, Michael explained that you needed to make a hasty departure, but he never actually explained how you met."

"I'm sure you are interested in the circumstances." Gabby understood Lady Rathbourne's interest in Gabby's sudden appearance. Did the proper English lady believe Gabby wanted to manipulate her brother into marriage?

The door swung open, and a stunning raven-haired woman rushed into the room. "Brompton told me the good news, Henrietta. I'm so happy Michael is back safely— Oh, my goodness. I do apologize. I didn't know you had a visitor."

"Please come in and meet Mademoiselle Gabrielle. She made the journey with Michael from France."

Gabby stood and curtsied to the lady who appeared to be of the same age.

"How exciting. You journeyed with Lord Kendal?"

The curvaceous young woman, breathless from excitement, spoke in gushes. Not at all what Gabby would have expected from an English lady, but more like her friend Jeanine at the convent. A textile merchant's daughter, Jeanine had not been trained in restraint and the finer attitudes of a lady, and Gabby liked her for it. Until the death of her parents, Gabby had shown the same uninhibited spirit, unrestrained in her curiosity.

Lady Rathbourne smiled indulgently. "This is my husband's sister, Lady Gwyneth Ashworth. Did you come with your husband?"

Lady Ashworth sat in the chair across from Gabby. "Yes. Since he had to meet with your brother, I accompanied him. I wanted to see Uncle Charles and Edward. I miss everyone. Our household is very quiet in comparison to Rathbourne House. You must be so delighted to finally have your brother home."

Lady Rathbourne toyed with a strand of flyway hair resting on her cheek. "It's been quite a shock for Michael to discover that I've married and moved the entire household to Rathbourne House. Cord is talking with him now."

"I hope Michael isn't too upset, since I'm so very glad to have you as a sister. And I'm sure my brother is pleased to finally meet him."

"There was a bit of male one-upmanship, but I'm sure..." Lady Rathbourne looked down at her feet. "But by now, Michael is regaling them with his adventure in France."

Lady Gwyneth rolled her exotic black eyes toward the ceiling. "Most likely drinking brandy. Is Brinsley here too?"

"I'm not sure," Lady Rathbourne said too quickly.

If Gabby hadn't been paying attention she might have missed the silent communication of the rounded eyes and raised eyebrows between the women. Whatever Lord Rathbourne was discussing with the men, his wife knew but didn't want to share.

"Will you be staying at Rathbourne House long? It will be delightful to have another woman in this household," Lady Gwyneth said.

"No, I don't want to impose. I will talk to Lord Kendal about moving immediately to my brother's house."

Gabby was exhausted from her travels and would have liked to avoid getting into a carriage for a very long time. Her stomach growled, reminding her how hungry she was, and she hoped the tray would soon arrive. Lord Kendal had been too excited to return home to stop for a midday repast and then refused to take tea at Kendal House.

The door swung open, and Gabby sat forward in expectation of the tea tray's arrival. Instead, a large dog rushed into the room with a young boy who must be Lord Kendal's younger brother. The golden curls, wide light eyes, and the dimpled smile were identical to his older brother.

"Hen, has the tea tray arrived? Gus and I are starving."

Lady Rathbourne and Lady Gwyneth laughed at the same

time. "I swear Gus and Edward can divine the arrival of the tray before Mrs. Brompton has brought it."

"We're growing." Edward bent down and patted his dog's head, while his canine friend sniffed around the table in the center of the seating arrangement.

"Gus, the tray has not arrived yet. Please sit down." Lady Henrietta pointed to the floor.

The retriever cocked his broad head to one side and then dropped to the floor in a pivotal position next to the table, demonstrating his knowledge of where the tray would be placed.

"Edward, come meet Mademoiselle Gabrielle, our guest."

The young imp tilted his head in courtly fashion and bowed grandly from his waist, as if meeting a royal. "My lady."

"How do you, my lord. I admire your fine, stout companion."

Edward grinned, emphasizing the Harcourt family charm and the same mischievous twinkle she had seen in Lord Kendal's eyes. Like his older brother, Edward was destined to break many hearts. But she would never give her heart to a man who confused her with Yvette or Mimi. Or that was what she told herself.

"Edward, is Uncle Charles up from his nap yet?"

"I'm not sure, Hen. He didn't join me and Mr. Marlow in the library."

The door opened again, admitting two burly footmen with trays laden with food. Another footman carried a tray with cups, saucers, and two teapots.

She wouldn't impose any longer once she had eaten. Then she would insist on being taken to Lucien's home.

CHAPTER SEVEN

Michael was hungry, tired, and more than a little irritated with his new brother-in-law. He didn't want to act like an ass in front of Ashworth, but he'd really like to settle a few things with Rathbourne in the way of men.

Michael always had imagined that Hen would marry someone he could relate to, someone easy to joke with, and, more importantly, someone who cared about linguistics. There was nothing humorous or relaxed in the way Lord Rathbourne pulled back his shoulders into a rigid posture or the way he stared at Michael, as if he were some strange foreigner from Arabia.

"What can one innocent young woman do in your home?" Michael demanded.

"Go through my office or your sister's. Pick Uncle Charles's mind for codes." Rathbourne's tone was condescending.

Michael wasn't used to being treated like an idiot. His intellectual prowess was well respected in both the academic and espionage circles. Some considered him a genius; not that he would ever use that term in describing himself. Uncle Charles and Henrietta, though, were definitely in the genius category.

"Does she know about your work as a code breaker or about your mission in France?" Rathbourne questioned.

"No. I told no one."

"But the woman tended to you when you were delirious. Was Denby always with you? How do we know that you didn't disclose your code breaking role in England?" Rathbourne asked in a steely voice as if he was interrogating a treasonous spy.

Michael sucked in his breath and tried for civility. "She knows nothing. She told me I spoke about Hen and our mother."

"You don't know what you might have shared in your delirium. We will have to keep her under surveillance."

"This is ridiculous." Michael had enough. He walked toward the door. "Gabby will not be treated badly after saving my life. I will take her back to Kendal House where she is no threat to England's secrets."

Rathbourne bolted from his chair, his harsh jaw clenched again. He spoke in a precise, clipped manner. "I won't allow it. You'll upset Henrietta."

Michael spun around. He was known for his easygoing manner, but since arriving at Rathbourne House he was a cauldron of seething frustration. With his hands fisted at his sides, he was ready to inflict physical harm. "Allow it?" he shouted. "You might have stolen my entire family, but you have no control over me or my actions!"

"Stolen your family?" Rathbourne's face contorted into rage. "Of all the asinine comments. You would separate Edward and Uncle Charles from your sister?"

Michael stepped closer, ready for an altercation. "As asinine as thinking Mademoiselle Gabby is a spy. Uncle Charles and Edward are my responsibilities. And I don't shirk my responsibilities."

Ashworth, now standing, waved his arms in the air. "Gentlemen, please. Kendal, sit down. Let's discuss this like the English gentlemen we are. You don't want Lady Henrietta rushing back in here when she hears the shouting, do you? You both promised her to try to get along."

"As long as he didn't provoke me," Michael protested.

Lord Rathbourne pinned Michael with a damning glare. "Provoke you?"

"You're the one who has accused Gabby of being a French spy."

"Gentlemen!" Ashworth raised his voice. "Think of Lady Henrietta."

"You're right. It's best not to get Hen riled." Michael sat down in the chair next to Ashworth. "Hen doesn't lose her temper easily, but when she does, watch out. With one glib remark she can level a man."

Lord Rathbourne sat back down at his desk. "She does have a sharp and deadly precise way with words."

Michael laughed at Rathbourne's tone of awe in regard to Hen.

"You two are pathetic." Ash shook his head. "Lady Henrietta, like Gwyneth, is a most gentle and accommodating woman."

"Gwyneth, accommodating? Since when?" Rathbourne chortled.

"My wife is always reasonable in her demands."

Michael was shocked to hear Rathbourne hoot with laughter. Was it possible that his sister's husband had a sense of humor?

"My sister doesn't have a reasonable bone in her body."

Michael looked back and forth between the two men, trying to grasp the connections. "You're married to Lord Rathbourne's sister?"

"Yes, and Cord is married to your sister. Cozy, isn't it?"

And, struck by their mutual bonds and fueled by the brandy, the men chuckled together—a tentative sense of camaraderie.

When the door opened, all three men jumped to their feet. Michael found it difficult to control his laughter. Exhaustion and brandy might not be the best combination.

A giant of a man, broad-faced, with longish black hair and piercing eyes, stood at the door. "What is so humorous?"

Ashworth said, "These men were cowering because they thought Lady Henrietta had come to give them hell."

Examining the stranger's fierce face, Michael tried to remember where they had met.

"Glad to have you back on British soil." A wide grin spread across the man's face. He crossed the room and slapped Michael on the back. "You gave me a hell of scare in Paris."

Michael shook his head in disbelief and pointed. "You're

the man who was hiding behind the tree."

The giant's thick eyebrows slashed together. "It's called 'covert operations.'"

"It must have been one hell of a big tree," Ashworth added irreverently.

"If you were on our side, why in the hell did you chase my man and me out of France?" Michael asked.

"I wasn't after you. I was guarding you. I left a false trail for Fouché and Napoleon's men to give you time to make your getaway."

"You could have fooled me."

"When you were playing a nun?" the amused man asked.

"Then, sir, I'm in your debt." Michael offered his hand. "As you already know. I'm Kendal."

He tilted his head to the side. "Brinsley, at your service."

"Brinsley has shared your daring escape dressed as nuns, but how did you end up wearing religious garb?" Ashworth inquired.

Rathbourne moaned aloud. Obviously his brother-in-law didn't appreciate how sticky the situation had become in France.

"Both Fouché and Napoleon's men were after us," Michael said.

"After you stole the French code book from Le Chiffre, which wasn't included in your assignment," Rathbourne added.

"I wasn't planning on stealing the book, but as you already know, I was shot returning home."

"Yes, ruined your cover, forcing Fouché and Napoleon to come after you. Then you almost got your sister killed by sending the damn code book to her." Rathbourne's sharp voice matched his harsh stare.

Michael jumped out of his chair. "Who tried to kill Hen?"

Rathbourne gestured for Michael to sit back down. "I'll explain later."

Michael stared at Rathbourne's implacable expression. He refused to believe Rathbourne's hyperbole that his sister had been in danger. This was England, not France. To keep the peace with Rathbourne, Michael kept quiet, but he was growing tired of his brother-in-law's insinuations about his competency. Henrietta would tell him everything and wouldn't be judgmental like her husband. After all, Hen had never held his escapades against him.

"Look on the bright side, Cord. You rescued Lady Henrietta, gaining her trust so that she was willing to marry you. I would say it all ended well."

Cord leaned back in his chair, his face relaxing in pleasurable memories. Michael didn't want to see the face of a satisfied male reflecting on his sister.

Ashworth drank from his glass. "Now that we've put all that behind us, please explain your disguise as nuns. I've been in many disguises undercover, but never anything as intriguing as a nun."

Brinsley effortlessly lifted a heavy mahogany chair that stood in front of the fireplace and placed it next to Ashworth. "Yes, do tell how you got the nuns to cooperate." Brinsley ambled to the side table and poured himself a glass of brandy. Clearly he was part of the inner circle. "I wanted to go to the nunnery and ask them why they assisted you, but with both Fouché's and Napoleon's men watching the convent, I couldn't risk it."

"Fouché's men followed Denby from our home. He escaped by hiding behind a statue of the Blessed Virgin in Notre Dame Cathedral. Mother Therese came to his rescue. In exchange for their wimples and dresses, we had to agree to escort a boy, Pierre, out of France."

"What happened to the lad who was with you?" Brinsley's enormous hands held the brandy glass to his mouth.

"It turns out that the lad wasn't a lad, but Mademoiselle Gabrielle escaping the clutches of Napoleon."

"The boy was not a boy?" Brinsley took a big swallow of his brandy. "You really do get into the most interesting situations."

"Why is Napoleon after this young woman?" Ash asked.

"He wants to marry her off to his brother and keep her fortune for his war coffers."

"Well, then, it was a good thing you got her away from

France," Brinsley said. "But what of her family?"

"Very tragic. Her parents were guillotined during the Reign of Terror."

"An orphan with a large inheritance?" Brinsley asked. "I'm glad I assisted her escape."

"The Sisters sent Gabby to join her brother in England."

"Then her brother will protect her from the fortune seekers in England." Brinsley reclined back in his chair.

Rathbourne cleared his throat. "Unfortunately her brother was the former Comte De Valmont."

"Valmont's sister?" Ash sat up straight. "This is the first we've heard that he had a sister."

"I was aware of a sister, but it was assumed she died in the Revolution," Rathbourne said.

"He hid his sister in a convent," Michael added.

"Valmont, the French spy?" Brinsley asked.

"Yes, the one who was shot by an unidentified assassin," Ash added.

"Gabby knows nothing about her brother's activities in England. She is an innocent. And I will honor my promise to Mother Therese to help her get situated in England," Michael said.

"How can we be sure?" Brinsley asked.

"We cannot assume. We'll have to keep her under surveillance," Ashworth said.

Michael watched all three men nod in agreement.

"For God's sake, she's been in a convent. She's not a spy."

"He does have a good point." Ashworth looked at Rathbourne and shrugged his shoulders. "I think we've been in this spy business too long, Cord. We suspect everyone."

"When it comes to the secrecy of my wife's work, I will not take any risks. Mademoiselle De Valmont can't stay in this house."

Discovery of Hen and his secret work could cost British lives. Their work as code breakers needed to be carefully guarded. He took a big gulp of his brandy. What a conundrum.

Rathbourne's concerns about Gabby were legitimate. But his brother-in-law didn't know Gabby like Michael did. She was not a mastermind spy. "She is going to be devastated to learn about her brother. She knows no one else in England."

"My wife is very savvy about guarding the secrecy of her work, but I worry more about Charles letting something slip." Rathbourne rubbed his jaw with one finger. "His discretion is questionable."

Michael sat up. "Be careful what you say about my uncle."

Rathbourne gave him a compassionate look. "Your uncle has changed. Once you see him again, you'll understand. I mean no disrespect to the old gentleman."

Michael hated to admit that Rathbourne was correct about Uncle Charles's lack of discretion with the change in his mental status.

"She'll move in with Ash and Gwyneth. Ash can keep an eye on her," Rathbourne announced.

Ash laughed. "You're not worried about my wife's safety? She is your sister."

Michael protested. "My God, she is a twenty-two-year-old woman, not some French assassin."

"What say you, Ash?" Rathbourne looked at his friend. "This will give us a perfect chance to discover if she has been sent here by Talleyrand, her brother's handler."

"This is ridiculous. She is escaping France. The nuns brought her to my home in Paris and asked me to help her escape. She's not working for anyone," Michael protested.

Rathbourne shrugged his shoulder. "Then it won't be a problem if she stays with Ash."

"Gwyneth will be delighted to have the mademoiselle stay with us. I know Gwyneth misses all the activity of the Rathbourne household."

"I would also like to ask my Aunt Euphemia to stay with you as an added precaution," Rathbourne added.

A strange, combustible mix of outrage by Rathbourne's overbearing plans and fear for Gabby left Michael taut with emotion. "Gabby will not be treated like a traitor because her brother was a spy. She has done nothing wrong."

"My God, man. Have you considered that her life might be in danger? Napoleon wants her back in France. You don't think he'll give up a fortune that easily? He probably has men looking for her in London at this very moment," Rathbourne said.

Michael hadn't had time to consider the possibility, having been hell-bent in getting them all out of France. "You really think that Napoleon would come after her here?"

"I think Cord has a valid point. What prevents Napoleon from kidnapping her in England?" Ashworth asked.

Rathbourne stood, dismissing them. "Tomorrow she'll be moved to Ashworth House. Tonight she can rest before learning of her brother's demise."

Michael's gut churned with unfamiliar feelings of protectiveness and tenderness. In her short life, Gabby had suffered and now she was left alone. And she wasn't safe, not even in England. He'd do anything to protect her. Unfortunately, he couldn't protect her from the trauma of tomorrow's terrible news.

CHAPTER EIGHT

The next afternoon Michael pulled his horses to a halt in the circular driveway at Rathbourne House. Still unable to sit comfortably in a saddle, he had driven his curricle. Inhaling the warm summer air filled with the scent of freshly mown grass revived him after his fitful sleep. After returning to an empty Kendal House last night, he wandered the halls and the bedrooms alone, lost in his own home. The task of informing Gabby of her brother's demise weighed heavily on him.

"Hen." He shouted across the sloping grass hill to his sister, bent over her garden on the south side of the house.

Henrietta stood and waved, her face relaxed and bright in what he hoped was anticipation of seeing him.

He picked up his pace, his mood lightened by the sight of his sister's smiling face.

"Aren't you industrious this morning?" he teased. His sister, like their mother, spent a great deal of time in the garden.

"Morning? It's afternoon." Henrietta pulled her gardening gloves off and dropped them into the basket at her feet before she hugged him. "I'll stop hugging you soon. I promise."

He gave his sister one last embrace before releasing her. "I'm sorry I'm so late, but I had a rough time of it last night. I couldn't sleep, knowing…" He shrugged his shoulders. "I'm going to shatter Gabby's happiness."

"The poor woman. And I can't help but feel a bit guilty for my happiness at your safe return."

He understood Hen's feelings. He also was glad to have returned home to his family—a joy that Gabby would never enjoy. "She has been so blasted happy, anticipating her reunion with her brother."

"She is a very gentle woman." Hen patted his arm. "Exactly as you said."

"Not a French spy plotting to extract secrets from you?"

"With the war heating up, Cord is correct to be cautious. But after last night's interactions, I don't believe she is a risk to our work. And I like her."

"I told Gabby that you would enjoy each other's company."

"If there weren't new changes in our household, I'd insist on having her stay with us."

Michael stared at his sister. "What is wrong? Your face is flushed. Did you exert yourself with the gardening? Shall I take you inside?"

"I'm fine, but let's remain outside to talk. When the sun is shining, I want to enjoy the last moments before the rain resumes."

Michael looked up at the clear blue sky. "I don't think it will rain."

"Oh, that would be delightful, except my plantings need the rain."

Michael led his sister to a bench under a large old elm tree.

Hen sat down and leaned her head against the mighty tree trunk. She closed her eyes and raised her face upward, basking in the sun's heat.

Michael sat down next to her. "Tell me how you came to marry that old stick-in-the-mud."

Hen popped her eyes open and then covered her mouth to suppress her laughter. "He's not old and not a stick-in-the-mud. He really isn't always so…persnickety, but Gabby's appearance did upset him. He is very protective of me and our work."

Michael chuckled out loud. "Don't let Rathbourne hear you call him 'persnickety.' Not exactly a manly description."

"He is quite confident in his manly pursuits." His sister kept her eyes down and fiddled with her dress. She finally looked up. "I didn't mean what you're thinking."

"How do you know what I'm thinking?" he joked.

"I meant… This is so embarrassing. There is no easy way to say this… You're going to be an uncle."

"Uncle?" Michael grabbed Hen's hands and pulled her off the bench into a tight embrace. Swinging her around in a wide circle, he laughed aloud. "Hen, you know how to level a chap. I'm just getting used to the idea that my baby sister is a married woman." He spun her in another circle. "But a mother…"

Hen laughed gleefully. "Honestly, I can't believe it myself."

He put her down and held her at arm's length to examine her face. "I'm thrilled for you. You deserve all the happiness, even with the dark-haired ogre. But why did you marry so quickly?"

Hen batted at his arms. "He's really not an ogre. Cord refused to wait. And with the end of the peace treaty, we both felt with uncertain times we wanted to be married. He is a gentle and devoted husband, and if you give him a chance, you'll like him."

"He's growing on me."

"Fine praise, I'm sure."

"But I always thought you'd marry a fellow linguist."

"I thought so too. But the ways of the heart aren't exactly logical, as you'll soon learn." Hen sat down and placed her hand on her stomach in a telling way.

"I didn't spin you too much?"

"No, I'm finally over those symptoms. But these days I need a nap every day."

"Of course, you must rest. But you're in good health? Your doctor allows you to garden?"

"Oh, not you too. Cord is driving me insane with his worries. You have to promise me you won't start treating me as an invalid."

Michael took his sister's hand into his. "Grant me permission to worry about you. I promise to keep my thoughts to myself."

Hen squeezed his hand and giggled. "You silent? That will be a first."

"You should be resting, not taking care of Edward and Uncle Charles. Maybe they should come home with me now."

Henrietta rolled her eyes to the sky. "We're managing fine. Brompton looks after Uncle Charles, Mr. Marlow is still Edward's tutor, and Cord is good with both of them."

Michael had witnessed Rathbourne's obvious concern for his sister, brother, and Uncle Charles at dinner last night. "He is very patient with Uncle Charles and Edward."

"I wouldn't marry him unless he accepted my entire family." Hen tucked her fly-away hair behind her ear. "I know this has been a shock for you. I'm sorry I didn't wait for your return, but I didn't know when you would come home and I couldn't expect Uncle Charles and Edward to live in Kendal house without me."

Michael had not yet adjusted to all the changes. His thoughts in turmoil, he couldn't sit still. He did some of his best thinking when he paced. He jumped off the bench and went into motion.

"It wasn't the homecoming I had expected." Michael didn't mention his hurt feelings. "During my sleepless night, I realized how poorly I behaved last night. I knew at some point you would marry and leave Kendal House and that Uncle Charles and Edward would need to move with you. And even though Rathbourne does seem a bit peeved about the code book, I'm sure we'll bump along fine."

"But you know no one will ever replace you in all our affections?"

"Not yours, I hope," he teased.

Henrietta's face flushed a deeper pink. "There are different affections for those we love."

This must be the effects of her pregnancy. Hen wasn't the sort who blushed.

"It is obvious that the stick-in-the-mud makes you very happy. And I saw at dinner how protective he is of you and the Harcourt family."

"When I finally got word that you were..." Hen brushed away her tears. "Since my pregnancy, I cry all the time." She gulped. "When I learned you were on your way home, I planned that Uncle Charles, Edward, and I, with the Bromptons, would greet you at Kendal House and have a big dinner party to celebrate your return. But you didn't tell us of your arrival. I hate that there was no family to greet you."

"It is totally my fault. I wanted to surprise you. And see the shock on your and Mrs. Brompton's faces."

Hen's eyes again filled with tears. "Can you forgive me for all the changes?"

Hen didn't need to ask his forgiveness for marrying Rathbourne. It was evident that his sister was deeply in love with her husband.

"I also planned that you would come and work with us each morning like we did at Kendal House. I could use the help, since the load has gotten pretty heavy, thanks to the end of the peace treaty. And, in that way, you'd be part of our daily lives. You'd still have your gentleman's life in the evenings."

He looked forward to the hours discussing the codes, Greek particles, and all the linguistic intricacies with his family.

"But will Rathbourne approve of me in his daily life?"

"With the war escalating, Cord is at Upchurch offices a great deal of the time. It will almost be like old times, except a different library."

"You'll have to catch me up on the work. With my gunshot wound and then fever, I've been out of the game a long time."

"I'm glad you had Mademoiselle Gabrielle to tend to you. When you told me last night of her singing in French, I got goose bumps. I think our dear mama sent the lady to you."

"It is strange. I had the very same thought." He didn't add that he also thought his mother would have been very pleased to have Gabby as her daughter-in-law.

Hen giggled. "I agree, but you must give her time."

"What are you talking about?"

"Don't pretend to me. You also thought that Mama would have been pleased to see you make a match with Mademoiselle Gabrielle, a gentle, beautiful French woman."

"Do you do this to your husband?"

"Excuse me?"

"Tell him what he is thinking?"

Hen's green eyes, so much like his own, danced in amusement. "Sometimes, but Cord can be quite opaque after all the years he worked as a spy. You are very easy to read."

"That makes me sound quite boring."

Hen tittered. "I'd never describe you as boring. But, truly, you cannot pursue Mademoiselle Gabrielle. She will be grieving and needs us all to act as a supportive family."

Supportive family—he didn't want to break it to his sister, but he was in no way close to thinking of Gabby as family. He felt like the ogre now. The poor woman was going to soon learn about the loss of her only family and he didn't seem able to contain his male thoughts.

"Of course, you're right. This is not the time."

He had planned he would pursue his attachment with Gabby once she was established and living with her brother, demonstrating to Gabby that he knew how to behave like a gentleman. Now everything had changed. And he wanted to take care of her, shelter her from hurt. He understood that his feelings for Gabby weren't logical or precise, and couldn't be deciphered like a substitution code.

CHAPTER NINE

Gabby rushed down the stairs and out the front door to speak with Lord Kendal. All morning she had been watching from her bedroom for him to arrive. Finally, she would be reunited with Lucien.

She had been separated from her only family for long years. She knew it wasn't ladylike to rush after the gentleman, but she didn't care.

She was wearing one of Lady Henrietta's simple day dresses, nothing in her usual French style. After the exhausting travel and then with the changes in Lord Kendal's household, she was grateful to have been spared dinner with the family. She begged off since she had no proper clothes, and Lady Henrietta allowed her to use the flimsy excuse to escape.

She awoke refreshed, knowing she was safe and that soon she would be with her brother. She'd be happy to finally resume her true identity as a sophisticated woman, not the schoolgirl in a convent or a young boy. Dressed in a stylish wardrobe, she would never be confused with a Mimi or Yvette.

Gabby followed a path that wound between the hedges, leading to the back of the house. She quickly arrived at the garden where Lord Kendal and Lady Henrietta were sitting.

Lord Kendal was bent over his sister, his body turned in concern and brotherly love. She felt a deep yearning in witnessing his obvious care.

Lucien was much older than Gabby and they had never spent enough time together to become really close, but now they needed each other. They were each other's only family. She wanted to be a loving sister to him. And despite how hardened he had become with the murder of their parents, he had always been a protective brother.

As if he sensed her approach, Lord Kendal twisted on the bench where he was seated next to his sister. He rose and bowed over her hand. "Good afternoon, Mademoiselle Gabrielle."

His face was closely shaven. The golden stubble gone. Although dressed as a proper English gentleman in his buff riding breeches and perfectly fit forest-green riding coat, he exuded a boyish air. Maybe it was his disheveled curls that never stayed in place, or the way his eyes always were bright with curiosity.

Gabby curtsied. "Good afternoon, my lord."

The formality between them hurt her. The adventure with Michael had ended. They were back in proper society. They would meet as polite strangers—Lord Kendal and Mademoiselle Gabrielle. She would assume her new life, and Lord Kendal would go back to his.

Last night she tried to reconcile her excitement to be reunited with her brother with the loss of being in Michael's company. She didn't want to give up his easy, light-hearted teasing or the promises in his touch and his intense stares.

They would meet in London, since she assumed the English aristocracy would be a small, intimate world as in Paris. Of course, with the war between England and France, she couldn't be sure how often they would meet as polite strangers.

Gabby curtsied again. "Good day, Lady Henrietta."

Lady Henrietta's face glowed in the afternoon sunshine. "I hope that you slept well."

"I did, my lady. Thank you for your generous hospitality."

Not known for her patience, Gabby had to bite her lip to prevent blurting out questions about her brother.

"It is a fine summer day."

Lord Kendal's teasing manner was gone. His eyes studied

her, not flirting or laughing with her, but keeping a distance. He also recognized the end of their time together.

She had known this moment would come, when she would have to give up her fantasies of a simple and happy life with him. The sorrow in his eyes was no less than what she was feeling. It was time for her to take her place with her brother. Time to say good-bye to the only man she had ever dreamed about.

"Do you have news?" She tried to not sound as impatient as she felt.

He took her arm and led her to the bench where his sister sat. "I do have news. I think it best if you sit down."

Gabby startled at the grave tone in Lord Kendal's voice. His usually mischievous eyes were dim and filled with concern and pity. A chill swept over her skin. A foreboding. The same look her servants had given her when her mother had been escorted from their home, and she'd had to show no emotion at her mother's suffering.

Lady Henrietta took Gabby's hand. Her glowing countenance now was clouded. Her eyes watery. Gabby trembled with the lady's pitying expression. Her heart beat harder, faster.

She looked back and forth between the grave and sympathetic looks. Deep dread settled into Gabby's heart.

No, this couldn't be happening. She woke up this morning for the first time in a long time not afraid, without fear for her future.

"Lucien?" The fear was strangling her voice. "Tell me."

She watched Lord Kendal swallow hard before he spoke. "I'm so sorry."

Gabby's mind halted.

"Your brother…" Lord Kendal shook his head. "He is dead."

It couldn't possibly be true.

"There has been a mistake." The words echoed in her head as if she were speaking down a long tunnel.

Lady Henrietta took her hand. "I'm sorry. Your brother was killed in a duel."

"Lucien is an amazing marksman." Not able to look at the awful truth in their eyes, Gabby twisted the material of her skirt. Her mind refusing to believe anything these strangers said. "My brother never would have lost a duel."

Lord Kendal's eyes and face were flat, contorted in sorrow. She looked away, not able to bear this world of loss and suffering.

"Who told you this lie? How did you discover...?" Her voice quivered.

"It is common knowledge in London," Lady Henrietta said.

Lord Kendal knelt on one knee before her. He took her hands between his. "I wish it weren't true. If I could make your brother's death not true, I would. I know how hard this terrible news is for you."

The dark, empty abyss was opening in front of her. Memories flashed before her. The screams. She opened her eyes wide, not looking at their faces, but looking up at the bright blue sky. Lucien was gone. There was nothing to do. The crippling pain would come later, like after her parents' deaths. She had to do something right now or she would shatter into a thousand shards.

"Can you take me to my brother's residence?" She was alone. No family. Where would she go? "I'd like to speak to his servants."

Lady Henrietta squeezed her hand. Her voice was slow and comforting. "We will try to find where your brother resided and where his servants have gone. It will take time."

"Then I must speak to his solicitor. I'd like to go now." She had to do something. She couldn't be helpless again, waiting for everyone to decide her fate.

"Today isn't the day." Lord Kendal voice had a commanding quality she had never heard before.

"Why not?" She could feel the panic rising in her throat. "I've no money. No place to go."

"You're not alone. You have Michael and me and our family. You needn't worry about the future right now." Lady Henrietta spoke in a soothing tone.

Future. What future? She knew what happened when everyone you loved was taken from you. The hollowness and pain carved deep holes in your heart and in your soul.

Lord Kendal spoke in a soft, soothing voice as if speaking to a child. "I'm not going to allow anything to happen to you. I will find the solicitor and bring him to you. I promise. You trust me, don't you?"

Gabby looked into his eyes, the color of the first spring leaves. "Sister and I had no other plans except to get me out of England and to Lucien."

"Neither you nor Mother Therese could have anticipated this. But Mother Therese trusted me, and I hope you will too."

Lady Henrietta stood. "Let's go back to the house and get you tea."

Michael took Gabby's arm. "Let me escort you inside."

She didn't want to be alone right now, but how could they understand her fear and loneliness? Their future, their world, hadn't just exploded. Yesterday Michael was upset because his sister got married and moved. How absolutely simple and normal.

"If you wouldn't mind, my lady, I'd like to spend time in the gardens."

"Of course. I'll have Mrs. Brompton prepare a tray for you when you come inside."

"Thank you." Gabby's voice cracked, responding to the gentle understanding.

Michael took her hand and placed it on his arm. "Let me accompany you. This isn't a time to be alone."

"Thank you. But I want to be alone." She didn't want words of comfort or soft platitudes. It was her brother, her loss, and her pain gnawing on her insides.

"But you're pale and shaking."

She hadn't realized her hands were shaking. She just had to move. The day her mother was killed, she rode her horse, risking everything, but she couldn't just sit and let them know they had beaten her. "I'm fine."

She saw the surprise and then the hurt flash across his face. "I'll wait for you in the drawing room."

She shook her head in refusal. She wanted to lean on him, gather her strength from him, as she had done with the idea that Lucien waited for her, for a new life. She wouldn't think about her brother right now. Lucien had taught her how to bury her feelings so no one could detect her vulnerability. As she had done when she was orphaned and had to pretend she wasn't related to her dead parents. She coped then. She would again.

"Gabby, please let me help you."

Staring into his undefended and open eyes was too painful for her.

"No, please, can you find my brother's solicitor?"

"Now?"

"Yes." It was hard to breathe, hard to go on. "I must know the circumstances of his death." She wasn't surprised that Lucien had fought a duel. He had a quicksilver temper and was offended easily, much like her father. "Gallic pride" her mother had called it.

She couldn't keep her voice from quaking. "I'd like to know where he is buried."

She turned quickly and walked toward a path that would take her down the slope and away.

CHAPTER TEN

Gabby had endured the scattered rain long enough. She returned to the house, hoping to pass undetected. Despite Lady Henrietta's pelisse and the warmth of the day, her hands and feet were wet and numb. Climbing the stairs, she hoped to avoid everyone's pitying looks and words. She didn't want to reassure them that she was fine when she wasn't.

Relieved to have escaped anyone's notice, she walked quickly toward her bedroom. A door on her right opened.

"I've been waiting for you, my dear. The tea tray is here."

Gabby floundered for a moment. The older woman spoke as if she knew Gabby, but they had never been introduced. Gabby curtsied. "My lady." She would remember this white-haired, doughty woman dressed in bright fuchsia with orange piping, who made quite a dramatic statement with her élan in color choices.

Breaking all rules of polite society, the woman put her arm around her shoulder and led Gabby into a warm, cozy lady's parlor. "Come along."

The smallish room was overflowing with flowered drapes and upholstery that assaulted the eye with their boldness and ghastly mismatch of colors, much like the lady in front of her.

Gabby quickly checked to make sure her mouth was closed and her face betrayed none of the disorienting surprise she was feeling.

"I can see by your reaction that you weren't informed of my presence. I'm Aunt Euphemia."

The warm room was like a furnace blast for her chilled body and her shocked state. Gabby unbuttoned her pelisse, basking in the heat. The woman closed the door. As a guest of the house, Gabby didn't feel she could refuse to take tea with the family's aunt.

Gabby placed her pelisse on the back of a chair and waited.

The older woman marched ahead to the settee in front of the fire. She gestured to Gabby toward the tea tray placed on the table. "You must eat a little even though you don't feel like it. I find a warm, buttery crumpet is quite the thing to settle an upset stomach and mood."

Gabby moved from behind her chair toward the table. "Yes, my lady."

"Tut, tut. None of that." The lady took Gabby's cold hands into her own. "You must call me Aunt Euphemia."

Gabby had been taught to respect her elders; she would never be rude to the lady. But call this stranger 'aunt'?

"You've had a rough time of it." Her rheumy eyes searched Gabby's face. "Too much loss for someone so young."

Had they shared her personal news with everyone in the household?

Aunt Euphemia led Gabby to the settee. "You needn't worry that you must converse. The benefits of my age...no need for silly chitchat on such a horrendous day." She adjusted her orange turban which was adorned with nesting birds and which had fallen over one eye. "We will not speak of your brother or your pain today. Come sit. We'll do nothing but sit together in front of the fire. I find the rainy weather chills my bones."

Gabby sat erect on the corner of the settee, her ankles crossed and her hands folded in her lap. Aunt Euphemia plopped down next to Gabby and leaned against the back of the settee, her legs splayed out in front of her. "In my sitting room, I don't hold to polite manners or polite conversation."

Gabby had no idea how to respond to such a claim. Already feeling off kilter, she could only nod.

The warmth of the fire penetrated through her damp walking

dress. The only sound in the small, toasty room was the ticking of the ormolu clock that looked very similar to the one that had been her grandmother's sitting room. A peaceful contentment settled into Gabby from the strange woman's presence. She felt none of the cloying pity or the invasive scrutiny from those wondering how a child her age was handling the murder of her parents. Or now how she was dealing with the news of her brother.

Aunt Euphemia bent over the tray filled with biscuits, breads, cheeses, meats, and fruit. The tray had enough food to feed ten people. Gabby hoped the entire family wasn't going to appear for tea. She couldn't face making conversation. But she didn't want to be by herself—dreading to be alone with her thoughts.

"I believe the tea is ready. Shall I serve you?" Aunt Euphemia asked in French. "Do you prefer I speak to you in French?"

"Thank you, but I'm fine with English."

"Why don't you make your own plate while I tend to the tea? Would you prefer chocolate? Shall I ring for chocolate?"

"We always drank chocolate in the morning." Gabby surprised herself by sharing a moment of her past.

"It is the same with me. I love the aroma of the chocolate when I'm first awake. And I add honey to mine."

Gabby smiled at the stout woman. "I also always add honey. My father liked to tease me about my sweet tooth."

"Gwyneth has always loved sweets, but not Cord. To grow as large as he did, he ate endlessly. I always was envious of his ability to eat everything and just get taller and stronger. Not like some of us." She patted her plump stomach. "He definitely takes after his mother's side of the family."

Gabby wanted to giggle. Aunt Euphemia's conversation was nothing that Gabby had previously experienced—twisted and contorted, rather like the turban she favored, which was precariously cocked to one side.

"Am I running on? I am. Cord...I mean... I am Lord Rathbourne's and Lady Gwyneth's aunt. I was told you met Gwyneth at tea?"

"Yes, I met the lady yesterday. A congenial woman." Gabby didn't want to tell Aunt Euphemia that she had been delighted by her niece's lack of propriety.

"I see Gwyneth has had the same effect on you as she always does when meeting new people. I was responsible for Gwyneth's upbringing after her dear mother died. I encouraged Gwyneth to express her opinions and to think for herself. She is open and spontaneous. In polite society, there are other descriptions for a woman who isn't held back by society's silly rules." Aunt Euphemia raised her eyebrows, her eyes twinkling. "Heresy, I know."

"I've spent two years in a convent. Not particularly conducive to expressing opinions… More about how a proper lady must always behave."

"Yes, I've always found it baffling that the nuns have chosen a life independent of the society's expectation of marriage then train young women to become good wives—preparation for an institution they've rejected."

Gabby sipped her tea, thinking about her childhood. Aunt Euphemia had encouraged Lady Gwyneth to think for herself. Since Gabby had been alone for these past years, she had been forced to rely on her own judgement rather like Lady Gwyneth.

"You've had to make your own way after the loss of your parents, which made you strong and independent. I admire that in a woman, but I hope you won't mind an old woman giving you some advice."

Well, maybe Aunt Euphemia wasn't so unique. Her preface sounded exactly the way Mother Therese began her lectures on self-improvement. "Yes, my lady."

Aunt Euphemia shook her head vigorously, making the bird on her turban wobble. "No need to be formal here. I feel it is important to know when to follow the rules and when not to. In my sitting room, there is no need."

She had been wrong. Aunt Euphemia wasn't anything like Mother Therese. Aunt Euphemia was definitely different. No one had ever given her permission to ignore the rules. Even

Lucien expected her to follow the rules, despite his own blatant refusal. "Yes, Aunt Euphemia."

"My dear, I want you to learn from my mistakes." Aunt Euphemia reached across the settee and took her hand. "I am a big proponent of self-reliance. But sometimes even strong women need to depend on other people. It doesn't make you weak to need help from others."

Gabby felt the grief jamming into her throat and behind her eyes. She needed her brother. Now, she had no one to rely on but herself.

"After the shock you've received today, you feel alone. But, my dear, you're not. I know we aren't your family and we won't try to be. But I hope you let all of us help lessen your grief. Like you, Gwyneth has lost her parents and her older brother. And I am told the death of Lord Kendal's mother was very difficult for him."

Tears formed in Gabby's eyes. She hadn't shed any tears up to this point, but now they wouldn't stop. And she had no handkerchief to wipe her eyes.

Aunt Euphemia pulled a lavender-scented, orange cloth from her bosom. "Here, my dear." She handed the handkerchief to Gabby. "It is fine to cry for all you've lost."

Aunt Euphemia leaned back on the couch. She offered no other condolences. She sat in silence, allowing Gabby to cry for the loss of her brother, her parents, her home.

CHAPTER ELEVEN

Embarrassment was a familiar feeling to Michael. He often got himself into a pickle, but his usual predicaments had never caused life-threatening danger to his family. He shifted in his chair as he had as a schoolboy called down at Eton. He definitely felt at a disadvantage with his brother-in-law since Henrietta had shared what had transpired because of his rash behavior.

"I need to speak with you." Lord Rathbourne leaned across his massive desk.

"Rathbourne, I believe we've gotten off on the wrong foot. And now that Henrietta's explained the entire mess I caused, I hope you will first let me apologize for my actions in France. I never anticipated the danger I would cause to my family by stealing the code book. I'm impressed that you didn't skewer me."

"Trust me, the idea did cross my mind. But that would have made your sister very unhappy." Lord Rathbourne tapped his chin with his index finger. "Your decision to take the book did set off an interesting chain of events."

"I was a damn fool."

And something he didn't expect from this meeting was Lord Rathbourne's hearty laugh. "Well, there is that possibility."

"I had no idea of the repercussions. I had hoped to decipher the code and send the results back to England." His work as a linguist hadn't prepared him for covert work.

"Not an unreasonable approach, but my men didn't appreciate how closely you were being watched. You should never have been assigned to France; you're not a trained field agent. It isn't a criticism of my predecessor, Sir Ramsay. He made the best decision at the time. Your talents are much better suited to Abchurch."

"Thank you for your generous attitude. I appreciate your willingness to forgive, even if it is due to my sister."

"Your sister can be quite convincing." Rathbourne's haughty manner softened. "But I am grateful for your willingness to share your incredible talent for the sake of England."

And damn if Michael didn't feel embarrassed again to receive such high praise.

"I plan to begin my work with Henrietta deciphering codes from Abchurch." Michael was a bit disappointed to be returning to the challenging but predictable work of code breaking. After escaping Paris, they had travelled under constant threat of discovery. Although his work in England was top secret and carried inherent danger, he found it thrilling to be chased by assassins throughout France.

"I've got another assignment for you."

"Undercover again?" A rush of excitement coursed through him. Although he'd definitely ruined his cover in France, he had the opportunity to prove himself to his new superior.

"Rather. We have suspicions that the opera singer, Madame Abney, may be a French agent, working for Talleyrand. After her acclaim in France, she has become very popular in London and has attracted royal interest. I want you to get close to Madame Abney."

"In what way?"

"What *way*? In the standard way a single man gets to know a woman. She is married to a Frenchman and the rumor is that they are not close."

"But, I'm…"

"She has loads of gentlemen pursuing her, and she is known to take lovers. You need to gain her trust. We also have suspicions about one of her favorite gentleman pursuers; we believe he might be part of a network of spies."

Before Gabby, he would have relished this assignment. "Aren't there any other single men who might be available?"

"Not with your title and skills."

"Sk-skills?" Michael stammered. This was Hen's husband. Had he heard the rumors? Michael didn't feel he was much different in his pursuit of women than any of the other unmarried gentlemen. He battled between embarrassment and defensiveness over the fact that women found him appealing and chased him.

Rathbourne laughed again. "Your linguistic skills."

"My linguistic skills?"

"You speak Italian and German, isn't that correct?"

"The Romance languages aren't much of a challenge. Mastering the Middle High German dialects and the Low German dialects was more of a challenge, but it helped my understanding of German, Russian, and the Scandinavian languages. Of course, my first love was the old Saxon tongue."

His brother-in-law raised his eyebrow.

"I digress. Yes, I have a command of the languages you mentioned. As does my sister."

"Your sister is not to be involved in this matter."

"Of course not. I would never want to place Hen at risk…"

Rathbourne raised his eyebrow again in that annoying supercilious manner.

"Again," Michael added, chastened.

"Exactly. Madame Abney became very close to Josephine Bonaparte during her time in Paris. Madame has spent a great deal of time in both Germany and Italy and made many connections. We believe she has been passing on messages to these contacts for Napoleon. We don't know how she is passing the messages, but we've assumed they are embedded in the music."

"Codes written in music have been used for centuries. It is a painstakingly slow method, but feasible. You are familiar enough with opera to know that the composer allows total leeway to the diva to sing her arias to showcase her vocal power and skills."

"I am aware. And it's exactly why I need someone with both language and musical knowledge. Madame favors Italian opera, but she also sings in German."

"It means attending all of her performances to detect a change in her arias," Michael added.

"Precisely."

"And to get close enough to look at her written music to see if there are any discrepancies."

"Henrietta has explained that you also studied music." Rathbourne stared at him.

"That is very generous of my sister. Music, like codes, consists of mathematical patterns, and I see and hear patterns very easily. I lack the passion of an artist to be called a true musician."

"You are perfect. Your sister wants to help in the analysis of the music, but she has enough work. Abchurch has kept her very busy while you were gone. She needs to rest and must avoid taking on too much."

"I agree. I've offered to move Edward and Uncle Charles back to Kendal House, but she won't hear of it. Of course, Edward will head off to Eton next year, but I worry about the stress of another change for Uncle Charles."

"I don't want your sister worried about your uncle. Please, for your sister's peace of mind, Uncle Charles must remain at Rathbourne House. You will be a regular visitor with your work for Abchurch. But you will have the freedom to pursue Madame Abney."

Michael shifted in his chair and cleared his throat. "Since arriving home, I hadn't planned on pursuing any liaisons."

Up went Rathbourne's eyebrow. The man used his damn eyebrow like a form of punctuation. Maybe Michael should pursue the study of facial movements in different languages. He wondered whether Rathbourne used his eyebrow in his inquisitions of spies. What a weapon! He could be known in spy circles as The English Eyebrow.

"You're worried about how your liaison with the beautiful

opera singer might affect your relationship with Mademoiselle De Valmont?"

"Yes, she'll get the wrong idea of what sort of man I am if I'm in pursuit of an opera singer."

"You already have a reputation of pursuing opera..." Rathbourne coughed behind his hand. "The lady is bound to hear of your past once she goes out in society. Women ferret out that type of information readily. Has she made the move to Ashworth House yet?"

Until Rathbourne mentioned Gabby, Michael realized they had been conversing in an easy manner. Rathbourne had even sympathized with the conflict of his assignment but still expected him to do his duty. And Michael acknowledged that he was the best choice to pursue the possibility of coded messages. Amazing. Hen would be pleased. He just wished he could explain everything to Gabby.

"She has arrived safely at your sister's home. Your aunt accompanied her." Michael didn't want to admit to anyone how disappointed he had been by Gabby's rejection of his help.

She had asked him to find her brother's solicitor. And once he had accomplished the task, Ashworth had stepped into the role of Gabby's protector. A single man couldn't serve as her protector. As if he didn't understand the rules of propriety, both Aunt Euphemia and Ashworth had explained how he must distance himself from Gabby to stop any rumors about the coincidence of his return from France and her arrival. A plan had been agreed upon. Her new identity was to be that of a family friend of the Rathbourne family.

He wanted to call on her, but he remembered Hen's words about not pushing her when she was grieving. But he missed her. He wanted to take care of her, comfort her utterly in the way men knew how to offer ease.

"Yes, I understand that Aunt Euphemia and Gwyneth have been helpful. And tomorrow the lady will be meeting her brother's solicitor?"

"Yes, Gabby and your aunt will be meeting with him. Ashworth has also volunteered to accompany them, but the ladies didn't feel it was necessary."

"My aunt has managed her own estate for many years. I'm sure she will be of great assistance."

Michael leaned forward in his chair. "Gabby has asked me to look into the circumstances of her brother's duel and where his body is buried. But this is the tricky part. How can I lie to her about something so important?"

"You will be protecting her by lying to her. How will it help the lady to know that her brother was assassinated, possibly by the same men who are pursuing her? The story is that Valmont was killed in a duel with the Duke of Wycliffe."

Michael sat forward. "I can't believe Wycliffe was a traitor. By Jove, I encouraged Hen to marry him."

Rathbourne stroked his chin with his index finger. "Appears he had gambling and opium problems."

"My mother and I thought it was an excellent match. My God, he was a duke. But thankfully, Hen had more sense."

"Your sister is a very discerning woman. She did tell me that you supported her decision to refuse him, despite the social pressures."

Michael raised his eyebrow in the same supercilious manner as his brother-in-law. "And, despite your reputation, she married you."

Rathbourne stiffened, his manner all taut and pompous, ready to take on the challenge. His brother-in-law really was a prickly sort of chap.

Michael grinned. "And I can see how happy she is."

Rathbourne gave a small smile, his body relaxing slightly. "It took some time convincing her to look past my reputation." He shrugged his shoulders. "But hell, a lot of it was a cover that I had established to hide my covert activities in France. And what Ash said is correct. If you hadn't stolen the code book, I'm not sure Henrietta would have had the opportunity to see me in a favorable light."

"But that's my point. Gabby will never see me in a favorable light if I am pursuing an opera singer."

"Your sister got past my reputation once I was able to share my work. Mademoiselle Gabby seems like a very sensible woman. And since my wife has convinced me that mademoiselle is a gently bred woman with no hidden or devious agendas, you will be able to share your work with her in the future. But presently, you must keep your distance from the mademoiselle. It won't take long for Napoleon's men to make the connection between you and the lady. And you have a vital role to play in discovering what the French are planning."

"But if only I could tell Gabby about the mission."

"Think, man. If you told her of your mission, you'd be putting her at risk."

"But you agree that...Gabby is not a French spy?"

"What I believe is that she is at risk to either be kidnapped or to be used by the French as a pawn, possibly to spy for them since her brother's death left her with no protector."

Michael sat up straight with the tension running up and down his spine. "But what if Napoleon and his men find her?"

"That is what I'm hoping for. We will be observing her very closely to protect her and to also see who makes contact."

"You're the one putting Gabby at risk!" Michael jumped up. "I won't allow it."

And there was the damn raised eyebrow. Michael was trying to get along with his brother-in-law for his sister's sake, but how did she tolerate his condescending manner?

Rathbourne spoke calmly. "Mademoiselle Gabby is already at risk. This will give us the opportunity to capture whomever is after her. Do you have the story straight on what happened to her brother?"

He hated to have to admit that Rathbourne might be right. But Michael couldn't separate logic from his feelings. Not when it came to Gabby and her safety. He should be the one to guard her. He should be the one comforting her. He should be the one she looked to for protection.

Michael couldn't remain still. He began to pace in the library. "Yes, Hen explained that both men killed each other over their shared mistress. Valmont killed the Duke in revenge for killing Isabelle."

"The truth is that all three, including a duke of the realm, were French spies. Isabelle was a double agent and worked for me. Valmont was shot by an unknown assassin, not by Wycliffe."

Michael stopped and looked at Rathbourne. "And what of his body?"

"Honestly, I don't know what happened to the body. But lie to mademoiselle, say you believe he is buried in Highgate cemetery."

"I can't lie to Gabby," Michael protested.

"This work is based on lies and subterfuge. To safeguard everyone you care about, you're going to have learn to lie to them."

"And you lie to my sister?"

"I try not to, but if her life were at stake, I wouldn't hesitate."

CHAPTER TWELVE

Grateful to escape Ashworth's house after two days of long solitary hours with nothing but her grief, Gabby followed Lady Gwyneth into the modiste shop.

"Haloooh, Amelia!" Lady Gwyneth called loudly in a sing-song voice.

The hanging ivory silk on the walls, the vibrant cut roses in Sevres vases, and the gilded ladies' chairs were exactly like a Parisian shop or a French boudoir. A tinkling of the entry bell flooded Gabby with memories of visiting a lady's shop with her dear mama. She fought the melancholic feeling bubbling up, along with the bittersweet memory. In her dreams last night, she was with Lucien in France, and everyone spoke in French, not English. She hated waking up this morning to the sound of the harsh English language.

Like the years in the convent, she was marking time, waiting. She must face reality, that there was no going back. She must make a new life in this new country. But how to go about this new life? Living with Lady Gwyneth and Aunt Euphemia was a temporary situation. She didn't want to be a burden to anyone, including Michael, who seemed to believe he was responsible for her.

A slender, ravishing woman with flame-red hair emerged from behind the curtain. "Gwyneth…and Mademoiselle Gabrielle."

Gabby had mixed feelings about meeting this lady after Lady Gwyneth's disclosure that the lady had believed herself to be in love with Michael until she met her fiancé. Gabby wasn't quite sure if Gwyneth was warning her off Michael or confirming what a rake Michael had been. Or still was? Gwyneth needn't bother since Gabby still stung with the memory of Michael's delirious confusion about with whom he was sharing his bed.

Gabby didn't want to admit that she missed the attractive rake and continued to call him Michael in her thoughts. She told herself over and over that the only reason she missed his company was because he was the most familiar person in all of London with everything and everyone else new. She privately wished that, despite the risk, he would call on her—to have a few moments when she felt hopeful and alive, inspired by his sunny, warm presence.

"Gabby, this is my dearest friend Amelia Bonnington, soon to be Lady Brinsley."

Gabby curtsied. "Thank you for your willingness to see me on short notice, Miss Bonnington."

The beauty curtsied. "I would have come to Ashworth House, but Gwyneth insisted that you both needed to get out of the house. Gwyneth does like to stay busy."

"After the last two dreary days, stuck inside by the rain, Gabby and I needed an adventure. And what can be more fun than seeing fabrics and discussing a new wardrobe," Lady Gwyneth said.

Gabby's only break had been with Aunt Euphemia, two days before, to meet with the solicitor. She had become a very wealthy woman in her own right. With great foresight, Lucien had transferred most of his funds to England and had left her a sizable fortune.

"Lady Gwyneth and Lady Henrietta have kindly provided my clothing for the past days. But I am in need of an entirely new wardrobe," Gabby said.

"An entirely new wardrobe. Are there any better words spoken by a woman?" Miss Bonnington spread her arms out, encompassing the entire room.

A young woman, with her chestnut-colored hair pulled back

into a tight chignon, in a plain muslin dress, entered the anteroom. She carried a small silver tray with flutes of champagne. Her blushing cheeks and round face reminded Gabby of Lisette, her *mémé's* daughter, a fresh country miss.

"Mademoiselle Gabrielle, this is Elodie. And this is her shop," Miss Bonnington said.

Gabby hid her surprise that this young woman was the modiste. In Paris, the dressmakers were highly sophisticated women who attracted customers with their haughty attitude and panache.

The shy woman bowed her head and curtsied. "May I serve you all champagne?"

The ladies sat in a semi-circle on diminutive ladies' chairs, their gowns overflowing around them.

Miss Bonnington chimed in, "I give advice on color, design, and the choice of fabrics, but it is Elodie who does all the magic, transforming my ideas into beautiful gowns."

Elodie said in a small voice, "Thank you, my lady," and curtsied again.

"Champagne would be delightful." Lady Gwyneth accepted the filled flute. "And, Elodie, you shouldn't be embarrassed. You are becoming the most stylish modiste in London."

"Because of patronage from you and Miss Amelia, my lady," Elodie said.

Gabby experienced another flash of memory of sitting with her mother and her cousin in Madame Beauchamp's salon, gossiping and being allowed to sip champagne. That had been her first adult woman experience, in a more lighthearted time of her youth…of another lifetime.

Miss Amelia, looking over her glass, carefully inspected Gabby. "Gwyneth didn't exaggerate your beauty. And, no matter what you wear, you'll look divine." No wonder Miss Amelia was Lady Gwyneth's close friend. They both shared an unfettered enthusiasm.

Gabby wasn't accustomed to such effusive praise. "Thank you. The only dress I possess is the one I travelled in. And after living in a convent and then being disguised… I'm ready to have a new wardrobe." She didn't know how much Miss Amelia was aware of her circumstances.

Acquiring a wardrobe was a much easier task than the painful meeting with Lucien's solicitor. Signing the official documents had made her brother's death final.

The next decisions were very difficult without her brother's guidance—where to live, whom to trust, and how to protect herself against Napoleon's men. She had never lived on her own, but she must now learn quickly.

Lady Amelia leaned closer to Gabby. "Gwyneth shared how you travelled out of France. You can trust me with your secret, but you must not share the information with anyone else. It would be disastrous for your reputation. Now, having given you that sensible and proper advice, Gwyneth and I are very envious of the adventure and want all the details." Miss Amelia clapped her hands together in anticipation.

"I'm very aware of the censure of society for such an unorthodox method of travelling, but expediency was the priority. And of course, I would never want to embarrass Lord Kendal."

"Embarrass Michael!" Miss Bonnington laughed, covering her mouth. "You surely must know that Michael is known for getting into all sorts of misadventures and causing havoc."

"No, he never shared that part of his past." But Gabby recognized that his appealing, boyish curiosity might lead him into trouble. His high spirits were new and attractive. His genuine manner was refreshing, especially after the affected French men who flaunted their importance. "The first time I met Lord Kendal he fell off the settee, spilled brandy in his boots, and swore in front of Mother Superior."

"Sounds like Michael. Oh, the stories, I could tell. Did Gwyneth explain that my family estate borders the Harcourt estate? My brothers and I grew up with Michael and Henrietta."

"No, I hadn't realized that you were childhood friends, my lady. How fortunate to be surrounded by other children."

Gwyneth crossed her legs in the same manner as Aunt Euphemia. "Gabby, you don't have to 'lady' us when we're alone. We're of the same age, not some dowdy dowagers."

"I'll try, Gwyneth, but all my training in a convent isn't easy to overcome."

"It must have been dreadful living in a convent. All the rules." Gwyneth gestured with her free hand. "I would have probably run away."

"I had no choice. It was the only safe place."

Gwyneth uncrossed her legs and leaned forward. "I'm sorry. How insensitive of me."

"You're not insensitive. You speak honestly and without artifice." Gabby admired Gwyneth and appreciated how openly caring and affectionate she was. "And there were many days in the convent that I wished I could run away."

"I'm not very good at following rules. I probably would have been beaten regularly." Gwyneth laughed.

Gabby joined her enjoyment. "We were never beaten. I can't imagine any of the sisters using physical punishment, but then again, none of us considered breaking the rules."

"I am glad that I had Aunt Euphemia to encourage me to look beyond society's restrictive rules for women. But, as my husband likes to point out, sometimes my behavior is not ladylike."

"That can't possibly be true." Amelia winked at Gabby as if they were co-conspirators. "I regularly wanted to run away from my five brothers. There were days when I wished I were an only child."

"I would love to have grown up with Amelia's brothers." Gwyneth sipped her champagne. "I hardly got to play with my brothers. They both were much older."

"Five brothers?"

"Yes, it does sometimes boggle the brain," Amelia admitted.

"I'm envious. Lucien was never home when I was growing up. And then he was forced to fulfill the role of both mother and father for me." Gabby was surprised by the quiver in her voice.

She had been enjoying the conversation until the mention of Lucien caused an unexpected rush of sorrow.

"I'm very sorry for your loss." Amelia patted Gabby's hand. "Gwyneth and I want to help you in any way we can."

"Thank you, my lady."

"And our first step is to start with a new wardrobe." Amelia stood. "I am to understand that you won't be wearing mourning."

Gwyneth turned to Gabby. "Amelia can be trusted."

"I am to be a friend of the Rathbourne family and not to publicly declare my true identity, although I do believe it won't be long before I'm recognized."

Gabby had to trust her new identity to Gwyneth and Aunt Euphemia, and now Amelia. After being chased by Napoleon's men across France, she had agreed to the plan of keeping her identity a secret. She had witnessed the lengths to which Napoleon would go to secure her fortune.

"For your protection," Gwyneth added.

"Yes, I understand, but I feel badly not to mourn my brother."

"But your brother would want you to be kept safe. He hid you away. It won't be forever, just until we know Napoleon has abandoned his efforts to take you back to France."

Amelia brought her hand to her chest. "How awful. I'm glad you're staying with Aunt Euphemia and Ash."

Gabby wondered how the elderly Aunt Euphemia could be of any assistance.

"I appreciate Gwyneth's hospitality, but I hope to soon establish my own residence." Both Aunt Euphemia and Gwyneth had been adamant that she remain with them to allow herself time to recover from her loss and to be assured it was safe to leave Ash's protection.

Gwyneth put her glass down. "Let's not get ahead of ourselves. Today, we're starting with the new wardrobe. Let me show you a few of the newest fabrics that have arrived."

"She must wear blue, don't you agree?" Gwyneth asked.

"Of course, and we've received a lovely lavender. Not an insipid pastel but the coolness of an amethyst."

"Amelia likes bold colors and bold designs. When she was going through a Greek phase, she designed a revealing toga for me. My aunt almost had a conniption. She was speechless, and for my Aunt Euphemia, that is no small feat."

Gabby giggled with the ladies, her spirits buoyed by the easy company and possibly the champagne she had consumed.

The tinkling bell disrupted their amusement.

A reed-slender lady with a narrow face, thin lips, and wide-set, prominent eyes entered on the arm of gentleman in a purple coat with a puce waistcoat. She wore a tightly-fitted, reddish-purple walking dress, almost the same color as her escort's coat. His darkish-brown hair was slicked back away from his high forehead with pomade. In the outmoded manner of a Frenchman of fashion, he stopped and produced a snuff box.

The lady did a slight curtsy. "Miss Bonnington, just the person I had hoped to meet today. And Lady Gwyneth. Such a pleasure." The lady drew out the word "pleasure" in a dusky, seductive voice.

Amelia curtsied. "Lady Sauvage and Lord Weston."

Gwyneth and Gabby remained seated.

"Miss Amelia." Lord Weston bowed then turned to them. "Lady Gwyneth." He bowed again. "You are looking in grand spirits. Marriage must agree with you."

"Thank you, Lord Weston."

Lord Weston searched Gabby's face in interest. Gabby lowered her eyes at the officious man's flagrant perusal.

"I haven't had the pleasure, my lady," Lord Weston said.

"Where are my manners? Lady Sauvage and Lord Weston, this is my dear friend, Lady Gigot."

"Gigot? I don't recall hearing that name." Lady Sauvage's voice dripped with arrogance. "Are you new to society?"

The thin woman's penetrating scrutiny of Gabby's borrowed, ill-fitting dress and bonnet should have made Gabby squirm in the chair. But after her years under Mother Therese's critical scrutiny, this one woman had no effect on her.

"I've just arrived from France," Gabby said.

Knowing the woman wanted her pedigree to decide whether Gabby was worthy of her attention, Gabby tilted her head with insouciance. Because she was an unknown French woman with connections to a very old and powerful English family, she would draw interest and speculation in the very closed society. She wasn't in the least intimidated by the woman's curiosity. She was, after all, the daughter of a marquis.

"My Aunt Euphemia and Lady Gigot's grandmother were close friends. We are bringing our dear family friend into London society," Gwyneth said.

The stylish gentleman bowed grandiosely. "It is a pleasure to meet you, Lady Gigot. I've not seen you at any events. I would remember such a fair flower amongst the ladies."

She wanted to laugh at his exaggerated flatteries. She neither liked nor trusted outrageous adulation. It seemed she preferred straightforward and teasing gentlemen. "I've not been out in society yet."

"Will you be attending the opera to hear Madame Abney sing this week?" He eyed her with hungry curiosity.

Gabby looked to Lady Gwyneth for guidance. "It will depend on my hostess's plans."

"I hope, Lady Gwyneth, you can be convinced to allow your guest time away from your company to attend Coventry Garden. Madame Abney is known throughout Europe for her incredible vocal range and dramatic presentation," he said.

"I've heard about the woman's skill. She was all the conversation," Gabby said.

"In Paris?" Lady Sauvage inquired innocently.

"Yes, my lady." Paris was a big city, and it was less easy to connect Gabby to her title and estate than pretending she was from the country.

"I'm not sure if we'll be attending." Gwyneth interrupted any further questions. "But once Miss Bonnington has assisted Lady Gigot in her wardrobe, she'll be in society."

"Then I hope Miss Bonnington will be speedy in her

assistance," Lord Weston droned as he tilted to one side in an affected manner.

Lady Sauvage's thin lips flattened into a hyphen of displeasure. "But Miss Bonnington, you told me you had no time to consult on my wardrobe."

"Oh, please do not scold Miss Bonnington. I should be the one to receive your reprimand," Gwyneth tittered. "I've imposed on Miss Bonnington's good nature to help our dear family friend."

Gabby suppressed her urge to turn and stare at this incarnation of the icy Lady Gwyneth. Having only seen Gwyneth interact with family and friends, Gabby realized her new friend was polished and very adept at handling prying members of "polite society."

Amelia interrupted. "I've already explained to Lady Sauvage that I've very little time for fashion because of my upcoming wedding."

"Good wishes are in order, Miss Bonnington. Lord Brinsley is a very fortunate man." Lord Weston bowed again.

Gabby found his bobbing up and down quite distracting.

Miss Amelia smiled and curtsied. "Thank you, Lord Weston."

"Miss Bonnington, Lord Kendal was at Lady Roscoe's soiree last night—quite unfortunate that you and the gentleman couldn't come to an agreement. Such a charming man."

Lady Sauvage looked directly at Gabby. "He is also recently arrived from France. Did you by chance meet the very dashing gentleman when you were in Paris, Mademoiselle Gigot?"

Amelia's face turned a blotchy crimson.

"I've not had the pleasure of meeting the gentleman yet. But since he is a relative by marriage to Lady Gwyneth, I'm sure I'll have the privilege soon."

Gabby felt Gwyneth stiffen next to her before Gwyneth brought her glass to her lips. After sipping her champagne, she said in an unrushed and languid tone, "Of course, we are all well pleased by his safe return. I will have to inform my brother of your kindness in mentioning Lord Kendal."

The conversation swirled around Gabby like a fast eddy and wasn't much different than in French drawing rooms, but she never before had to maintain a false identity. Did Lady Sauvage suspect that Gabby was hiding something, or was it the usual social banter in hopes of finding a scandal? And there was no doubt in Gabby's mind that Lady Sauvage would create a scandal if she discovered Gabby's travelling companion.

"Come, Cedric." The lady took the gentleman's arm. "We must not be late for Lady Billingsworth's at home."

Lord Weston bowed again with a great flourish. "I will look forward to seeing you at the opera, my lady." He took out his handkerchief and patted his sweating forehead, probably from the exertion of endless bowing. "A gentleman lives to hope."

Did Gwyneth just snort? Gabby kept her face placid, but she did want to giggle. Perhaps the champagne *was* having its effect.

Amelia's face still showed patches of color on her high cheekbones. After the guests had departed, Amelia reached for her champagne flute. "Of all the nerve for that woman to imply that I was a jilted woman."

Gwyneth snickered. "You really must not care what that vindictive woman believes. She did it for spite because you're not helping with her gowns."

"You're absolutely right, but I don't want her to spread rumors that Derrick wasn't my first choice to marry."

Now Gwyneth laughed heartily, with her mouth wide open in loud guffaws. "Derrick knows that you absolutely adore him."

"I'm sure you think I'm silly, Gabby. I was never in love with Michael. I confused our friendship with love until I met Derrick. But everyone believed we would make a match. There were unkind rumors of why we didn't become engaged. But you must know, Michael never was interested in me that way. We were friends and still are."

Gabby now felt her cheeks getting warm, and, fair-skinned like Amelia, her face became blotchy with embarrassment. "Lord Kendal and I are no more than acquaintances. I owe him a great deal for his assistance in my escape. But do you believe the lady knows about our trip together?"

Gwyneth reached for the champagne bottle to refill their glasses. "I did find Lady Sauvage's comments most interesting. I'm beginning to wonder if she purposefully came to meet Gabby."

"You're right." Amelia put her glass out for Gwyneth to refill. "I had already told her I didn't have time to consult. Why did she appear in the shop today? She didn't have an appointment with Elodie. And no one knew I was meeting you here. And her dress, although very beautiful, wasn't done by Elodie but by Madame Gaillard."

"All very suspicious. Now, I do believe we must make a point of going to the opera, don't you?" Gwyneth mused.

Gabby was surprised by Gwyneth's reaction. She assumed that Gwyneth would want to confer with her husband.

"I agree. It might be helpful to talk further with the inquisitive lady." Amelia nodded.

"It means we've got to pick fabric. Amelia, get to work."

"Yes, my lady." Amelia batted her eyelashes. "Why do I feel we're about to embark on an adventure?"

With French champagne and fine fashion, it seemed all in great fun, but Gabby knew how brutal and dangerous Napoleon's men could be. Intrusive English ladies didn't frighten her in the least. But the idea of returning as a prisoner to France constricted her throat in panic.

CHAPTER THIRTEEN

Gabby's fingers rushed over the keys, pouring her fear and worries into the melancholic melody. Afraid she might splinter and never regain her composure, she spent hours playing the piano, allowing herself a way to express her feelings.

She took a slow breath, trying to come back to herself after the intense outpouring of raw emotions.

Morley, a hefty man with a square chin and crooked nose, knocked then entered the music room. The Ashworth butler was unlike Gaston, their butler at home, who was the epitome of grace and refinement associated with servants in the estate of a French marquis. England was turning out to be a refreshing change from French snobbishness and pomposity.

"I'm sorry to interrupt. Lord Kendal said he was expected."

Gabby's stomach fluttered at the announcement of Michael's surprise visit. His beloved, animated face would be a welcome change from her lonely isolation. Did he have more news of her brother? There was no reason for his visit, since he had provided the news of her brother's duel and the solicitor's information that she had requested.

"Thank you, Morley. I was expecting Lord Kendal," Gabby lied as she stood and walked to the settee. Being seated would help her not rush into his arms. She straightened her dress around her ankles, keeping her hands busy and feeling like a debutante about to receive her first suitor.

"Shall I bring tea, my lady? And shall I summon Lady

Gwyneth?" Morley, likely an ex-soldier, was well trained in his role as butler.

"Tea would be lovely, but don't bother interrupting Lady Gwyneth. Lord Kendal won't be staying long."

Morley bowed. "Yes, my lady."

Pouring tea and observing the social ritual would help her cope if he brought bad news.

Gabby secured the pins holding the top knot of her curls and tugged on Lady Gwyneth's day dress that pulled too tightly across her chest. Although Gwyneth was taller, Gabby was endowed with the full bosom of her Grandmamma Bonnet. Gabby had the wrong shape for the slim lines that Josephine de Beauharnais had brought into style.

"Mademoiselle Gabrielle." Michael bowed.

He was dressed in a blue fitted coat and buff pantaloons that emphasized his strong, lean legs. The perfect gentleman's attire for an earl. Although dressed appropriately, he looked as if had been pulling on his collar, and his hair was windswept, not fixed with pomade like other gentlemen. The close-fitted tailoring of his clothes looked too constraining for his exuberant energy.

"Lord Kendal, a pleasure." It *was* a pleasure to bask in his warm, beaming smile. "Please, will you join me?" Gabby pointed to a chair across from the settee. "Thank you, Morley."

The butler nodded and closed the door.

Once the door was closed, Michael rushed to the settee and seated himself close to her. He took her hands into his, ignoring all rules of her proper behavior and all manners of propriety. "Gabby, I've been so worried about you. I couldn't stay away."

She tried not to respond, but the heat of his strong, calloused palms seeped into her and his fresh, out-of-doors scent soothed her jagged, lonely feelings.

There could be no secret visits between them after today, now that she was going into society. For one brief moment, she would enjoy the safety of his touch. She squeezed his hands back before she released them. "Lord Kendal. I hope you are well."

His words came out dashed and impatient. "How can I be well when all I can think about is you and what you must be enduring?"

Gabby couldn't breathe. She wanted to lean into him and pour her heart out. She wanted to be held and comforted by him. She wanted to go back to their time in France and enjoy the moments of simple pleasure when her future was hopeful and anything was possible between them. She stared at him, wanting him to feel the love and affection she felt.

"I want to help you. Protect you from any distress from your incredible loss."

Of course he wanted to help. He was a good man, but she wasn't his responsibility. It was only a slight chance of fate that brought them together. She couldn't allow herself these feelings. It was too dangerous. And although she would never admit it— too dangerous for her fragile heart.

"You have more news of my brother?"

"Oh, Gabby, please don't shut me out, not when we're alone like this."

She regretted pulling away; he was a dear friend and much more to her. But anyone close to her could be in danger. Napoleon and his men didn't care who they hurt. She didn't want Michael or his family harmed. She would never forgive herself if anything happened to the people he loved.

"But that's the point, we aren't supposed to be alone like this."

She watched his hopeful look fade.

"Please, only this brief moment. After this visit, we must separate and keep the charade up in society. I wouldn't do anything to jeopardize your safety."

Gabby felt the stinging burn behind her eyes. He was as bereft as she, victims of their forced separation and the roles they must play. She couldn't pretend she didn't know how alone and sad she would be after losing his companionship. She couldn't look away from his fervent stare.

"For one moment, I want us to be the two simple people who

unexpectedly came together in France, before I must play my role in keeping you protected. Once this terrible time is finished and we know you're safe, I plan to court you openly and outrageously so that all of London knows of our connection." His eyes gleamed with that wicked, devilish amusement.

She shook her head, but her heart bounded into a lively vivace Bach tempo. She opened her mouth to speak, but Michael placed his finger on her lips.

"Shhh. I'm not expecting you to pledge your feelings to me." His passionate stare held her trapped.

She placed her hand over his fingers. Happy to touch him again. When he was ill, she had become familiar with every part of his face, his bronzed arms, his strong hands. "It's only because of my brother... You feel responsible for me."

Michael pressed his lips to her palm. "Responsibility is not what I feel for you, dearest Gabby. I feel responsible for my sister, my brother, my uncle, and now for most of England. But what I feel for you isn't a responsibility. It's much more."

Gabby shook her head. "I..."

"Please say nothing. I know I have no claim on your feelings. But I want you to know that I will always be your friend, and much more if you let me. I will stand by you always as a friend if that is all you desire."

She couldn't stop the tremble in her voice or the joy bubbling up. "Thank you. I am grateful for your offer of friendship, since I have so few friends in England."

"Once you come out into society, you'll have more gentlemen friends than you could possibly wish for. It is going to be very difficult to see you in society and hide my feelings, but I promise I will be a man of judicious behavior and manner."

And then the charming, boyish smile, lethal to all ladies, crossed his face.

"Can you achieve such a thing?" she teased. "Judicious behavior? I've only witnessed outrageous behavior."

It felt good to joke and laugh together again. He made her forget the gravity of her circumstances and her grief. She loved his open nature. She loved his lightheartedness, despite his title and wealth. She loved him. She'd fallen in love with his *joie de vivre* during their escape from Paris.

No matter how she tried to deny her feelings, he would always own her heart. But, like him, she must make the choice to protect him, because she cared too.

"You wretch!" He pulled on one of the curls that had fallen down from her topknot. "How little faith. But you must promise me."

"Michael, I can't promise…" She shook her head again. How could she make promises?

"Wait to hear my request. It's not what you think. Promise me you won't marry anyone else until I have a chance to court you too. I want you to be the belle of the season. And enjoy all the things you've missed in the convent. You deserve happiness, but promise me that I'll get a chance when our association isn't dangerous."

Happiness. Was it possible? Her life had only been about surviving. "I've thought if I married right away, Napoleon's men wouldn't pursue me. But then I realized Napoleon wouldn't honor an English marriage and would just have it annulled in France."

Michael took both her hands between his. "Exactly. It's why we must keep you hidden until he gives up pursuing you and has married his brother to another woman."

Michael caressed her hands. "I won't let anyone hurt you, Gabby."

She lowered her eyes since she didn't want to betray her tender feelings for him.

"And then I'm going to enjoy being your persistent, tenacious suitor."

Whatever the future brought, she would always hold this day and his pledge close to her heart. "I don't plan to marry anytime soon."

"You haven't been out in society. Once you make your appearance, you're going to cause a riot in the *ton*."

She scoffed. She was French, with no title now and past the

age of debutantes. "And while I'm being the belle of the season, what will you be doing? Pursuing Yvette or Mimi?"

"Forget Yvette and Mimi. I never would have…" He shook his head and gave her his lost puppy look that always softened her. He didn't know the potent effect his sorrowful, apologetic looks did to her insides…to her heart.

"Oh, Gabby, you're too innocent. All men have pasts."

"And is your past filled with a lot of Yvettes and Mimis?"

"Gabby." He leaned forward and pushed one of her errant curls behind her ear.

His tender touch sent tremors and shivers through her body, making her heart sing.

"The past doesn't matter. It is only the future that matters. And my future is only filled with Gabby." His voice lowered while he gently touched her cheek.

She leaned into his rough, warm hand. She wanted to believe the past made no difference, but she could never escape her past. She would always be pursued for her lineage and wealth while Napoleon was in power. Was it too much to hope for a future together with Michael. "We must stay apart." If she didn't love him, the separation wouldn't hurt this much.

The door swung open. Gabby pulled away from Michael as he jumped to his feet.

Gwyneth, with Amelia, swept into the room. "Morley told me of your arrival, Lord Kendal." Gwyneth looked between them. "Did I dally long enough?"

"Lady Gwyneth." Michael bowed, missing Gwyneth's raised eyebrows, which were directed at Gabby.

"And Miss Bonnington." Michael's voice had turned to teasing. "About to be married? I go away for a few months, and my sister marries a humorless chap and you're about to marry a brute."

Amelia snickered. "Derrick isn't a brute. He is just a very large man."

Gwyneth sat next to Gabby. She whispered, "Everything all right?"

Gabby smiled and nodded.

"A large man, you say?" Michael walked toward Amelia as if stalking her. "Amelia, how risqué!"

Amelia tried to punch Michael's shoulder, but he dodged her arm and lifted her in his arms and swung her in a circle. "Now, there's my favorite tomboy."

Watching the easy friendship between Michael and Amelia stirred Gabby's feelings of envy and loss. All her friends lucky enough to escape the guillotine had fled France or were in hiding.

Amelia laughed heartily.

He swung her once more. "My sister with a man who doesn't care about linguistics. And you with a man who doesn't look like he can run between the Cricket posts."

"Incorrigible." Amelia huffed when Michael put her down. She straightened the bandeau holding her flowing red hair. "I can see your adventure in France hasn't made any difference in your sense of propriety. Miss Gabby has her work cut out for her."

Michael turned and winked at Gabby as if she were used to twirling and laughing in drawing rooms. And, in that moment, she wanted a lifetime of twirling and laughing with Michael.

CHAPTER FOURTEEN

Michael held his position in front of the mirror until he could no longer stand it. He exhaled loudly, impatient for his ham-fisted valet to tie his cravat. "Too tight, old man."

"It wouldn't be if you didn't jump around like a dog with ticks."

"Tut, tut. Manners, Denby."

"Yes, my lord." Denby pulled hard on the white linen, causing Michael to jerk his head back, as his valet intended.

"Denby, pack your bags. Your services are not needed now that we've left France."

"That's not what Lord Rathbourne said." Denby assisted Michael into his jacket. "He said I was to keep an eye on you with your new assignment."

"My new assignment is to entertain an opera singer. How dangerous can that be?"

"Women can be more treacherous than men," Denby growled. "They use their erotic charms on you, and before you know it you're believing everything they say."

Michael had only met one dangerous woman, a crafty woman disguised as a schoolboy. Gabby's gentle nature and sweet voluptuous body were a formidable and irresistible trial. Her rounded derriere in breeches appeared repeatedly in his daydreams.

He sighed out loud. "Sounds like you were burned by a woman, Denby."

Denby winked at Michael in the mirror. "Lucky you've

recovered from your injury. Might be a bit awkward with your new assignment, you know what I mean."

Michael noticed how adroitly Denby changed topics. "Yes, I get your meaning."

"Speaking of your injuries, when do you plan to see Miss Gabby?" Denby brushed off the shoulders of Michael's evening jacket. "Really tough about her brother. And after all her solicitous care of you. You owe her."

"I'm very aware of what I owe her." He stepped away from Denby's ministrations, irritated that even his valet-cum-bodyguard reminded him of his need to maintain his distance from Gabby.

"I'm glad she's got Ashworth to protect her." Denby grunted. "She's a brave little thing. But we know Napoleon's henchmen are treacherous."

"Your guilt-inducing tactics are not going to work, Denby. You trying to make me feel bad doesn't matter. I already do, but everyone has warned me off, including Gabby."

"She probably doesn't want you to feel responsible for her, independent as she is."

"Damn you. Of course, I feel responsible for her."

Denby handed white gloves to Michael. "There must be something we could do."

If Denby only knew how often Michael considered the ways to help Gabby. He was trying to only think about her safety, but no matter, all he did was think of Gabby.

He considered allowing the rumors to circulate that he had travelled with Gabby. She then would be forced to marry him. But that was no solution, as Gabby pointed out—Napoleon would never honor an English marriage. Besides, he could never promote any rumor besmirching Gabby's reputation. It could blow her cover. And his, for that matter.

She deserved time to decide what she wanted. She was very clear she didn't want to escape one forced marriage only to have another forced upon her. He wanted her to have choices. As long as she chose him.

"Is the carriage ready?"

"Yes, my lord." Denby faked his punctilious servant's mode. "Remember I'll be at the tavern right across from Covent Garden, if you need me tonight."

"Why in earth would I need you tonight?"

"In case the lady takes you captive. Or decides to shoot you in the arse."

"Very humorous, I'm sure." Michael walked out of the room.

Michael leaned back in the velvet seat and crossed his legs, playing the part of a bored gentleman, to see and to be seen by his fellow members of the *ton*. He had never before attended the opera to enjoy the music. He and his fellow chums came for the dancers who flitted across the stage in flimsy costumes.

He pulled at his constricting collar. Damn Denby for making it so tight. Although he threatened regularly to fire his bodyguard, he had enjoyed the close comradery of the ex-army officer. Michael hadn't known until he had been shot that Denby had been assigned to protect him during his time in France.

And Denby was still guarding him. Another reminder that the French spies who had infiltrated the opera company were dangerous. He could be offended that his new brother-in-law didn't think he could handle himself, but this wasn't a time for vanity. England was at war. He had a unique and important skill set to help win the war. No one except Henrietta had his skills, and like Rathbourne, he didn't want his sister to put herself in harm's way.

The usual boisterous crowd hushed suddenly. Michael moved forward to look over the balcony to see who or what had prompted the self-absorbed aristocrats to cease their conversation and draw their attention away from themselves. The main floor was crowded with the usual young bucks, all of them staring up at a box across from him.

He followed their enraptured gazes to see who had captured

their drunken interest and had them staring with their mouths open. In a box across from him, three women, conversing together, sat down, unaware of the dramatic entrance they had made.

Michael's heart thumped against his chest at the sight of Gabby, her long curls in a bandeau with blue feathers and matching gown. Although he couldn't see her eyes, he knew the blue in her feathers and in her dress exactly matched the cerulean color of her eyes. He also knew her smooth cheeks would be flushed with spots of color.

Gabby moved forward to look at the stage. Her generous bosom pressed against the balcony railing when she leaned forward in her low-cut gown, causing an uproar. The young bucks in the pits cheered with raucous hoots and whoops. Jealousy and outrage combusted in a fiery flash through Michael's body. He was going to skewer Ashworth for bringing her out into society in this outrageous manner. And what was the purpose of subterfuge if she had every man in London wanting to know her and just plain wanting her?

Amelia and Lady Gwyneth sat on either side of Gabby. Three gentlemen stood in the shadows, behind the women. Of course, Ashworth and Brinsley didn't want to draw attention to themselves. Michael couldn't see the third gentleman, who must be Gabby's escort. Gritty, dark jealousy writhed in his gut. Another man was close to Gabby, who was dressed in that revealing, indecent gown.

Michael was interrupted in his deadly musings when there was a smattering of applause as the orchestra members entered the pit. The maestro took up his baton and the music started as polite society went back to their conversation, blissfully ignoring the Prologue. More interested in themselves, they all waited for Madame Abney and her arias and her dramatic acting.

Michael tried to turn away from watching Gabby and focus on the task of listening to Giacomelli's opera of the Greek myth, *Merope.* But he couldn't look away from Gabby. Thoughts of another man escorting her, touching her, twisted in him like a sharp and deadly knife blade.

Unable to help himself, he stared at Gabby, wanting her to feel the connection between them—that she knew he was nearby, that she belonged to him, only him. He watched her flutter her fan in front of her face.

Amelia leaned over and spoke to Gabby. He watched Gabby abruptly look up and then across at him. He held his breath. She gave a quick and barely discernable nod before turning toward the stage.

He wanted to go to her at intermission and make it clear to everyone she was his. He gave himself a good mental shake about why he had to keep his distance. His overwhelming need for this one woman couldn't trump his mission to find the French spies. But above all, Gabby's safety was his first priority.

And, unlike Ashworth and Brinsley, he wasn't at the opera to guard Gabby. It burned him to realize that other men were responsible for her. But he would do everything he could to protect her, even if it meant ignoring her. He leaned back in his seat and tried to clear his mind of the soft desirable woman across the theater.

He took a slow, deep breath and tried to replace his fantasy of undressing Gabby to the intricate pattern of the singing. What a crack assignment! Gabby threw off his game—his superior skill to focus and analyze data. And what a dangerous and delightful distraction, his gentle Gabby.

Involved in visualizing the trills from the horn section, he jumped when he heard the door to his box open.

Damnation. He hadn't planned on the appearance of his friends from university. With his rummy friends' entrance came the pungent smell of whiskey and cigar smoke. Swirling his cane, the Earl of Felton sauntered into the box, his cravat and thick hair askew. "Kendal, why are you up here alone?"

The enormous Baron Chalmers barely fit when he plopped down in the ornamental chair next to Michael. Chalmers was a solid mass of muscle, which made him a good man to have around in the event of a tavern brawl. "Are you here to see her too?"

Michael stared at his Oxford compatriots, whose life interests were women, gambling, and boxing. Neither of them were remotely interested in opera or Madame Abney. Their tastes ran more to voluptuous opera dancers. Only a new opera dancer would have enticed these two to abandon a gambling den.

"I'm here to see her too," Michael joked. "I've heard her high C is spectacular."

Fenton snorted and Chalmers guffawed loudly, drawing the entire audience's attention to their box. Being in the company of his rakish friends would work well in hiding his real purpose in pursuing the prima donna.

Fenton bent over and placed his hand on Michael's forehead. "Did you suffer a brain fever while in France?"

Michael tried not to show any reaction to how close Fenton was to the truth.

Chalmers turned his chair to face Michael with his back to the stage. "You always were cagey." Chalmers pointed to Gabby's box. "He has the perfect view. Pretending he came for the music..." Chalmers shook his head. "His box is directly across from the delicate flower."

Fenton indolently sat back in the chair and crossed his legs. "He wants her for himself."

Chalmers guffawed again. Had his friend always been this loud?

Michael's irritation with his friends was mounting at a pace with their loathsome implications. These two idiots couldn't possibly have attended the opera because of Gabby.

"Hate to break it you, old chap, but Weston beat you."

"Would either of you muffleheads tell me about whom you're talking?"

Fenton clapped him on the back. "As if you don't know."

Chalmers leaned out of the box, looking down in the pit. "You're trying to make us believe you didn't just see the display of those fine womanly attributes." Chalmers turned back with his hands held in front of him as if holding two oranges.

Although Chalmers outweighed and outsized him, Michael was going to mangle the giant before he killed him.

Fenton took a whiskey flask out of his pocket. "I thought Hopwood was going to have a heart seizure."

"If you two pop-in-jays don't explain what you're talking about, I swear I'll…"

"No need to name call." Chalmers then took out his flask and guzzled whiskey. He handed the silver flask to Michael, who now was in need of strong alcohol. Chalmers took another swig after Michael. "You'll what?"

"Tell me who you are referring to now." His face must be turning purple by now from the strain of "communicating" with his dense friends.

Fenton slowly inspected Michael's face. "You really don't know?"

"Would I be asking you if I knew?"

"Mademoiselle Gigot, newly arrived from Paris."

Barbarity and violence conflagrated into a hot, fiery ball in Michael's chest. He had never in all the years of friendship hated his friends as he did at this moment.

Fenton pulled at his cravat. "Why aren't you escorting mademoiselle for her first night in society? She lives with Rathbourne's sister, and with your sister being married to Rathbourne you should have beat Weston out."

"He's keeping his distance, obviously, since he's worried he'll get caught in the marriage trap," Chalmers ventured.

"Weston is looking for a wife?" Fenton untied his cravat. "But what about Weston's affair with Lady Sauvage?"

"I never believed it would last. Weston wasn't the lady's usual type. Rumor is that she has unique interests," Chalmers added.

"I bet I could get her to sing high C." Fenton chuckled before he took another swig of whiskey.

Michael didn't need to say anything, which at this moment

was a good thing. Fenton and Chalmers kept the conversation going without any response from him.

"Confess, Kendal. Too close for comfort? Worried Rathbourne will force you to get leg shackled?" Fenton squinted, trying to get Michael's face in focus and clearly not at all in tune to Michael's foul mood.

"Might not be a problem. I heard Ashworth is her protector," Chalmers said.

"Damn, Chalmers, you're an idiot. Ashworth will kill you if you repeat that to anyone else," Fenton said.

Michael was going to kill Chalmers so it didn't matter. Michael took a slow breath, trying to bring his out-of-control feelings back into control. He didn't want to show any reaction and alert his friends to his interest in Gabby, since they would spread that gossip throughout London tomorrow. "How do you know so much about the lady?"

"I told you he was a cagey one." Chalmers beamed in pleasure as if he had translated a Greek cypher.

Fenton ran his hand through his disheveled locks. "I can't remember. Can you, Chalmers?"

Chalmers shifted in the small chair that barely accommodated him. "Weston. He's been going on about her beauty in the clubs. He met her at a dress shop while he was with Lady Sauvage. The mademoiselle was with Lady Gwyneth and Miss Amelia."

"You're wrong, Chalmers. The first time we heard about her was at Mrs. Billingsworth's home. Weston went on about how ravishing she was. I heard him say it was love at first sight," Felton added.

"And he didn't care if Lady Sauvage heard him," Chalmers added.

"So you've met the chit at Rathbourne's house? I was told her mother was friends with Rathbourne's aunt," Fenton said.

"I've not met her." Michael adjusted the cuffs on his shirt. "I've been very busy with my own estate, since I was gone for months."

"Then why are you here? And don't try to hoodwink us that you like opera."

"To meet Madame Abney. I've been told she's a very attractive and unique woman." Michael waggled his eyebrows. The implication would never be lost on those two, not after all their shared adventures.

Chalmers guffawed again. And Fenton said, "Now that sounds more like you, old man. For a while you had me worried."

CHAPTER FIFTEEN

Irritated by the interruption to the salacious details of Josephine de Beauharnais's latest affair, Joseph Fouché, barked, "I'm going to run you through."

Lesser men, *most* men in fact, would have been screaming for their mothers in the line of fire of the Minister of Police's ire. But not his assistant, who walked stiffly but quickly into the center of the spacious office.

Fouché looked across his ornate Louis XIV desk. "I told you I was not to be disturbed unless it was Napoleon himself."

His efficient and ruthless assistant bowed. "Sir, I apologize..."

And right on the heels of his assistant was his rival, Charles Talleyrand, the Foreign Minister, who was as adroit as Fouché in retaining power during the constantly changing politics in France.

The look of shock on his assistant's face at the Minister's effrontery was worth the interruption. Anatole, a cold-blooded assassin, intimidated most of Paris, but obviously not Charles Talleyrand.

Fouché nodded to Anatole, who promptly turned and closed the door.

Confident that he was untouchable, even to Fouché, Talleyrand strode into the office. Fouché couldn't chance disfavor with Napoleon by physically harming his top diplomat, but it didn't stop Fouché from blatantly spying on Talleyrand's activities and attempting at every opportunity to discredit the arrogant aristocrat.

Fouché quickly closed the report on his desk and placed the

document in the drawer and locked it. His rapid actions weren't lost on the observant Talleyrand.

"To what do I owe the honor of a visit from the Foreign Minister? It must be of great import to have you scurry away from your peace negotiations."

His arch nemesis smiled. It never was fun to bait Talleyrand since he never responded, but it didn't stop Fouché from trying to rattle the poised diplomat.

"The First Consul has sent me to express his concern over a matter he considers to be of vital importance."

Fouché was always entertained by the diplomat's indirect manner of speaking. In contrast, Fouché's manner was direct—blackmail, assassins, torture.

"Indeed, please be seated. A brandy?"

Talleyrand inspected the Fragonard pastoral scene mounted behind Fouché's desk. Fouché, adroit at reading people, saw the flicker of surprise in Talleyrand's eyes. Talleyrand assumed that he was too uncouth to appreciate a masterpiece. The Foreign Minister most likely assumed that Fouché, with his violent nature, would have scenes from the Spanish inquisition. Fouché favored those graphic and gory depictions for his bedroom.

"No brandy." Talleyrand flicked his wrist. "I won't be long."

Fouché sat behind his desk with his Baccarat glass filled with the heavy Armagnac. He leaned back against his chair with a practiced nonchalance despite his heart pounding, searching his mind for what would have precipitated the sudden appearance of the Foreign Minister.

"Bonaparte wants information from your vast resources."

"Of course, I am at the First Consul's service."

As Minister of Police, his network of spies kept him informed on everything that happened in France and throughout Europe. Napoleon might be the First Consul, but Fouché, with his humble beginnings, had amassed an empire of spies, thieves, criminals, and aristocrats, all of whom reported to him. Nothing of significance escaped his notice.

"You have detained Mother Therese for questioning. Why?"

His suddenly sweaty palms made him grip the glass tighter. "A nun? For questioning?"

"Don't act like a coy virgin with me."

Fouché took a slow sip, giving him time to consider the ramifications and possibilities of leverage with the information he possessed. "The First Consul is very interested in finding Mademoiselle de Valmont, isn't that correct?"

Talleyrand fingered the enormous gold bishop's ring he continued to wear, despite the fact that he openly lived with a married woman. Oh, yes. Fouché knew all the details of his affair.

"Now I recall. I thought the nun might know the location of Mademoiselle de Valmont."

Here was the tricky part. Valmont had hidden his sister in the convent to protect her from Fouché. Did Talleyrand know that Fouché had tried to use the mademoiselle to blackmail Valmont to work against Talleyrand and his espionage plans in England? He used Valmont, Talleyrand's agent, as part of a bigger scheme to discredit Talleyrand in Napoleon's eyes. If the First Consul ever learned of Fouché's treason…

"Surely you know that Mademoiselle Gabrielle was placed in the convent for the last years by Valmont while he spied for you in England?" Fouché asked.

"No, I was not aware. And the reason why her brother felt a need to hide her?"

"I've no idea." Fouché would never confess. This was the game of cat and mouse they played.

Stroking his weak chin, the Foreign Minister scrutinized Fouché's face. Talleyrand and his spies probably already knew the reason.

"And has Mother Therese told you who Valmont was protecting his sister from?"

"No, she won't speak."

"You realize Mother Therese is from the Gascony family. Her brother is a high-ranking official. The First Consul is most displeased. You are to release her immediately."

Fouché shrugged. He was finished with her anyway since he

hadn't been able to extract any useful information from her. Not that he would ever admit defeat by a nun.

"Did the sister give you leads on Mademoiselle de Valmont's whereabouts?"

This was the tricky part. If he admitted he didn't have anything, Talleyrand would never believe the lie and, at the same time, he needed to redeem himself in Napoleon's eyes and give all appearances as if he were sharing vital information.

"The First Consul is still interested in marrying the girl to Jerome?"

"Yes, her brother's fortune was taken out of the country. Napoleon wants the money and the girl."

Fouché wanted to find the girl to prevent her from revealing that he had threatened to harm her if her brother didn't do the dirty work in England. There was a small chance the girl didn't know of his involvement.

"My belief is that she escaped with the English spy, Lord Kendal. It is the connection that would tie the nun to Mademoiselle's disappearance. I've had my men looking for her and Kendal since they both disappeared from Paris."

Talleyrand never wavered in his direct inspection of Fouché, watching for any indication of falsehood. "Yes, I believe that is the best avenue of inquiry."

Not surprising. Talleyrand's league of spies was also following Kendal.

"Anything else you'd like to share with the First Consul? He is most impatient to get this situation resolved."

Definitely not his plan of killing the girl after he had gained access to her fortune. Since there were no remaining family members, it would be easy to convince the young girl to sign over the funds.

"Of course you will keep me informed of your activities and any information you've gleaned from your contacts." Talleyrand stood, dismissing him.

Over his dead body. "I will serve the First Consul in every task."

CHAPTER SIXTEEN

With the end of the first act of *La Merope*, the ladies rose from the velvet-covered gilt chairs. Gwyneth linked her arm with Gabby's. "Let's see if my husband remembered to order the champagne."

"Ash wouldn't forget." Amelia exited the box right behind Gabby and Gwyneth.

The gentlemen waited for them in the lavishly decorated hallway. The hallway matched the ornate fashion in the red velvet boxes, hung with heavy crimson drapes tied back with gold tassels.

The men had escaped the opera fifteen minutes into the performance with the excuse that they didn't want the ladies to be exposed to their cigar smoke.

Lord Ashworth handed his wife a glass of champagne from a heavy silver tray held patiently by a waiter.

"I thought you might be thirsty after all your serious attention to the music," Lord Ashworth said.

"Very humorous, husband of mine," Gwyneth teased.

Lord Ashworth handed flutes to both Gabby and Amelia. "Did my wife listen to any of the music?"

Gwyneth poked her husband in the side with her elbow. "Not fair. Amelia and I had a lot to tell Gabby, since she is new to society."

"Are you enjoying the opera?" Lord Weston moved next to Gabby.

What could Gabby say? She could barely listen to the music

with Gwyneth and Amelia pointing out notables and gossiping. Amelia liked discussing everyone's clothing choices, and Gwyneth knew how everyone was related and whether they had speaking relationships or were estranged.

Neither woman was catty. Their only criticisms were reserved for the men who treated their wives harshly. And the ladies' conversation had given her plenty of time to watch Michael. She snuck peeks at him and his friends, who seemed to be having a grand time. Michael never looked back at her once his friends joined him. She needed to become accustomed to seeing him out in society. Tonight was easy with Michael at a distance and only in the company of men. He was back to his old life, his old ways.

"Yes, I'm finding Giacomelli's *La Merope* very enjoyable. Do you enjoy opera?" Gabby asked.

Since Lord Brinsley had pressured Lord Weston to join the men in the hallway, neither Gabby nor Lord Weston had heard very much of the music.

"How often did you attend the opera in Paris?" Lord Weston examined Gabby's face closely.

Avoiding any personal disclosures, Gabby took her time answering, fluttering her fan in front of her face. Lord Weston had shared that his mother was French and he had spent a great deal of time in France as a child. He also persisted in asking questions about Gabby's past.

"I'm very fond of all music, and I especially enjoy the lush orchestration of French opera."

The noise in the hallway was getting louder as people gathered outside their boxes. Gwyneth and Lord Ashworth were surrounded by a large group of people, mainly gentlemen. Gabby heard her name mentioned several times. She hoped these weren't the same gentlemen from the main floor who stared at her throughout the entire first act. It had been quite disconcerting to draw such attention when she was trying to avoid scrutiny. She hadn't realized it, but the chatting with Gwyneth and Amelia had helped her relax and briefly forget that a kidnapper could be lurking among these men.

She looked toward Lord Ashworth, who had been tasked with protecting her. Laughing with a gentleman, his posture was relaxed, but his eyes were vigilant, scanning the crowd.

Lord Brinsley, with his massive shoulder propped against the wall in relaxed posture, looked down at his fiancée's face, seemingly unaware of anyone but Amelia. The still manner with which he held himself didn't fool Gabby. He was ready to react if needed.

Lord Weston had slowly maneuvered their position, turning so that Gabby's back was away from the crowd and she was separated from her friends.

"I was too young when we used to visit our French relatives. I know very little of French opera," Lord Weston said.

Gwyneth came from behind and touched Gabby's arm, causing her to startle. "Pardon me, but there are two gentlemen who wish to make your acquaintance." Gwyneth whispered to Gabby so that Lord Weston wouldn't overhear. "The entire male population of London wants to meet you, but these two are actually trustworthy." She smiled and nodded to a gentleman who stood nearby.

"Mademoiselle Gigot, may I present Lord Fenton."

A very handsome man with disheveled chestnut-brown hair, as if he had run his fingers through his thick locks, and a wrinkled and loosely tied cravat, took her hand and bowed. "A pleasure, my lady." His devilish grin told her that he knew his ruffled appearance didn't lessen his appeal with the ladies.

"And Lord Chalmers," Gwyneth said before turning back to her husband who had taken her arm.

Lord Chalmers bowed only his head, since the crowd around them had grown, preventing him bending his immense size. The massive gentleman had been in the box with Michael. These men were Michael's friends.

Lord Felton nodded. "Weston."

Lord Weston tilted his head. "Felton. Chalmers. Surprising to find you two at the opera. You came to hear Madame Abney?"

By the strong smell of whiskey and their jovial manner during the performance, Gabby doubted either was interested in music. Most likely they shared Michael's interest in Yvettes and Mimis, the usual reason men of their caliber came to the opera.

Lord Felton leaned on his onyx-head cane. "We came to celebrate with our good friend Kendal, who has been out of the country."

"And he came to see Madame Abney." Chalmers winked at Weston.

Gabby fanned her face, hiding her jealousy at hearing about Michael's interest in the very attractive and very dramatic diva.

"That sounds more like Kendal." Weston laughed, but neither man joined him. "Couldn't imagine any of you attending the opera to enjoy the beauty of music."

Before Lord Weston's patronizing conversation, Gabby had been enjoying his company.

Lord Felton gazed at Gabby. "Weston, you're right. I hadn't realized how much beauty could be found at the opera."

Lord Felton was a very attractive man, but his flatteries had no effect on her. She was partial to dimpled smiles.

A gong sounded in the hallway.

Lord Chalmers leaned down and directed his conversation to Gabby. "Will you be attending Lady Burney's party after the opera?"

"Not tonight. I'll be retiring after the performance."

Lord Felton placed his hand over his heart. "I'm heartbroken. Until we meet again, fair lady."

Chalmers chuckled. "Fenton and I will look forward to our next meeting, my lady."

The gong sounded again, warning the patrons to promptly return to their seats.

Lord Weston clasped her elbow. For a brief moment, Gabby was jostled closer to him when the throng of people surrounded her.

Lord Weston kept a tight grip on her elbow while he directed her into the box, trying to negotiate around all the gentlemen who wanted to meet her.

Oblivious to the bumping, Lord Weston asked, "Were you able to hear Madame Abney sing in Paris? She reportedly was a favored choice of Josephine de Beauharnais."

Gabby felt like the air was trapped in her lungs, as if she were confined under water. This reference to Napoleon's wife. Did Lord Weston know who she was? Gabby had been enjoying the evening despite the public attention. But now fear flitted across her skin causing her to shiver despite the hot, crowded space.

She swallowed and tried to answer in a normal voice. "Tonight is the first time I've heard Madame Abney sing. She is a very talented and very dramatic singer."

Gwyneth smiled at Gabby when they entered the box and patted the chair next to her.

Gabby sat, focusing careful attention to spreading her gown around her feet in order to hide her apprehension.

Lord Ashworth leaned down and whispered to his wife, "You're more beautiful and definitely more dramatic than any opera singer."

Lady Gwyneth giggled. "Me? Dramatic? To whom have you been talking?"

Lord Ashworth gave his wife a tender, possessive look that made Gabby look away. She was beginning to like these people. They were good people and very generous in welcoming her, a stranger who was dangerous to know.

CHAPTER SEVENTEEN

Gabby hurried into her bedroom after the long evening, relieved to finally be free of the demands of polite society. She was a strange combustion of unfamiliar emotions after dinner and the opera. Not being able to speak to Michael, Lord Weston pressing his attentions on her, and the forced gaiety was too much. She had spent hours in the convent longing for the society of witty conversation, beautiful gowns, and handsome gentlemen, but tonight's experience left only a hollow feeling.

"Mademoiselle, you look tired. The evening was too much?" Melie, her maid, spoke in rapid French. The daughter of a French baron, Melie was left a penniless orphan after the Terror. The young woman had escaped France and now survived by sewing for Elodie's modiste shop.

Amelia had sent Melie to be Gabby's maid—a sympathetic gesture that touched Gabby deeply. Amelia had understood how alone Gabby felt in in a new country, in an English household. Having a French maid who had also lived through the terrible time helped Gabby's homesickness.

"It was a wonderful evening." It wasn't a total lie. Gabby had enjoyed hearing Madame Abney sing. The prima donna had a commanding control of her voice and understood the nuances of the music. "But you are correct, I am tired."

Melie assisted Gabby out of her pelisse. With the satin and lace pelisse draped over her arm, Melie took the garment to be hung. Speaking aloud in French, Melie admired the fine workmanship of Gabby's clothing.

Gabby sat down in front of the intricately carved lady's vanity to remove the reticule from her wrist. She opened the delicate blue satin bag for her rose petal lip pomade. Expecting to find extra hairpins and her handkerchief, she felt a slip of paper. She opened the string purse wider and removed the folded sheet.

She unfolded the mysterious note. In bold French script, the words burned through her brain. *Your life is in danger. Trust no one. The English are lying to you.*

Her heart pounded sharp blows inside her chest, making it difficult for her to breathe.

Returning to the bedroom, Melie asked, "What were the other ladies' gowns like? As beautiful as yours? I wonder how many were wearing Elodie's creations."

Gabby startled with Melie's sudden appearance. Her hands shook and she struggled to quickly place the note back into the reticule.

She couldn't think. Her speeding heart resonated in her ears. Her whole world shifted. Desperate to be alone, she wanted to dismiss Melie and examine the note more carefully.

Gabby stood slowly, her knees shaky. To not cause any suspicion, she needed to endure the painstaking nighttime ritual of undressing. Suppressing the need to hurry the earnest maid, Gabby stood still while her mind raced like the furious prestissimo tempo. The long row of pearl buttons in the back of her evening gown would take forever to unbutton.

Gabby already knew she was in danger, but who would send such an ominous warning and for what purpose? A letter in French, a cautioning against trusting the English—the writer must be French. Or was that the deduction the writer intended?

Afraid of harming the fine stitching around each button hole, Melie carefully slipped her finger underneath the fabric before she unfastened each button.

Constrained and frustrated by this newest threat, Gabby fidgeted. What had the French been advising her against? And what had the English lied to her about?

"I won't be too much longer, mademoiselle. Only two more buttons."

Of course, Melie wouldn't miss Gabby's agitation. And Gabby had felt she was doing a convincing job of standing still. Finally, exhaling a loud sigh, Gabby stepped out of her dress.

"I'll wear my chemise for now. My robe, please."

"Yes, mademoiselle."

Wrapped in her new silk robe, Gabby sat on the tiny lady's chair covered in midnight blue satin, perfectly matching the blue damask drapes and bedclothes. After seeing the color of Gabby's eyes, Gwyneth had been adamant that she stay in the blue room. Gwyneth and Amelia were kind and ingenious women. Gabby couldn't believe her new friends were lying to her and for what reason or benefit. But which English could the letter be referring to?

Melie began the process of undoing the hairstyle she had earlier spent hours creating. Slowly the maid removed the pins and then the bandeau, then she reached for the hairbrush.

Gabby's impatience combusted. "It won't be necessary, Melie. I'll brush my hair myself." Gabby tried to sound blasé, but the beating panic made her desperate. She would never be free, never escape Napoleon and his manipulations.

"But mademoiselle, I must brush your locks."

Melie was new as a lady's maid and took her position very seriously. "I've a headache, Melie. I'd like to be alone now."

Melie's cheeks flushed with color. "Yes, my lady."

She didn't want to hurt the young woman's fragile feelings, but Gabby truly couldn't withstand any more consideration and concern.

Gabby softened her voice and smiled at Melie. "A lady should brush her hair each night, but there are nights when I am too tired to care about the beauty ritual. It will be our little secret."

"Your hair is shiny and thick, mademoiselle. You needn't worry if you skip some nights." Melie's sunny, heart-shaped face shone back at Gabby in the mirror.

Melie's diligent efforts to succeed at her new job was a reminder to Gabby that she wasn't the only one who had suffered and was still suffering from the chaos and violence in France. The innocent always suffered in these wars waged over men's need for power.

"Melie, you have been a tremendous help, but I'm ready to retire."

"Of course, my lady. I could make you a tisane to help you sleep."

"No, no. It's not necessary."

"If there is anything else you need?"

"No, Melie, you may retire too. It's been a long evening for both of us."

"Thank you, mademoiselle. I wish you a restful sleep."

When Melie wished Gabby a restful sleep, Gabby felt a giggle rise up inside her. She covered her mouth with her hands. Maybe she was closer to hysteria than she realized. When Melie finally closed the door, Gabby grabbed the reticule and retrieved the note.

She couldn't stop her hands from shaking while she unfolded the paper. She moved the candle closer to examine the vellum. The writer's script had dramatic flourishes, most likely the handwriting of a woman.

How had someone been able to place the letter in her reticule without her noticing? She reviewed the events of her evening. She had returned to her room after dinner so that Melie could attend to her toilet. Melie had helped her slip the reticule on her wrist after she had donned her pelisse. And for the rest of the evening the reticule had been securely on her wrist. Only Lord Weston had been close enough to be able to slip a note into her reticule. He was the most likely candidate since it seemed unlikely that her English friends would warn her against themselves.

There had been a brief moment in the crowded hallway when it was possible for another one of the gentlemen to have placed the note. Lord Fenton had stood close to her when she turned to speak with Lord Chalmers. Was it possible he had placed the note? Were they working together and Lord Chalmers had been a distraction?

The only logical suspect was Lord Weston, since he had spent the most time with Gabby. But if he had concerns, why hadn't he spoken them aloud? And how could she ask him about the English lies without revealing the existence of the letter?

Gabby dropped on her bed, her thoughts spinning with possibilities. She tried to think logically, but the bleak knowledge that she had no one she could trust agitated her. Why had Lucien died? How was she supposed to go on?

She thought of the only person she truly trusted in England. How could she tell Michael when the note implied his friends and family were liars?

Gabby held the note to her heart, trying to stop the dark thoughts from overwhelming her. Tomorrow she wouldn't be so overwhelmed. Tomorrow she would search for the writer of the note. Tomorrow had to be easier.

CHAPTER EIGHTEEN

Michael bowed over Madame Abney's hand. The diva reclined across a purple sofa in a brightly colored, revealing dressing robe. "A pleasure, Madame."

Michael wanted to bite his tongue. What was he thinking?

Already he couldn't breathe in the stifling airless room with closed windows. The drawing room, as was the entrance way of her townhouse, was overflowing with heavily scented bouquets of roses, lilies, and freesia. His bouquet from last night, one of many, was lost in the sea of blossoms.

A grand piano was the centerpiece of the room, almost outshining the lounging diva. Michael had learned that the louder and more powerfully constructed piano was replacing the pianoforte. The new piano was known for its effulgent and commanding tone.

The voluptuous lady was definitely not planning a drive in the park by her state of dishabille. The red and purple dressing gown, the same grape color as the divan, was belted loosely around her waist and clung to her rounded stomach and thighs, revealing a generous amount of cleavage. She was exactly the kind of woman Michael had always found attractive—plush and soft. He tried to suppress the thought of his past enjoyment when he thought of his pledge to Gabby. His tastes, it seemed, had changed forever to petite, curvy women. No, just a single petite, curvy woman.

"I'm sorry I wasn't able to give you proper attention last night." Her lips pouted, and Michael's mind went wild with the implications of her O-shaped lips.

He had only been there five minutes and already he was in a pickle. How was he going to accomplish his mission without...?

He had anticipated a drive around Hyde Park with the diva, not an afternoon of seduction. His plan was to make his association known in the park without committing a real assignation. Or that had been his thinking late last night when he pondered his assignment and how to succeed without betraying Gabby. He wasn't made of the covert spy stuff that relied on deception and lies and hurting innocent people. And Gabby was the innocent. After all that she'd lost, she needed constancy. And once he could end the charade, he planned to be the constant in her unsettled life.

"Please make yourself comfortable. Brandy and port are on the side table." Madame stretched back, giving him an eyeful of her womanly flesh.

Bloody hell! He had believed that he had weeks of pursuing the lady before she would expect...

"It is a beautiful summer day, and I had hoped to entice you with a drive in the park, as I said in my note."

"After my performance last night, I find I really don't want company or more adoration of my fans. I usually spend my day in leisure before the next performance." Madame raised one knee, allowing her dressing robe to fall open to a view of her white thigh.

Deciphering Madame Abney's message didn't require a skilled code breaker. Her intentions were as clear as Eve communicated to Adam.

"I need to unwind, relieve myself of the tension." She wiggled and jiggled on the sofa.

Before his trip to France, and Gabby, Michael would have welcomed an afternoon romp with this sultry woman.

She ran her finger along the outer rim of her robe, drawing Michael's attention to her finger and all that creamy skin.

There had to be a solution to his problem...he knew many men who would wish to face such a carnal challenge. He tried to look away from the woman who smiled slyly at him. How not to meet the lady's wishes? There had to be a solution. He was considered one of the smartest men in England.

He sat down and crossed his leg. He was at a total loss on how to proceed. There were certain dictates that a gentleman followed in these circumstances, but he wasn't going to proceed. "I see that your piano is the new grand. Does it have more than five octaves? Fifth interval? Does the more robust sound help you prepare for such an arduous role?" He uncrossed and crossed his legs. "And I must say you performed magnificently last night." He couldn't stop himself from talking.

The lady laughed, her tone dark and full, like her singing voice. "You actually know about music?"

"I'm not an artist like you, but I have a slight knowledge of music. My mother was a very talented musician."

He found nothing stopped the ardor of women more than when men spoke of their mothers.

"You're an interesting man, Lord Kendal. Come sit here so we can discuss my performance more closely." She patted the divan next to her luscious hip. He was finding her performance today quite compelling, as long as he wasn't required to perform a duet.

Michael swallowed. "Of course, I would love to discuss music."

She gave a rich, husky laugh, the kind that all men recognized and responded to. He preferred a light, tittering laugh and the glittering sparkle in cornflower-blue eyes.

Michael remained seated. "You don't wish to discuss the complexities of the Giacomelli's opera? I must say the use of the trills of the horn section were quite interesting, and the repetition of your line truly increased the drama."

"You are turning out to be not what I had expected."

He gulped. Not what he wanted to hear.

"I've only heard of your talents with the ladies. But you are a man who knows and loves music and is not afraid to speak of his mother. How unique and quite appealing," she purred.

Oh, holy dung pile. Not what he was trying to accomplish.

"Can you describe how you prepare for your role? I'd be most interested to hear how you learn the music. Do you sing from a written sheet or from ear?"

Her lips pinched together. "Is that really what you want to discuss?"

Now he was in it. He knew women and this was no simple question. The lady definitely wouldn't be pleased if he was seen as rejecting her obvious advances. And if she felt spurned by him, then he wouldn't be able to accomplish his mission. Blast it. Women were harder to untangle than Greek participles. Give him hieroglyphics any day.

Why was she so hell bent on seducing him? Last night when he went back to her dressing room, it had been filled with gentlemen admirers, including many old titles, and men of wealth and power, all ready to accommodate the woman. Had she gone home with one of them? Should he be suspicious?

He stood and gave her his best dimpled smile, the one that worked miracles on disgruntled ladies. He didn't want to think about how his smile hadn't affected Gabby after he had mistaken her for a French dancer.

Madame's eyes never left his face, but her breath hitched and drew him again to review her abundant plenitude of womanhood.

She slid a little further back on the divan to give him room to sit, causing her gown to slide further down her shoulder. And dammit, the blasted woman didn't adjust it. And he was expected to sit next to her.

"Right here." She patted the spot would easily give him access to all of her.

He used his teasing voice. "But, Madame, we barely know each other."

"Barely." She pulled the other side of her robe down. "Which I hope we can remedy today." She licked her full, lower lip, which was painted a crimson red, and all he could think of was the lush, pink lip of a French minx.

Michael sat down, spreading his legs underneath the low table in front of the divan, trying hard to strike a casual pose, trying hard *not* to have his hip touch her hip. It was a farce, a ridiculous French farce, which led to thoughts of Gabby and what she would think if she ever learned of this afternoon. His throat felt parched and his palms were sweaty. It was good that Gabby was off with Lady Gwyneth.

Madame Abney's hand went immediately to his knee. What was wrong with this woman? Didn't she know anything about subtlety in the art of lovemaking?

Of course not. She was a dramatic diva who sang big, gestured big, and dramatically emoted for hundreds of people. And by the way her lips were parted, she wanted to do some loud singing with him this afternoon.

He took her hand and brought it to his lips. "You have the voice of an angel. I've had the distinct pleasure of hearing Madame Bianucci. She doesn't compare to you." In researching Madame Abney, he had learned of her intense rivalry with the famed Italian opera singer.

Her lips snapped shut and her eyes narrowed. And now all he had to do was fuel the fire of jealousy instead of the fire of passion…enabling him to make his escape.

Suddenly, to his amazement, the door opened. Without any preamble, the stiff butler announced Lady Ashworth, Miss Amelia Bonnington, and Mademoiselle Gigot.

What kind of crack household was this to usher gentle ladies of good breeding into this room, with Madame in a definite state of dishabille?

His brain rushed for a way to extricate himself, but his superior mind abandoned him in the shock of Gabby finding him entangled with Madame Abney. At the same time his body froze, unable to move.

He tried to jump up but his legs were sprawled under the low table. His knees slammed into the table, shooting bloody pain through his legs. Wanting to curse aloud at the sharp pain, he stumbled backward. He righted himself and tried to get off the damn sofa as Madame Abney grabbed hold of his jacket, for what purpose he didn't understand.

He fell back against her, causing her to scream, in her forte operatic voice, right next to his ear.

His heart and mind raced, but all ingenuity abandoned him.

Gabby, standing still, stared in disbelief at him spread across Madame Abney's cushiony bosom with her robe partially down. Could it get any worse?

He struggled to disengage from his ignominious position, which was made more difficult since he didn't want to touch any part of the lady. During the melee, he heard giggles from Lady Gwyneth and Amelia, but all that rang in his ears was the sound of Gabby's gasp.

He finally stood, tugging down his waistcoat, then he bowed. The tops of his ears burned in embarrassment and shame. How could he ever explain to Gabby that he was innocent in this ridiculous tableau?

"Pardon me, my ladies."

Gabby's eyes were wide, and she tugged on her lower lip. He wanted to take her in his arms and reassure that he wasn't involved with the opera singer.

Lady Gwyneth, his new sister-in-law by marriage, spoke in a quiet, restrained manner, but her eyes were filled with laughter. "We didn't mean to intrude. Your butler said you were at home."

Why in blazes were the ladies visiting the singer? Why weren't they out at Hyde Park like all the rest of London?

Amelia added, "I'm happy to meet with you another day, Madame Abney, since you are engaged." Then Amelia sniggered. He gave her a dark look, which didn't seem to have an effect on his childhood friend, who smirked back at him. "At the modiste shop?"

"No, no. Please come in." The lady sat up and straightened her robe. "Lord Kendal and I were discussing my performance last night."

The silence in the drawing room was ripe with speculation. Lady Gwyneth raised her eyebrows when she walked past him to a side chair.

Michael waited, unsure of his role in this comedy of errors. With Gabby so near, he wanted to touch and reassure her. Her close proximity was a feast to his senses and strained his patience—never his strong point. He blew out the air and the frustration trapped in his lungs. He couldn't risk Gabby's safety. He had to keep up the charade that she was a stranger to him.

"Please come and be seated. I see you've brought drawings, Miss Bonnington."

Distracted, Michael hadn't noticed that Amelia carried a leather portfolio. And now he understood the ladies' appearance. Amelia loved to draw fashion. Madame Abney was most likely interested in new gowns.

"Lord Kendal, be a lamb and ring for tea." Madame pointed to the damask pull next to the fireplace.

He had to pass in front of Gabby to get to the fireplace. When he walked past, he gave her the most plaintive look, begging her with his eyes to have faith in him. Her immediate dismissal, averting her eyes, was easy to understand but still pained him.

Gabby and Amelia moved forward toward Madame Abney.

"May I present Mademoiselle Gigot, Madame Abney," Lady Gwyneth said.

Gabby did a slight curtsy before she sat down. She kept her eyes turned away from the singer.

"My pleasure, mademoiselle."

Gabby didn't respond. Of course, she didn't. She believed she had interrupted his liaison.

After pulling the bell, Michael walked to stand in front of Gabby's chair. He smiled at her. "I've not had the pleasure of an introduction to Mademoiselle Gigot, Lady Gwyneth."

"My apologies. I thought you had met Mademoiselle Gigot at last night's performance."

Michael bowed. He felt her resistance when he took her hand, but he had to touch her. He raised her hand to his lips. "Enchanted."

Gabby kept her eyes down, but nodded. "Thank you, Lord Kendal."

Madame Abney gave the same husky laugh. "Be careful, mademoiselle, Lord Kendal is quite the rogue."

Gabby's eyes shot up to Michael. He beseeched her again with his eyes, trying to express his devotion to her. His heart plummeted at the glimpse of vulnerability in her bright face before she looked down.

Madame Abney pressed her hand against her chest. "Oh, my. What an amazing blush. Charming. I've never been able to effect a blush."

Michael couldn't decipher whether Madame was astute enough to perceive his blinding attraction to Gabby and was jealous, or whether she was just used to commanding the center of attention.

"I've known Lord Kendal since childhood, and I know him to be a steadfast and loyal friend. Not a rogue in any way." Amelia stared at Madame Abney, challenging her to contradict.

Gratitude to Amelia brought a grin to his face. He looked back down at Gabby, whose color was still high, but she was looking at Amelia in open interest. Maybe Amelia's words would help lessen Gabby's suspicions.

"I think your loyalty to Lord Kendal is laudable, but I believe you're too innocent to know of gentlemen's activities and their well-deserved reputations."

Would this conversation never end? Michael never was embarrassed around women—or at least not recently—but now his face felt as if it was a glowing ember.

Amelia's fair skin turned a brighter shade of red than his, and she looked ready to combust. Madame had no idea that Amelia had five brothers and knew all about men, and also had a very fiery redhead temper.

Lady Gwyneth harrumphed. "Miss Amelia, why don't you show Madame Abney your drawings, particularly your choice of colors to emphasize the lady's dramatic looks?"

Michael didn't know if Lady Gwyneth was rescuing him or Amelia, but he was grateful to both ladies and would thank them directly when he had the opportunity.

Now, if only he could devise a plan to speak with Gabby and explain. But there lay the problem; he couldn't. Not yet.

Michael was about to make his excuses when the door opened.

A wiry man in a mustard-yellow waistcoat and an elaborate cravat strolled into the room. Brown curls, artfully held in place with heavy pomade, covered his receding hairline. "Madame Wife."

He stopped his entry into the room when he spotted Gabby, and he turned sharply, like a retriever on the scent of a fox.

Michael bristled, blood surging into his male, possessive muscles, ready to stop the flamboyant codpiece from touching Gabby.

"And who might this delectable ray of sunshine be?" He leered over Gabby.

Gabby leaned back in her chair away from the jackass.

Madame Abney threw her arms in the air. "Francois, leave the poor girl alone. She is my guest, not one of your...I shall leave the rest unsaid in front of gentle company."

Lady Gwyneth and Amelia had both turned their heads to watch the drama unfolding.

"As always, a warm greeting from my harridan of a wife." The lecherous man did a blatant perusal of Gabby. "I am Monsieur Falient."

Michael was ready to spring on Monsieur Falient and teach him a few manners in the presence of Gabby, his lady, when he remembered his role. Monsieur Falient might be part of the spy ring and required further scrutiny. And he couldn't risk exposing Gabby's identity.

"Monsieur." Gabby gave a slight nod of her head and looked away.

"Lady Gwyneth Ashworth and Miss Bonnington, this is my husband, Monsieur Falient."

Both ladies nodded their heads. "Ladies." He bowed deeply as if being presented to a royal. "What a spectacular surprise to have so many fair ladies in my wife's drawing room. It is usually filled with adoring fops."

Madame Abney hissed before she flipped her dark tresses over her shoulder. "Lord Kendal, my husband."

Monsieur Falient inspected Michael's appearance, looking closely at his cravat. Michael knew why the husband's focus was on his clothing. A gentleman wouldn't be able to retie his cravat if he had undressed. Michael's perfectly tied cravat meant that no activity of the prurient sort had gone on with Madame Abney.

Michael exhaled mentally, grateful to have avoided any dealings with a potentially hotheaded husband. Reminding himself that he was on an assignment, Michael stepped forward and offered his hand. "Kendal."

Falient's palms were soft and moist from sweat. And the man reeked of liquor.

"Is there a reason for your unexpected visit, monsieur?" Madame queried as if asking about the weather.

"Nothing of any importance that cannot wait. I will not importune your esteemed guests."

He bowed again from his waist. "Ladies; Kendal." And left the room.

Madame Abney fluttered back to the settee. She muttered under her breath in a theatrical sotto voce for all to hear. "Strutting popinjay. Comes every afternoon for my guests to see him."

"I think that is my cue to leave," Michael said.

Madame Abney threw her head back and chortled. "Men are such cowards."

Michael bowed. "Or very astute."

He wanted to touch Gabby again before he left, but it would require him to take Madame Abney's hand as well.

He bowed generously, keeping his distance from the dramatic diva. "Good afternoon, ladies."

He caught himself before he said his usual parting line, "Pleasure was all mine." He got no pleasure from this afternoon, only painful torture of the Spanish Inquisition type.

CHAPTER NINETEEN

Gabby couldn't control the burn she felt on her face, and in her heart. The cad was back at his old ways, pursuing an opera singer, just as Lord Felton and Chalmers had suggested last night. Michael's attendance at the opera wasn't for the music.

She wanted to crumble into a heap and cry, but she refused to allow that fleshy, self-absorbed singer to detect any reaction to Michael's perfidy. She was a Valmont, centuries of nobility and pride. No, she wouldn't allow one British earl to undermine generations of pragmatic French women. One British earl who had pledged his devotion to her.

She wasn't experienced when it came to the sophisticated society games of flirtations and dallying, but she wouldn't accept that Michael was fickle or dishonorable. There had to be more to his appearance this afternoon than a bored gentleman pursuing…

She ignored the conversation of colors and fabrics. Her new friends sensed her upset and didn't try to engage her in the conversation. Amelia had been thrilled to be invited to consult with the opera singer on her costumes for the opera, and she wouldn't allow her gloomy feelings to interfere with her friend's happiness. Then Gabby remembered the note warning her against the English. The creeping doubt—were these women truly friends?

Madame Abney, thrilled to talk about herself and her gowns, didn't really require engagement from an unknown French woman.

Gabby looked yearningly at the piano, wanting to pour her distraught and lonely feelings into the receptive instrument. After receiving the threatening note, she had decided the only person she could trust with the contents was Michael. She believed his pledge that he would never betray her. He was a sincere man who didn't seem to be capable of deceit. He was upset by Mother Therese's joke on him. What a fool she had been since the joke was on her, poor orphan Gabby de Valmont, heartsick for an English rake. She missed her brother. He would have protected from unscrupulous gentlemen who confused and confounded.

"You keep looking at my new piano, mademoiselle, with such admiration and longing. Are you familiar with this newest piano?"

Madame was correct. It was painful longing, but for more than music—longing for a place to belong, longing for someone trustworthy of her love.

"Yes, Madame. The sound is magnificent."

"Where could you possibly have heard the grand? Mine is the only one in London."

"In Paris."

"In Paris? But the only person who received the grand piano is Monsieur la Toure, the finest pianist in all of Europe." Madame stared at Gabby and waited.

Gabby's mind raced. She hadn't been thinking when she answered. Would Madame Abney be able to make the association to Gabrielle De Valmont and Monsieur la Toure?

An impatient Madame Abney wanted an answer to the mystery. "You are too young to have heard him in concert. And with Monsieur la Toure's advanced age, he stopped touring and only took the most exceptional musicians as students."

Gwyneth stiffened in her chair. Amelia turned and gave her a quizzical look.

Madame Abney scrutinized Gabby. "You were a student of Monsieur la Toure?"

How should she answer? She had been caught off guard, lost in pity for herself and her loss of everything she cherished, including her artistry. "I was his student for a short period of time."

"But I don't remember him ever speaking of a Mademoiselle Gigot. I believe I would remember someone so young, a prodigy... Did you ever perform at Madame le Querq's salon?"

Gabby shouldn't have come today. After receiving the note and then seeing Michael, she didn't feel capable to handle the probing questions. Madame Abney was getting too close to the dangerous truth. It had been her performance at Madame le Querq's salon that brought her to Josephine Bonaparte's attention, and subsequently to Napoleon's.

Gabby had to stop this line of questioning. "I'm not surprised that Monsieur la Toure never mentioned me. He would forget everything. His head always engulfed in a cloud of music."

Madame's voice softened and she leaned her head back against the divan. "Yes, he never remembered what day it was or if he remembered to eat that day."

"His cook would have to scold him, reminding him to eat. He would laugh and say he sustained himself on music," Gabby added. Her mentor's passion for music and his expectation of her had given her a structure to her life when everything had crumpled around her.

Madame looked up at the ceiling, lost in reverie. "A true artist. He shared his passion for music with me."

Watching the change in Madame's face and the reverence in her voice for Gabby's beloved teacher, the pain in Gabby's chest eased. "It was a privilege to have him as a teacher."

Madame sat forward and clapped her hands. The woman was definitely mercurial, as expected of an emoting diva.

"This is fabulous. I've no one in London who challenges me. Everyone is intimidated and tries to please me instead of pushing me like the Monsieur."

"You continue to play, even with the demands of your singing career?" Despite her distrust of the diva, Gabby was interested.

"I find I can almost express myself more in my playing than my singing."

Although Gabby had been distracted at last night's performance, Madame's passion and gift for music as a singer was abundant.

"I don't truly understand since I love singing, but I've decided it is because I first started as a child, pouring my heart into the pianoforte."

Losing herself into the music, as Gabby had done. Mother Therese had always given the reassurance that when one door closed another one would open. Finding someone at this low-spirited moment who understood the need to express passion in music was a balm to Gabby's aching heart.

She smiled openly at the lady, enjoying suddenly this astonishing connection. "I understand. I am lost if I'm not able to play."

"Have you found anyone in London to study with that can compare with Monsieur la Toure? I find I am most impatient since no one else inspires me."

Gwyneth interjected. "Mademoiselle has just joined us in London."

Gabby had been so lost in the enlightening conversation that she had completely forgotten about her need to hide her identity, and the threatening note.

Gabby looked between her friends "Ladies, I do beg your pardon for my meanderings. We are here to discuss fashion."

"I'm very much enjoying this conversation." Amelia sat forward on the edge of her chair. "I feel the same way about my painting. It is important to find a way to express yourself."

Lady Gwyneth harrumphed again. "I'm feeling quite bereft amongst three talented artists. I don't possess the soul of an artist."

Miss Amelia chided her. "You have your own talents." A conspiratorial smile between the two friends followed, but it was lost on Gabby where Gwyneth's talents lay.

Madame Abney pulled her robe together and stood. "Please, you must play for me."

Gabby wanted to play on the grand piano after all the misery she had experienced seeing Michael entangled with the singer. And with her feelings in tumult, pounding the stronger action keys, imagining the keys to be a pair of duplicitous green eyes, would give her great satisfaction. And how unexpected that the lady who brought about her unhappiness also brought a way to rid herself of the gnawing insecurity.

"Please, will you stay and play for me? My man can take you home in my carriage."

Gabby looked to Gwyneth. This didn't have the makings of any devious plan by someone who meant her harm. She would be able to detect insincerity in Madame Abney wouldn't she? She had a good sense of people and their motives, but since her life had been threatened and uprooted she didn't feel she could totally trust her judgement.

Gwyneth shook her head. "It isn't possible today. We have Lady Bostwick's garden party to attend next. Possibly another day, Madame."

Gabby stood. "I will play for you, Madame, but only if you will play for me. I see there is music on the piano, may I see what you are working on before we must depart?" Gabby looked to Gwyneth for approval. The lady nodded.

Madame walked to the piano and lifted the music sheet. "Bach's *Jauchzet Gott in allen Landen*. I have never performed this piece written for singer and trumpet."

Gabby followed the singer to the piano, delighted to talk about music. "'Shout for joy to God in every land.' But a sacred cantata for an opera house performance?"

Madame handed the music to Gabby. "It is written to showcase the virtuosity of the soprano."

Gabby studied the notes written next to the music. Madame had made notations about the orchestration. The revisions were changing the duration of the notes.

Gwyneth stood. "I'm sorry to interrupt, but Mademoiselle Gabby, we must leave for Lady Bostwick's."

Gabby placed the music on the piano. "Of course, Lady Gwyneth."

Madame Abney took Gabby's hands into her own and squeezed tightly. "I am so delighted to have made a new friend. You must come to my performance tomorrow night—backstage. And you must meet my brother. He is in the orchestra, a skilled musician and pianist. He also studied with Monsieur la Toure."

Surprised by the lady's unrestrained demonstration, Gabby looked to Gwyneth, who now stood at the door. The lady shrugged her shoulders and then nodded.

"It would be a pleasure," Gabby said.

The singer definitely was comfortable expressing her strong passion for her art. Gabby had been the same reveling in her passion for music until the Committee of Public Safety began their killing purge. She had learned to hide anything and everything about herself to survive when a mere association to music was enough to be sentenced to the guillotine.

CHAPTER TWENTY

Gabby sat across from Gwyneth in the carriage on their way to Lady Bostwick's garden party. The ladies of London were no different than those in Paris, filling their days with social visits and parties.

Gwyneth crossed her leg over the other in the same manner as her Aunt Euphemia and reclined against the leather seat. "The season's demands are usually tedious, but today…"

Gabby and Amelia fanned themselves, attempting in vain to keep the overpowering odors away. The afternoon heat increased the pungent smells of garbage and horse manure from the street. Also similar to summer days in Paris.

"Devil of an afternoon. I never enjoyed myself more. I hope Lady Bostwick's party will be as intriguing." Gwyneth looked between Gabby and Amelia. "Which topic should we start with? Kendal or Madame Abney's association with Josephine de Beauharnais or Josephine Bonaparte, or whatever she is calling herself these days. But I think the way Amelia was about to go off like a bonfire on Guy Fawkes Day, I think it will have to be Kendal."

Amelia wheezed, "That…"

Gabby did wonder if Amelia had curbed her tongue because of her presence. She would have liked to hear Amelia's choice of blasphemy. After her years in the convent, she was getting an education she never acquired from the nuns. These unconventional women were nothing like the women she had known in France, although they did engage in silliness similar to

French girls when the nuns weren't about. But those were young girls, not esteemed women of the English peerage.

Amelia shuddered visibly, her skin coloring to a bright pink that clashed terribly with her deep-purple dress. "That woman...I'd have liked to tell her." Amelia's voice shook in indignation. "What is there not to know? I have four older brothers. Their escapades with ladies and not-so-ladies would shock most women."

Gabby was grateful that she sat next to Amelia so the lady couldn't detect her interest in the conversation. Gabby's experience with men was very limited, her years in Paris ending abruptly. Her most recent encounter with a golden gentleman left her sleepless, reliving the moment when Michael had pulled her down on top of his hard body, her soft curves melting around him, cradling his obvious desire. She always became breathless, imagining what he would have done next to wring new and exhilarating sensations from her body.

"I wanted to blacken that woman's eye for implying Michael uses women, like some of the cads we know."

Gwyneth snorted. "Amelia, I was quite impressed with your restraint."

"Well, thank you for directing me to my drawings."

The friends laughed together. Like Michael, these women were too open and ingenuous for her to believe they were lying to her. What could they possibly be lying to her about?

Gwyneth looked at Gabby. "Amelia is the only of my acquaintances able to blacken anyone's eyes. She has an amazingly strong right arm."

"The benefits of learning to defend yourself against brothers who solve all their problems with punches."

"And I thought it came from your cricket playing."

Amelia twisted on the seat to look at Gabby. "Michael isn't a rake, not in the way Madame Abney suggested. He spends most of his time in scholarly pursuits."

Gabby sat up straight. "Scholarly pursuits?"

"Michael is a brilliant linguist. I do believe he would have been happy to spend his days at Oxford studying ancient languages."

Gwyneth shifted closer across the aisle. "I don't know this about Kendal."

"When his father died, Michael was bereft. He was very close to his father, a jovial sort who doted on his wife and children. They were a very happy and loving family. With the death of his father, Michael became the new earl with all the associated responsibilities. He had to leave Oxford and his studies to come to London. Suddenly the sweet scholar was now an earl, garnering all the attention from the ladies."

"And what man could resist such temptation?" Gabby tried not to sound peevish, but the memory of "Yvette" and "Mimi" and how many more made her resentful and jealous.

Gwyneth glanced at Amelia. "This is when Amelia believed she was in love with him."

"It was a young girl's infatuation. But when I came to London for my debut, Michael had changed. A man-about-town, no longer the gentle boy with whom I had grown up and who loved to get into endless trouble with my brothers."

"It was the same for me with Ash." Gwyneth uncrossed her leg. "The rogue always sported a different lady on his arm."

"Gabby doesn't know about your past with Ash," Amelia interjected.

"Like Amelia, I've known Ash since I was a little girl. He and Cord are the best of friends. And of course, he never saw me as anything but Cord's younger sister."

Gwyneth and Amelia were talking to her as friends, sharing their trials in their courtships. Their consideration of her tender and bewildered feelings made her weepy. She had to fight the tears gathering behind her eyes.

"Like Ash and Derrick, Michael is experienced. Women love him; he is charming to the fairer sex because of his wit and boyish looks. And underneath his roguish manner, he is very sensitive. The reason I believed I was in love with him wasn't because he's handsome or charming. Although a young boy himself, he comforted me after the death of my mother."

Gabby recognized his sensitive nature, much like her own. And despite his newest escapade with Madame, she had witnessed his open love and care for his family. She had never seen a gentleman so willing to express his tender feelings.

"He is loyal and caring toward everyone. Derrick told me that Michael was going to call out Cord because he thought Cord had taken advantage of his sister."

Gwyneth laughed, her mouth wide open, showing her sparkling teeth. "Take advantage of Henrietta? I still can't believe the change in my brother since he married Henrietta. And talk about reputations; Cord had the worst, and well-earned if the rumors are true."

Amelia took Gabby's hand. "Don't give up on Michael. I've known him for a very long time and have never seen him look at a lady like he does you. In my silly childhood, I had hoped he would look at me in that desperate, hungry way."

Gabby's stomach fluttered as if there were a horde of butterflies wildly flapping.

"Instead you have a besotted Derrick."

Miss Amelia's rosy lips curved into a knowing smile.

"The point is, don't be too hard on Kendal. I am sure there is more than meets the eye to today's escapade," Gwyneth added.

Gabby's face warmed with the conspiratorial look Gwyneth shot her. "But you must make him suffer a little for his newest outing with Madame Abney. It is what I did to Ash when he was pursuing a certain lady. Men's ardent way of apologizing is very rewarding."

Gwyneth watched out the window. "We've only got another ten minutes before arriving at the Bostwick's estate. Let's get to Madame Abney."

"Before we dissect if the opera singer knows who Gabby really is, we must discuss the secret you've been keeping from your friends. Confess, Gabby." Amelia searched Gabby's face.

Gabby's heart leapt into her throat. Could they know about the note?

No, they couldn't. These intrepid ladies would have confronted her immediately. Neither would have been able to contain their curiosity. She wanted to share the contents of the note, but the threat held her back.

Gwyneth teased, "You have that many secrets? Amelia is referring to your musical genius."

"Of course! What else has you worried? You know Gwyneth and I wouldn't let anyone hurt you."

Shame burned and curled inside Gabby. How could she mistrust these woman, who both had only been supportive and protective of her?

"I'm sorry. There is so much to take in. I made a mistake sharing my past with Madame Abney. But I was distracted."

"Of course you were. Finding Michael in a compromising situation was definitely distressing. And then it was obvious you were enthralled with her piano. I look at fabric the same way, wanting to touch it, explore all the possibilities of the material," Amelia crooned.

"I couldn't hide my fascination with the piano. I tried not to tell her much about myself, but when she spoke of Monsieur la Toure..." Gabby felt the familiar burn behind her eyes and the sharp pain in her throat. She wasn't the kind of woman who gave in to bouts of feeling maudlin. But recently she had succumbed to *pleurer comme une madeleine*. She couldn't seem to stop crying.

Gwyneth clicked her tongue. "You did well, keeping the information to a minimum and diverting her to discuss music. And no one can fault you for wanting to talk about home and your beloved teacher. No one in England is familiar to you and no one shares your past. It has to be lonely and disconcerting."

Gabby clenched her lips together, refusing to cry. She nodded.

Her friends seemed to appreciate her distress. Amelia squeezed her hand but looked at Gwyneth, allowing Gabby a moment to compose herself.

"Gwyneth, do you believe Madame's mention of Josephine

Bonaparte was an attempt to see how Gabby would react?"

"I cannot know. But it is suspicious that the day after Gabby comes out in society, Madame requested to consult with you about new gowns. And then her mention of Josephine, and then the invitation for Gabby to be backstage."

"What a suspicious but methodical mind you have," Amelia said appreciatively.

"Well, thank you." Gwyneth bobbed her head. "The highest of compliments in my family."

"But I do believe Madame was genuine about her devotion to Monsieur la Toure and finding an artist of Gabby's caliber. She truly was moved."

Gwyneth shook her head again. "Do not forget, Madame Abney is a gifted actor. We saw last night her incredible dramatic skills. I also thought she was being honest, but we can't trust anyone with Gabby's safety in question."

"What do you think, Gabby? Do you think she was acting or sincere?" Amelia asked.

"I don't know what to think. It is all so confusing. But I need to go backstage to find out if the lady is a liar."

"It could be a trap and possibly dangerous." Gwyneth raised both eyebrows.

Gabby refused to be helpless, to allow her fearful circumstances to dictate her behavior, especially in front of these fearless ladies.

"As your chaperone, I must accompany you. I will bring my pistol," Gwyneth added gleefully.

Amelia burst into laughter. "There is no way Ash is going to allow you and Gabby to go backstage unaccompanied. I must go with you."

Then the ladies all hooted. As if the danger to her was a hilarious joke.

"Please excuse us, Gabby. We're not making light of the threat. We are entertained by our husbands. It's a game we play with them. Ash and Derrick have us guarded at all times. Neither will admit to it, but right now I'm sure Talley is following our carriage on horseback. You needn't worry. There will be plenty of protection backstage."

Amelia straightened the small hat flirtatiously perched on the side of her head. "What an eventful afternoon. And, unlike Gwyneth, I hope this is the usual boring party that Lady Bostwick hosts."

CHAPTER TWENTY-ONE

He watched from the garden hedgerow, hidden in the dense foliage, out of sight of all of London's society. He had followed her from Madame Abney's townhouse to the Bostwick estate. Now that he had found her, he wasn't going to let her out of his sight.

Ashworth stood to one side, away from the milling groups, his brow pinched together as a younger man spoke, most likely one of Rathbourne's underlings reporting. Ashworth, like Rathbourne, had worked undercover for years in France. Were they as tired as he was of the layers of lies, assignations, and deceptions?

He had one final mission, and then he was finished with the entire lunacy. He didn't care if France and England continued fighting for the entire next century.

There was a hush when she entered the garden, as if she were a member of the British royal family. Her French royal lineage had brought ample tragedy to her short and innocent life.

Pompous dandies with their extravagant cravats, bright colored jackets, and tight lips crowded around her. She had grown into a beautiful woman and all the London coxcombs noticed.

From the way she stiffened in response to the swarming men and their need to take her hand, she wasn't impressed with the English any more than he was. He was glad she didn't want the attention from all the men because his plans would put an end to this ridiculous farce.

A stunning redhead wearing a very stylish gown that looked more French than the tasteless English style, swept in and took Gabrielle's arm, extricating her from the hordes.

The blue ribbon tied at the side of her bonnet framed the Valmont's extraordinary eyes, white-blond curls, and her distinct Gallic chin, carved from centuries of superior breeding. Her graceful, confident manner was the epitome of French beauty and style.

The redhead's comment made Gabrielle smile. But as she moved closer to his position in the hedge, he noticed the forlorn slope of her small shoulders and air of dejection surrounding her. Was she aware of the treachery planned against her?

A lissome man pressed his lips to her small, gloved hand in familiarity.

The audacity of the Englishman touching her destroyed any of his newly acquired patience. He was going to run the English bastard through. He wasn't sure if he could wait until he extricated Gabrielle from London before he killed the "gentleman."

The redheaded woman squeezed Gabrielle's arm and then waved to a goliath with a harsh, square face. Another of Rathbourne's henchmen by the forceful stare he leveled at the gentility crowded in the garden.

All the party needed was Rathbourne to complete British intelligence.

Gabrielle was in the midst of a trove of English spies. Were they protecting her or using her as a pawn in the game with Fouché and Napoleon? Most likely using her, as he would have done in the past.

How her presence in the midst of the den of spies came about made no difference now. He didn't care how many men surrounded her. He'd get his revenge. And once he had tasted the sweet reward, he'd be finished.

Gabrielle kept her eyes downcast, listening intently to the animated English gentleman who spoke rapidly and expressively. By the way his eyes searched her face and the way he angled his body possessively toward her, he was pleading his cause as a jilted lover.

Whatever the blond Adonis had pleaded, Gabrielle was moved. Her skin flushed and she chewed anxiously on her lower lip. She had feelings for the persuasive Englishman. It couldn't be true. With her French lineage, how could she lower herself?

He'd tear the man apart. But only after he inflicted his retribution.

He couldn't risk anything today, with England's elite spies all around. He now was a changed man—he had almost learned patience over the last year. The right time would come. And when it did...

CHAPTER TWENTY-TWO

Fenton stepped closer and lowered his voice, showing some sense of propriety with two dowagers standing only a few feet from them. "Did you manage to get your diva singing last night?"

Hell, Michael didn't need a rehash of the absurd scene from just hours before with the demanding opera singer. He wished he had never heard of Madame Abney. Why couldn't he go back to deciphering codes with Hen?

But he had to maintain the appearance of pursuing Madame Abney, especially to bait his two blockhead friends who lived on the *ton*'s gossip.

He shrugged his shoulders. "I've just come from her townhouse."

Chalmers inspected Michael's impeccable blue coat and perfectly tied cravat, which he had worn to look upright and proper for Gabby. "You went home to change your clothes?"

Avoiding looking at his friends, Michael examined the cuffs on his sleeve. "Of course, couldn't come in the clothes from last night." Not really a total lie since no one wore their clothes from the previous night.

Fenton, more astute than Chalmers, kept his steely gaze on Michael. "Something's not right about you."

Michael pulled at his cravat. Fenton and Chalmers had shared many an adventure and might see through his pretense. "What the hell is that supposed to mean, Fenton?"

"You're not acting like your usual clever self. No witty rejoinders that fly right past Chalmers."

Chalmers elbowed Fenton. "Give the man a break. He's tired after his night with Madame."

He wasn't tired, but he was worried about Gabby's reaction when she saw him at the garden party. He had reasoned it would be strange if he didn't greet Amelia and Lady Gwyneth, hoping that would give him enough time for a moment with Gabby.

Fenton looked around and behind him before speaking. "You might have some competition for Madame's attention. She's attracted royal notice."

Michael shifted his weight and feigned curiosity in Lady Roscoe's arrival to hide his acute interest in Fenton's news. Fenton always knew the *on dit*, since he spent most of the time in clubs, hiding from his mother and three sisters.

Chalmers poked Michael in the ribs again. The damn poke hurt. The man had no idea of his strength. "Hope you impressed her last night."

Fenton crowded closer to Michael. "No snappy retort?"

"I never share my… It is ungentlemanly."

Chalmers snorted, causing guests to turn to look at them. "Since when did you become a prig?"

He had never regaled men with stories about women, but that didn't stop women from talking about him. Which led to today's misadventure. Madame Abney wanted either to test his reputation or to prove her own. Damn women and their gossip.

"I don't think you have any worries. The king only wants her to perform a sacred piece of music, a cantata by Bach, a royal performance."

The small hairs on Michael's neck stood on end. Could the threat to His Majesty be encoded in tonight's performance? He was glad that he planned to return to the opera tonight and glad that Gabby wouldn't be at the performance to watch his pursuit. He'd listen carefully to the music. He also needed to spend time with Madame to have access to her music, which wouldn't be too difficult.

"Do you know when this royal performance will happen?" Michael scanned the crowd, pretending interest in the party.

"You didn't want to talk about her performance last night?" Fenton grinned widely. "Or was it your performance that has you concerned?"

Michael rolled his eyes and waited for Chalmers's lewd retort when he spotted Gabby, Lady Gwyneth, and Amelia arrive in the garden.

"She's here," Fenton said. Chalmers whipped around. "Excuse me, old chap." And Chalmers, like all the other men in the garden, made straight for Gabby.

Fenton and Michael stood shoulder to shoulder and watched the gentlemen flock around Gabby.

"She doesn't look like a woman seeking male attention," Fenton observed.

Gabby's eyes were shuttered down, hidden by her adorable bonnet with a big blue bow.

Hope rekindled in Michael's chest. Gabby wasn't looking at any of the men with her eyes wide open in interest or enjoyment, not the way she looked at him, or at least had before this afternoon.

"I think I'll wait for a more private moment to regale the lady with my charms," Fenton jeered.

Michael wanted to plant a facer on Fenton's handsome visage. The storm of his possessiveness was growing exponentially, like a mathematical equation. He wasn't a violent man who derived pleasure from fighting or hurting others, but watching all the men of his acquaintance touch Gabby was a startling revelation. He would and could hurt anyone who wanted Gabby.

Lady Gwyneth took Gabby's arm. Michael couldn't hear Lady Gwyneth's comment, but whatever she said caused the men to back up and open a path for the ladies.

Out of the corner of his eye, Michael spotted Ashworth moving toward his wife.

Taking the opportunity to join Ashworth, Michael called out to him. There were some benefits to Hen's marriage to Rathbourne.

Ashworth turned and waited for Michael to accompany him.

Ashworth said quietly, "I didn't expect you to be here."

"A bit of confusion that I need to remedy."

"Already?" Ashworth's eyes glinted in amusement.

"Darling," Ashworth took his wife's arm and pulled her away from the crowd of gentlemen. He gave a possessive look that was clear to the men—she is mine.

Lady Gwyneth and Ash separated themselves, staring into each other's eyes. Ashworth ran his hand along Lady Gwyneth's arm in a tender lover's touch.

Michael couldn't wait for the day when he could touch Gabby publicly, declaring she was his and his only.

"Mademoiselle Gabrielle." Michael searched Gabby's face, looking for a clue into her feelings, hoping for a sign.

"Michael, what a pleasure to see you this afternoon," Amelia spoke loudly.

Gabby wouldn't meet his eyes. She had the same closed expression for him as for all the other gentlemen.

"We were making our way to the table for refreshments. Would you like to join us?"

Startled by Amelia's suggestion, he offered his arm to both ladies. "This way, ladies."

Bless Amelia. She had just given him a way to plead his cause to Gabby. He felt Gabby's hesitation before she placed her hand on his arm.

With her slim, white glove on his arm, heat and need washed over him.

Amelia said in a loud voice, "Lovely afternoon for a garden party, don't you agree?"

Michael had to control the urge to press Gabby's slight body closer to his side. Amelia walked to the far end of the table, giving Michael a brief moment to speak with Gabby.

Bending over the table piled with sweets, he pretended to be filling a plate for Gabby, choosing between the wide array of biscuits, tarts, small crème cakes, and assortment of fruit. He held up a lemon tart and showed the dessert to Gabby while he leaned closer and whispered, "Gabby, please let me explain about this afternoon. It isn't what you think. I haven't broken my pledge. I promise."

Gabby's eyes, darkening to the color of sapphire, searched his face as if trying to decipher a substitution code.

"Please Gabby. Let me explain. Meet me in Ashworth's garden tomorrow night at midnight." His voice grew rough with need at the idea of Gabby, alone with him in the dark.

Michael would have missed her slight nod if he weren't watching intently. He placed the lemon tart on her plate.

Gabby added a chocolate biscuit. His spirits vastly improved by Gabby's agreement, he was about to tease her about her sweet tooth but was interrupted by Weston's arrival at the table.

Michael's body locked in readiness to claim and protect. He was turning into a brute when in close proximity to Gabby.

Weston bowed grandly. "Mademoiselle Gabrielle, my mood is much improved by your appearance this afternoon."

Michael let out a slow breath of relief at Weston's flowery asinine flattery. Gabby wouldn't be impressed with such tomfoolery.

"Kendal." Weston's voice held a challenge that no male could miss.

Michael bristled, but he had to curb his primitive urges around Gabby. No easy feat for him, since he had never experienced these extreme and intense feelings before and he wanted to proclaim his devotion for Gabby to the entire world. He wasn't a man known for his subtlety.

"Weston." Michael nodded. And then, smiling down at Gabby, "I've taken too much of your time, mademoiselle, when your attention is in such high demand." He bowed. "Good afternoon, my lady. Weston."

And Michael walked away, leaving his Gabby. He'd do anything to protect her. Which at this moment meant walking away, releasing her to be admired and charmed by the entire male population of England. Bloody hell.

CHAPTER TWENTY-THREE

Fouché paced outside the office of the First Consul. The sound of his boots echoed in the long mirrored hallway. The most powerful man in Paris, the Minister of Police, waiting outside closed doors, like a servant anticipating his master. The delay was unbearable and untenable. Unable to sit patiently, he strode into the hall, away from the calculating glances of Monsieur Brugiere, the First Consul's confidante and chargé d'affaires, who was seated in the antechamber.

Brugiere wasn't intimidated by Fouché, and unlike most of Paris, chargé d'affaires had never been blackmailed. Fouché was paralyzed to threaten the man with no family ties and a spotless reputation.

Fouché stopped his pacing to stare at the long, perfect rows of blossoming roses in the gardens. He didn't need his skills as a statesman to read yet another sign of his weakening position of favor with Bonaparte. Had Talleyrand found out his plan to kill Mademoiselle de Valmont and reported his treacherous behavior to Bonaparte?

Never a man to be indecisive, Fouché always planned for all possible consequences of his actions, rather like anticipating five moves ahead in a chess game. His ability to maintain his powerful position over the chaotic years was also due to his training to become a priest. He recognized the evil lurking in men and used their dark needs to his benefit.

But what he had considered a minor problem, a gnat to swat away, had grown into trouble he hadn't foreseen. He needed to send a messenger to England to stop Anatole from killing the girl. He hoped he wasn't too late.

But if the messenger arrived too late, his latest intrigue would win him favor again. Within weeks, the English King would be dead, thus strengthening his power and reestablishing his favored dominant position with Bonaparte.

No one would be able to track the murder to him. The English might have theories but no proof of his culpability. The finesse of the plot would suggest Talleyrand's sophisticated touch. And if he were questioned by Bonaparte for his duplicity, he would claim ignorance. How could an unsophisticated man like him devise a plot around an Italian opera and a Bach cantata? In contrast, the Foreign Minister was well known as a connoisseur of the arts.

The outer door opened and out swept Talleyrand, as always dressed in velvet and lace, a great contrast to Fouché's utilitarian solid black uniform and black boots. Gold buttons were his only adornment. Hiding his surprise at the Foreign Minister's appearance, Fouché remained by the window.

Talleyrand, always a gentleman, gestured grandly with the sunlight glinting off his ostentatious ring. "Walk with me. I'm late for a meeting with the Austrian ambassador."

Fouché stiffened in response to Talleyrand's air of royal command and planted his feet wider apart, in a clear message that the skilled diplomat wouldn't misread.

"I've a meeting with the First Consul," Fouché said.

"No, the First Consul summoned you to meet with me."

Infuriated by Bonaparte's manipulation, Fouché resisted the urges that would give any indication of the blow Talleyrand had just delivered. He smiled broadly at Talleyrand. "Of course, it must be of great importance to take the time of the man who singlehandedly is keeping Europe from going to war."

Obviously harried and not in the mood for gamesmanship, Talleyrand ignored the comment and walked briskly down the long marble corridor. Talleyrand's sour mood made Fouché wonder what had transpired at the meeting with the First

Consul. Talleyrand's long strides didn't impede Fouché from keeping up with the taller man.

Talleyrand wasn't a fool and, although it was hard to admit, was a very skilled statesman and a man of great vision. He worked steadfastly trying to negotiate favorable treaties for France.

"My network hasn't been able to unearth your newest intrigue in London yet, but I want you to stop your machinations."

This was very straight talking for a man who never revealed his plans. "I'm trying to extend the terms of the Amiens Treaty with England, keeping peace between our countries. And I don't want your plans to disgrace me or ruin my negotiations to regain the First Consul's favor."

Bonaparte had no plans for peace with England. Talleyrand's plans must have been a way to distract and appease England while Bonaparte built his empire in the rest of Europe. Fouché recognized the greed, need for power, and manipulation in Bonaparte. It was the reason he supported Bonaparte's coup d'état of 18 Brumaire.

Bonaparte was an opportunist. Peace was one of many instruments to be used to gain his goal of complete world domination.

"I would never interfere with your plans for peace. I believe we are all in accord with the First Consul's plans for France."

Talleyrand paused. "I knew it was a fool's errand to even approach you, but the First Consul requested this discussion. Let's be very clear. I will do everything in my power, with the support of the First Consul, to stop whatever new plans you have with your circle of criminals in England."

Interesting approach by the silk-talking and silk-handed diplomat. Did Talleyrand recognize the challenge in his words? Of course, he did. Was this more of a manipulation to encourage Fouché to do the deed, enabling Talleyrand and Bonaparte to distance themselves and deny?

He wondered how much Talleyrand really knew of his plan

to kill George the Third. In the years of knowing the diplomat, Fouché had never had an honest confrontation with him. Neither man was capable of trustworthiness.

"And I won't brook any interference in the removal of Mademoiselle de Valmont from England. It is time to stop your intrigues on the greater European scene. This is not my warning. The order came directly from the First Consul. Restrict your conspiracies to France and your position as Minister of Police."

CHAPTER TWENTY-FOUR

Gabby avoided watching Michael's departure. Disappointment and longing sank heavily in her stomach, causing the lemon tart and chocolate biscuit to form a lump of misery. She placed her plate back on the table, unable to look at the sweets that had been tempting when Michael was near.

She had never felt this unsteady. The excitement and disappointment of love was more challenging than mastering a Beethoven sonata. The death of her brother, followed by the intimidating note, was the cause of her shakiness, not the green-eyed gentleman who devoured her with his eyes and made her pulse leap by his nearness.

Gabby didn't listen to Lord Weston wax on about her beauty. Her mind twirled on whether she should trust Michael. She mulled over her friends' honesty about the difference between the way women and men loved. She wanted to trust Michael. He was good man. It was her sadness over her brother and the unfamiliarity of this new world, as well as the note, that caused her to question her relationships with everyone.

Lost in her thoughts, she hadn't noticed that Lord Weston's voice had grown quiet, almost to a whisper. "Lady Sauvage wants to speak to you about your brother."

"Lady Sauvage was acquainted with my brother?" Gabby realized her mistake the moment the words left her mouth. But the shock that someone had known Lucien made her forget the ruse of her false identity.

"How does the lady know I have a brother?" Her voice

quivered like the strings of a violin hovering over a sharp note.

"She didn't share the information with me. She only asked me to escort you to her. She knew you'd be interested in hearing about your brother and she didn't want to discuss him in front of the English ladies."

Chills of heat and cold chased over every inch of her skin. "Why not? The ladies are my dear friends."

"Lady Sauvage didn't explain. You must ask her yourself."

Gabby nodded. "I'd love to speak with the lady."

Lord Weston offered his arm. "I believe she is in Lady Bostwick's salon. She avoids the outdoors in the warmer months."

Ignoring the shakiness behind her knees, Gabby weighed the danger of the lady's request. The lady couldn't be a threat to her safety in the middle of the party since Gabby wouldn't hesitate to scream and fight.

Gabby scanned the crowd for Gwyneth. She spotted her friend chatting with two gentlemen, her back to Gabby. The men were enthralled by Gwyneth's conversation or possibly by how stunning and voluptuous she looked in her ivory muslin dress with its cobalt blue ribbon under the bodice. The dress was in the French style, but with Gwyneth's jet black hair, ivory skin, and her womanly curves, she looked like a Madonna in a Raphael painting.

Lord Ashworth stood alone at the end of the refreshment table, watching the gentlemen who watched his wife. She found it hard to believe that Ashworth, a very perceptive man, had been slow in recognizing Gwyneth's beauty and generosity. By the way his eyes tracked her every movement, it was obvious he now reveled in his wife's beauty and wasn't pleased that other gentlemen also appreciated her natural gifts.

Gabby caught his eye to acknowledge her departure.

He gave her a slight nod. He must trust Lord Weston, despite the suspicions of Gwyneth and Amelia concerning the gentleman and Lady Sauvage. He'd allowed Lord Weston to accompany her to the opera and now to escort her through the house. Gabby dismissed the minor fact that Lord Ashworth didn't know Lord Weston was taking her to a secluded part of the Bostwick estate. She assumed if so, he or one of the men would follow her.

Walking into the cool, dark, and silent house was a dramatic change after the bright sunlight and plethora of sweet scents of the summer blossoms. Like its medieval history, the confiscated abbey smelled old and musty. Lord Weston guided her down a corridor to the right of the entrance and straight into the family quarters.

Her heart raced in surges against her chest. She could hear the noise of the outside party, but the cold silence, the dim walls, and the creaking dark wood floors unnerved her. She took small breaths through her mouth, trying to slow her choppy breathing.

Lord Weston opened a door into a drawing room where the lady of the house could entertain her family and closest friends.

Lady Sauvage, in a stunning magenta gown, sat in an armchair upholstered in Fragonard Blue Toile fabric. The hanging crystal chandelier, the Louis XV Rococo gilt wood console table, and the matching Fragonard Blue Sevres vases could have been taken out of any salon in Paris.

"Come, my dear. Join me." Lady Sauvage held a champagne flute in her hand. "Can't abide the sweet punch at these parties." She gave a husky laugh. "Please let me serve you a glass of bubbly."

Gabby released Lord Weston's arm and moved to the chair opposite Lady Sauvage. Her heartbeat thrummed an uneasy rhythm with each step she took.

The two chairs, turned away from their winter position in front of the fireplace, faced out to acres of manicured gardens outlined by gravel paths and carefully sculpted hedges. The blue skies, blooming roses, and the full sunshine didn't ease the sensation of her heart bounding out of her chest.

Lord Weston remained at the door. He bowed. "If you'll excuse me, ladies. I will return to the party."

Lady Sauvage stood and swept her billowing skirt around the small table separating the two chairs and lifted a flute from the side table. "French champagne."

Gabby took the goblet from the thin woman who stood over her. Gabby leaned back in the chair and saw the imposing woman. "Thank you, Lady Sauvage."

Gabby pretended to sip the chilled champagne and waited, to avoid blurting out her questions about her brother. The way the woman had arranged for Lord Weston to escort her to this separate room away from the party, and provided a comforting and familiar French room with exquisite French champagne was suspicious.

"You know you look a lot like him. Your eyes, the same turquoise blue, the same flaxen curls, and the full lower lip. You're beautiful, but he too was beautiful. Not effeminate in his beauty. It was probably the strength of his personality."

Lucien and she looked like their mother, but Lucien had inherited their father's mercurial temperament.

The need to speak of her brother fueled her longing to trust this woman, to learn the details of his death from someone who recently knew him. "I know not of whom you speak."

"Please, no games. You are Mademoiselle Gabrielle De Valmont. I'm not sure why you're hiding your identity, but it was obvious when I first met you that you were Lucien's sister."

"How did you know my brother?"

Lady Sauvage's eyes glowed. "I was a very good friend of his."

Gabby stared at the intense, thin woman who wasn't beautiful in any traditional sense, but her flair for style, her strong, almost harsh personality, and confident forcefulness would have attracted Lucien. But what did she really know of the kind of woman who could attract Lucien's attention?

"Do you understand what my relationship was with your brother?" Lady Sauvage's astute gaze tracked her.

"You were his mistress?" Gabby stared back at the woman. "His French liaison?"

Lady Sauvage's deep laugh was almost in the low male register. If she were a singer, she would have had to sing a man's part. And for some inexplicable reason, Gabby believed the woman would enjoy playing a male part.

"Lucien and I shared many of the same appetites."

Heat flooded Gabby's face. Her brother was dead. How dare this woman? Gabby didn't want to discuss his intimate relationship with this crude woman.

"Oh, I'm sorry. I've offended your sensibility. How insensitive of me, but I assumed you understood about men and their needs."

A calculating Madame Sauvage knew exactly what reaction she would get. "I will not discuss my deceased brother in this way. Is there anything else you wish to say to me?"

"Please, I didn't mean any offense."

Gabby stared at the woman's catlike, opaque eyes and the small smirk in the corner of her painted lips.

"I loved Lucien. And I feel it my duty to help you in England."

"That is very kind of you. But, as you know, I have family friends to assist me."

"You think I believe the story of your family being close with the Rathbournes? You're in the house of English spies. They're plotting against France. And you are a pawn to be used when Rathbourne needs a negotiating piece. They won't protect you from whatever threat you perceive that has caused you to side with the English."

Icy fear engulfed Gabby, a dark, sinister feeling pulling her down, like a forceful undercurrent of a rapid river. She couldn't breathe and couldn't calculate how to respond in this game with this cunning woman. "You sent me the note?"

"Yes. You must take your rightful place in society, not as some French emigre with no history, no lineage. Your father was a marquis. Your brother was proud to be French. Your brother worked for our country, not against it. How would he feel to learn you had aligned yourself with his enemies?"

Gabby's lungs constricted, making it impossible to move air in and out. Gabby stared at the sophisticated French woman, trying to comprehend everything that woman claimed. And what she said rang true of Lucien. He was proud of his heritage, as she was of their long line of distinguished ancestors. But why would he spy for France? He abhorred the brutality of the new regime. If he supported the New France, why had he hidden her away from Napoleon?

Gabby had to get out the oppressive room. She had to get away from this scheming woman. Panic fluttered around her. Her breath came faster while her heart jolted in an uneven rhythm. Gabby stood, wanting to escape outside where there was air, where she could breathe. She might not be as clever in playing games, but she knew that she couldn't allow this woman to see her as vulnerable.

She quickened her pace down the hallway, confused by the next hallway to take her outside away from the party and the staring eyes. The hallway twisted on itself. This ancient abbey was utterly confusing. She was about to turn around and retrace her footsteps, but she first needed to slow the pulsating panic. She held her hand to her chest, trying to ease the painful inspirations.

"It is quite a confusing, convoluted place. Don't you agree? Were you lost or exploring?"

Gabby stared at Aunt Euphemia marching down the hallway, brightening the dark and eerie space with her shocking chartreuse dress, turban, and the umbrella swinging on her arm. Gabby's chaotic mind wandered to the incongruity of the umbrella for a sunny day and Aunt Euphemia's sudden appearance.

"You've had more wretched news, if I'm not mistaken by your pallor and quickened breath." She took Gabby's elbow. "Come along, my dear. I'm going to take you home. We'll go out this side door so no one will see or learn of your distress."

CHAPTER TWENTY-FIVE

Michael had to steel himself and call on all of his self-discipline to leave Gabby at the party. She was well-guarded, and the sooner he figured out if codes were being passed at the opera the sooner his association with Madame Abney would be finished. He bumped along in a hired hackney on the dirt road to Covent Garden.

The leather seat of the hackney was cracked and the cab reeked of smoke and other odors he decided to avoid considering. He wasn't exactly going incognito to meet Pudgy, but he had decided the arrival of the Earl of Kendal in his own carriage so close to the opera house would attract unwarranted attention.

Finally, he alighted from the revolting hackney on Wellington Street and walked the few blocks to the Bountiful Cow Pub, located far enough away to avoid probing eyes.

Entering the dark and dingy tavern, he spotted Pudgy bent over reams of paper at a table near the window. The low hanging wood beams and the smell of ale and roasting meat assaulted his nostrils and flooded him with memories of their favorite Oxford pub, The Cock and The Camel. The young gentlemen of titles enjoyed mixing with the lowlife, avoiding the responsibility and respectability that faced them once they ascended to their family titles.

"Kendal." Pudgy stood and waved from his spot in the corner. Besides being a gifted musician, Pudgy composed. His ginger-brown hair was mussed, his cravat open at the neck, his shirt sleeves rolled up to his elbow. Pudgy never had time or care for his appearance.

"Composing?" Michael asked.

"A small string arrangement."

While most men would need to expound on their success, Pudgy was more interested in the work than the accolades. It was Pudgy's modesty that had laid the foundation for their unlikely friendship. Pudgy, the son of a clergyman, and Michael, an earl's son, were both prodigies at Oxford. Their extraordinary abilities separated them from most of the men at Uni. Michael and Pudgy were more interested in their fields of study than tavern wenches, gambling, and brawling.

"Pudgy, it is good to see you. Thank you for meeting on such short notice." Michael offered his hand.

Pudgy's protruding, crooked nose that didn't fit his thin face wrinkled in amusement. He shook Michael's hand.

"I haven't heard the name 'Pudgy' in a while. The nickname rather dates our friendship." Pudgy patted his lean stomach.

Michael sat and placed his elbows on the scarred wood table. "Still hard for me to reconcile the change in your appearance."

Pudgy chuckled. "I was quite a rollie-pollie before I grew."

Towering over most men, Pudgy had a long, thin torso, long neck and arms, unlike the round fat rolls and chubby face he'd had at Oxford.

"Thank God my fingers were never fat or I would have stopped eating." His long slender fingers helped his reach on the violin.

"You were the only one I knew who could consume two entire chickens in one sitting."

"Yes, I don't seem to have the extreme appetite of young men."

The men shared a convivial laugh, appreciating all the extremes they had pursued as young men at University.

A burly waiter approached, a jagged scar across his face, like a tomcat who spent his nights fighting in the grungy back alleys. "You gents be wanting ale?"

Michael looked to Pudgy, who shook his head. "Not yet. But we'll need some sustenance in a bit."

Pudgy waited until the waiter had moseyed away and leaned over the table, speaking in a hushed tone. "You have had me curious since receiving your note. Why are you suddenly interested in opera?"

"You know I've always been interested in the mathematical nature of music."

"Yes. How could I possibly forget the long hours of discussing the mathematical patterns of scales and harmony? But what does that have to do with this music?"

This was the tricky part for Michael. He trusted Pudgy completely, but Michael wasn't at liberty to divulge his work.

"I recently heard a linguist from Germany speak on the history of hiding messages in music. I found myself intrigued, unaware of the endless possibilities of altering patterns in music as a means to communicate."

Pudgy sat back in the narrow chair that barely held his long frame and crossed his arms over his flat abdomen. "Suddenly you're interested in this one piece of music, sung by Madame Abney, who, by coincidence, has spent a great deal of her career in France. And just happens to now appear in London when war has been declared."

Michael should have known Pudgy wouldn't accept his story. And would immediately draw all the correct conclusions.

"Dammit, Pudgy. Put that brilliant mind to rest."

"You can't tell me the real reason for your sudden interest?"

Michael wanted to confide in his close friend, but he would be putting Pudgy at risk with any information. "I cannot. But I would appreciate any help you can lend me in understanding how someone might send hidden messages in this opera."

Pudgy ran his long, narrow index finger back and forth between his dark shaggy brows. "An intriguing question theoretically. And I'm happy to offer my assistance to help my country."

Michael neither denied nor admitted anything. "Thank you. I knew I could count on you."

"I've one condition for my assistance."

Michael damn well hoped he wouldn't have to lie to Pudgy. "Of course. If I can, I will."

"When this is all over, you will tell me what this damn secret business is about."

Michael didn't want to speculate on how long his role as code breaker would be necessary, now that England was at war with France again.

"Of course, and you do know, Pudgy, if I could confide in you, I would."

"You don't need to explain any further. I've brought my copy of the orchestration of the opera."

"Outstanding." Having Pudgy's brilliant mind for assistance buoyed Michael's hope to solve the problem quickly.

"You realize that Madame Abney has her own music with her own notes."

"Yes, I'm working on it."

And Pudgy gave a loud bark of amusement. "I'm sure you are."

Michael pushed thoughts of Gabby to the back of his mind. He was on a mission for King and Country.

"I want to study your score and then I plan to listen to the opera to learn if there are messages that might be delivered in the performance rather than the written music."

"Of course, we might glean patterns in the written music. But we'll also need to listen to Madame Abney every night if she is the one delivering messages, since she can alter her lines and only she and a few others will know the changes."

Michael didn't want to contemplate how many hours he would have to listen to the arias.

"Pudgy, I appreciate your help. But I don't want to put you in danger. After you look over the score, I don't want you to be further involved."

"Dammit, Kendal. I want to be involved. Besides yourself, who else could be more fitting to figure this out?"

"I've already put you at risk by asking you for the score."

"I'm not the fat boy from Oxford. I can handle myself."

Michael realized he had unintentionally pricked Pudgy's sense of gentlemen's honor. "If you detect anything, get a message to me."

Pudgy barely nodded. But Michael didn't miss the grin before Pudgy looked down at the table.

"Before we start analyzing the music, can you share your impressions of Madame Abney and her brother?"

Pudgy leaned back on the back two legs of his chair. "I don't believe she or her brother are involved in espionage."

"I haven't said anything about espionage."

Pudgy rolled his eyes while shaking his head. "Hypothetically speaking, I'm having difficulty believing either of them would be involved."

"Hypothetically speaking, what are your reasons?"

"Both are consummate, dedicated musicians. Music is the center of their lives. Nothing else matters. I don't believe they care about whose country is at war as long as they can make music." Pudgy's ardent defense of the Abneys was interesting and very insightful.

"The one thing I've learned—" Michael caught himself before he said *in France*—"is that understanding people's motives is quite confounding. And wartime brings out the worst and the best in people." Michael considered how hurt Gabby would feel when she learned of her brother's role as a spy for the country that murdered her parents. He hadn't considered if Gabby would find it upsetting about his work on behalf of England. He hoped she would understand his own need to work and protect his country. "But tell me more of the brother."

"He is an excellent pianist like his sister. Her career is more acclaimed. He could have his own career, but he chooses to help his sister. He is her voice coach. They rehearse together, and I believe he manages her career. It is rumored that he is very savvy in promoting his sister's career, and that he negotiated a very high salary for the diva for her London appearance."

"Interesting. And what of the husband? Is he also a musician?"

"He was trained in music, but isn't involved. What I've heard is that he's more involved in the dancers."

Michael sat back and crossed his legs. "What else have you heard about the husband?"

"I only know the rumors. That neither are very interested in the marriage."

"Have you witnessed any discord between the couple?"

"Never. He escorts her to rehearsal every day. They barely speak and he often reads the *Morning Post* during rehearsal."

"If anything raises your suspicion around either man, will you contact me?"

"Of course. Is this interest in the men anything to do with Madame Abney's possible performance for King George?"

Michael sat forward and lowered his voice. "How do you know of the performance?"

"Nothing suspicious. Madame Abney approached me about the arrangement of the strings for a Bach cantata that she is planning to sing for the performance."

"Why did she contact you?"

"She wanted me to add more strings to the composition. And she wants me to perform with her."

Considering all the dangers involved with this concert, Michael was grateful his job wasn't guarding the king. But then, in a flash of insight, he realized that his deciphering of the codes was the best protection for the king. He exhaled and squared his shoulders. "I'll need to see the music for the cantata also."

"Of course. But if you believe that the messages are being sent by Madame Abney to others in the audience, I would wager it would be in her aria. The Castrati Farinelli made this aria famous with his amazing vocal technique. Every line is varied and every rest provides basis for interpretation. Everyone comes to hear what Madame Abney will do with the famous aria."

"Excellent. This is most helpful. Especially if I don't have to listen to the entire opera each night." Michael must have sounded desperate since Pudgy laughed heartily.

"But if the messages are in the written music then there are many painstaking ways of using the music to hide codes."

"Yes, trust me. I've been thinking of all the possibilities, but I also thought it might be helpful to consider who has access to her music. Besides her brother, her husband, her dresser, and the maestro, who else would have access?"

"Since she rehearses with her brother, who also is her manager, he is the person most in contact with it. The manager of the opera company is someone else who frequents her dressing room. And then all of her admiring fans, including hordes of gentlemen who flock backstage."

Michael hadn't really considered all the possibilities of how she could easily pass messages. It really wasn't his job to monitor her visitors, but to use his skill as a linguist to decipher the music. Rathbourne definitely would already have been watching her and her visitors.

Pudgy gathered the papers he had been working on and placed them in a leather satchel. He then retrieved the score for the opera. "I've only two hours before I must return for tonight's performance. We must get started."

"Of course, I also plan to attend tonight. Let's get to work. I believe the easiest and the most likely approach is to follow the pitches since they obviously have the letter names A to G. You could expand to the rest of the alphabet by saying a low octave is A-G, the next octave is H-N, and so on."

"But that would mean words with early and late letters would jump big intervals, which is unlikely. It might be better to use flats for the second octave, H-N, and sharps for the third octave O-U, and maybe double sharps for V-Z."

"You take the first act and I'll take the second act to see if that pattern is obvious."

Twenty minutes later, the men agreed that neither could see a pattern using either pitches or changes in key signature.

The waiter approached when they both stood up and

stretched. "You gents want anything to eat? Shepherd's pie is our specialty."

"We'll take two and two ales, please." Michael hadn't realized how hungry he was, and that he would be foregoing dining out tonight. He'd need sustenance for his own performance.

After a filling meal, they continued their search, but to no avail.

Pudgy sat down and shuffled through the papers. "Perhaps the note in the base line tells which section of the alphabet you are in for the vocal line. For example, an A with a C base note is the letter A, but an A with a G base note is the letter H?" Pudgy asked.

"I've already looked at that possibility. It doesn't exist."

"You are quick with patterns. Amazing for someone who doesn't play music."

"I play a bit. What about using the time signature?"

"I'm now obsessed with finding the pattern before you do. I should be better at this," Pudgy said.

"A little of the Oxford one-upmanship stirring in your soul?" Michael joked.

"Maybe a little, but it is an intriguing challenge to look at the music from a totally different perspective."

"One of us should have deduced a pattern by now." Michael ran his fingers through his hair. "Not to overrate our skills, but we are the best." Neither was accustomed to failure.

Laughing, Pudgy gathered the music back and handed it to Michael. "Nothing like a bit of modesty."

Michael stood and shook Pudgy's hand. "Thank you for the assistance. I really appreciate your help."

"Damn, I wish we had solved it. And, like you, I'm not used to failing. I will crack this."

"Pudgy, this is not a game, like at Oxford. You must be careful."

CHAPTER TWENTY-SIX

With her feet propped up on an ottoman, Gabby settled back into a giant cushioned chair in Aunt Euphemia's drawing room at Ashworth House. During the ride back from the party, Aunt Euphemia hadn't spoken, respectful of Gabby's need for silence. Gabby's mind was numb from trying to sort out the truth from the lies in Madame Sauvage's revelations.

Aunt Euphemia placed a hot buttered crumpet and a pile of ripe strawberries on a plate from the tray before them. She handed Gabby the full plate. "You must eat to maintain your strength."

Aunt Euphemia sat across from Gabby. "Are you able to talk about your conversation with Lady Sauvage? Or would you prefer for me to tell you what I know of Lady Sauvage and your brother?"

Gabby sat up and then nodded.

"Lady Sauvage and your brother had an affair. I'm not sure the lady's heart was involved, but for a while they were lovers. The rumor was that your brother ended the affair. And I believe the lady isn't used to such high-handed behavior. It is possible that what you heard today was the venom of a scorned woman."

Aunt Euphemia took a big bite of her crumpet. Butter dripped on her chin.

"If you're wondering how an old woman like myself would know of such goings-on, it was common knowledge in society." She wiped away the butter with a linen napkin. "Our society is a very small group of people. Quite boring, actually."

Gabby stared down at her plate, trying to force herself to

taste the food that Aunt Euphemia had thoughtfully organized. "Why would Lucien spend time with that woman? She gave me the shudders."

Aunt Euphemia laughed heartily with her mouth wide open. Seeing the look on Gabby's face, she stopped immediately.

"My dear, I didn't mean to offend you. Only enjoying a refreshing moment of innocence. I feel I've become quite jaded about men and their lust for women, money, and power."

"I didn't know what part I should believe of what she said. Or if it was all lies." Sipping the hot chocolate that Aunt Euphemia had remembered was her favorite brought back memories of mornings with her mother. She did find a sense of safety enveloping her when in Aunt Euphemia's company. "She didn't believe the story of our families being acquainted."

"You poor thing. So many deceptions whirling around you. It is very difficult to know whom to trust."

Gabby kept her eyes down on her plate. She didn't want Aunt Euphemia to realize the truth, that she had considered the grand old lady and her family as a potential threat.

"I've been remiss in not sharing the entire truth with you, but with the shocking upheaval of your loss, I didn't want you to have more upset."

Gabby stopped, unable to swallow the dry crumpet. She wasn't sure she could handle any more bad news. She didn't think there was anything of her life or memory left to destroy.

"Despite the lady's claims to the contrary, our families are acquainted. I was friends with your dear grandmother. You must understand before the chaos in France, people travelled between our countries frequently."

"You knew my grandmamma?" Gabby held her breath and waited, afraid of what she might learn next. How could there possibly be bad news about her dear grandmamma?

"Your grandmother was brought as a young debutante to London for a season, anticipating a possible match with the Earl of Falconbridge. Matches between the great families of France and England were common."

"I didn't know." Gabby stared at Aunt Euphemia.

"Of course not, it was before you were born. Your grandmother did not want the match and returned to France and married your grandfather, with whom she was very compatible. Your grandmother was very proud that your mother had made an advantageous match with the marquis."

Gabby placed her plate on the side table. She couldn't possibly eat.

"During that season, Delphine and I became dear friends. Your grandmamma was beautiful and popular. She had her pick of beaus and friends. And despite our differences, she was very kind to me when I didn't "take" with many of the gentlemen. I wasn't very amenable to twittering and pretending I didn't have my own opinions." Aunt Euphemia slapped her knee. "I always was a difficult gel as my father would say."

Gabby couldn't imagine Aunt Euphemia and her grandmother as debutantes.

"Delphine and I corresponded. And on a visit to France, I stayed with your grandparents."

Gabby shook her head. "It is too much to take in."

"Can you imagine my shock when you arrived at Rathbourne House? I felt my heart would stop." Aunt Euphemia chortled. "For a moment, I thought I was seeing Delphine's ghost."

Gabby smiled faintly. "My mother told me of the resemblance, but I never was able to appreciate the similarities because of the difference in our ages."

"I'm sure it was difficult to imagine your grandmother as a young woman. Cord and Gwyneth, I am sure, believe I have always looked this way." Aunt Euphemia patted her sagging jowls. Her voice suddenly turned grave. "Only a few people know what I am about to tell you."

The air moving in and out of Gabby's lungs stopped— trapped in worry.

"Your grandmother wrote begging for my help during the beginning of the unrest in Paris. She said she was too old to make the trip but wanted her daughter and grandchildren out of

Paris. She had tried to convince your father to leave, but he refused to believe the mob would touch a marquis."

Aunt Euphemia's voice grew quieter. "I arrived too late, too late to save your parents, but I arranged for you and your brother to escape to your relatives in the country."

Gabby was speechless with the extraordinary shock. It was extremely dangerous to be in Paris, but the risk to an aristocratic English woman was absolutely deadly.

"Lucien always wondered how our poor relatives in Aveyon were able to coordinate our escape. We learned later that the only way people got away was with hefty blackmail money. Our cousins were very afraid. I was forbidden to speak of our past life or our parents."

"It was a terrible time, not knowing who could be trusted. But I lost contact with you. I'm missing years of what happened to you after the Terror ended."

"Lucien stayed with me during the worst months. When the violence was over, he returned to Paris to find out about our estate. I remained in the country with our relatives until Lucien felt it was safe to bring me back to Paris. I was very happy to return and resume my study of music. And for several years, everything was stable, until Napoleon took interest in me."

"Yes, I can see his motivation. Like your grandmamma, you are a beautiful, gentle woman."

"Without any forewarning, Lucien whisked me out of Paris in the dark of night to be hidden in a convent. He promised me he would come back and take me to England."

"And if he could have returned for you, he would have."

Gabby thought of all the days and months of waiting and hoping for Lucien's return. How did Aunt Euphemia know of her brother?

"I'm sure you're wondering why, after your conversation with Lady Sauvage, that I'm now telling you of our connection. I didn't want to give you any more difficulties before I shared what had transpired with your brother."

"You know how he died?"

"I know how he became a French spy."

"Lady Sauvage was right? Lucien was a spy? I can't believe it. Lucien was very angry, rightfully so, about the changes in France and the murder of our parents. I can't believe he'd help Napoleon by spying."

"Your brother had to get his fortune out of France. Not an easy task. This aspect of the story is conjecture on my part. I believe that in exchange for his safe passage to England, and in order to take the majority of his fortune with him, your brother made a deal with the Foreign Minister, Talleyrand. And unlike Napoleon Bonaparte, who is only interested in his domination of the world, Talleyrand saw the benefit of having someone of your brother's caliber spying for France."

Gabby's body started to shake. If her brother was a spy, would she be sent to prison? England was at war with France and her brother was a French traitor. Would she be treated as a spy?

"My dear, it's been too much for you. You've lost all your color."

Unable to squeeze a single word out for fear it'd be a choking sob, Gabby took a deep breath before she uttered, "I will be sent to prison?"

Aunt Euphemia stood abruptly and sat next to Gabby. She placed her hefty arm around Gabby's shoulder. "Oh my. I have given you a terrible fright. I'm sorry. After all you've endured in France, I can see how you made the assumption. You are not going to prison because of your brother. But now you understand why I have not shared the information. I also don't believe for a minute that your brother ever told Lady Sauvage of his spying. Which leads us to a very interesting question of how the lady came to the information. But that is for another day."

"I can't stay here. I wouldn't want you or Lady Gwyneth or Lord Ashworth to be associated with me." Gabby's heart plummeted to her feet. She'd have to keep her distance from everyone. She had to protect Michael and his family. She had money. She could hide in the English countryside.

Aunt Euphemia spoke in a slow, measured voice. "Gabby, your presence is not a danger to any of us. But most importantly, you are safe in England."

"But why? My brother was a spy. In France, the association would be enough to imprison you or hang you."

"I would hope our country is a bit more open-minded about innocent women. But, most importantly, I am not a helpless woman in England. I would never allow anyone to harm you. You are safe here. No prison. I promise. Your appearance in England has appeased my long-suffering grief. I've always regretted that I couldn't save my dear friend's family. And now you are here. I will never allow anyone to harm you, including the English."

Aunt Euphemia's vehement promise washed over Gabby like a fresh spring rain clearing the stagnant air. And like her belief in Michael, she believed Aunt Euphemia's assurance.

Aunt Euphemia twisted to look at Gabby. "Because of your grandmother and her plea, I worked to help other women and children to escape Paris and the guillotine. Although we couldn't save your mother, we saved many lives."

Gabby had heard stories of the bravery and sacrifice of the people who refused to be cowed by the intimidation of the Public Committee. "I wish I could share with Lucien that it was our dear grandmamma's brave friend who helped us escape the guillotine. He always believed it was relatives on our father's side."

"I hope you can now understand why I've waited. And I would have waited longer, if it weren't for Lady Sauvage. There was nothing disrespectable about your brother's actions. He made every effort to get you away from France and Napoleon. Like all of us during this time of war with plots and deception, he made the best choice he could."

The burning sensation started behind her eyes and in her throat. Lucien. If she could only thank him for all he sacrificed to take care of her.

Her voice shook. "I wish... When Lucien left me at the

convent, I was very angry at being taken away from Paris, my music, my friends, and my mentor. I didn't get to tell him how much I loved him."

Aunt Euphemia took Gabby's hands between her own wrinkled ones. "Your brother knew you loved him. Never doubt that for a minute. Now, you must go for a lie down. You have the opera tonight. Gwyneth is very excited by all the intrigue and the romance." Aunt Euphemia waggled her bushy eyebrows. "You lift this old woman's spirit. And tomorrow we'll have tea and talk about better days. I'll regale you with stories about your grandmamma as a debutante. And if she could see how you are handling yourself with all these challenges, she would be proud. You come from a courageous stock of French women. Never forget that."

CHAPTER TWENTY-SEVEN

The carriage stopped at the end of a dark alley in front of the backstage entrance to the Royal Opera House. Only one lantern hung above the small wood lintel for the singers', musicians', and workers' entryway. A marked contrast to the front of the opera house, which was lit with a multitude of burning lanterns and chandeliers in the opulent, mirrored grand foyer.

Lord Ashworth assisted each lady down from the carriage.

A giant of a man, capable of moving the heavy scenery by the looks of his brawny arms and thick neck, stood by the door.

Lord Ashworth nodded to the man. "Crawford."

"Lord Ashworth. Good to see you again. Haven't been around backstage for a while."

Gwyneth twittered. "Yes, Lord Ashworth, explain to the nice gentleman why you haven't been spending your nights in the pursuit of opera dancers."

Gabby wondered if Crawford was as familiar with Michael's name and his pursuit of opera dancers as he was with Lord Ashworth.

Lord Ashworth cleared his throat and took Gwyneth's arm. "Lady Ashworth, what a wonderful sense of humor." He bent down and whispered something to Lady Gwyneth who looked up into his eyes, her smiling face suddenly serious and her eyes darkened with longing.

It was Amelia's turn to harrumph. "Shall we go in?"

Gwyneth pulled her arm away from her husband. "Of course, Amelia. My husband forgets himself."

Gabby followed the ladies into a small anteroom. A list of the names sat on a wood table positioned next to the door.

Despite the cracked walls and stacked boxes lining the long hallway, there was a burst of action. Men hustled back and forth. There was an air of excitement in the preparation for the performance. Ignoring the low thrum of fear vibrating through her, Gabby was still eager for Madame Abney's performance.

Lord Ashworth had warned the ladies they were to be vigilant regarding their surroundings and the people around them. He gave no other specifics for their behavior during the evening.

Crawford winked at Lord Ashworth. "My lord, I'm to escort the ladies to Madame Abney's dressing room. Madame doesn't like gentleman callers before the show. Says it distracts her."

"I agree with Madame Abney, Mr. Crawford. Men are irritating distractions," Gwyneth retorted in a too sweet contrite voice.

Lord Ashworth chuckled. "You will pay for that comment, wife."

Gwyneth grinned back at her husband and said in a saucy tone, "I look forward to my punishment."

The usually relaxed Lord Ashworth stiffened and his breath came out rushed. Gabby heard him whisper to Gwyneth. "You forget yourself, wife."

Gwyneth leaned into her husband while he slipped Crawford a coin. "I'll come back for my wife and the ladies at intermission, Crawford."

Everything was proceeding according to their plan. Lord Ashworth would pretend to be leaving, but in fact would be backstage observing. Gabby didn't know how Lord Ashworth would gain access to the backstage and he didn't volunteer any more information, except that the ladies would be protected at all times. Lord Ashworth hadn't hinted if he also suspected Madame Abney as a threat.

If Madame Abney was a French spy, Gabby would risk everything to apprehend her to protect her friends.

"Come this way, my ladies." Crawford pointed down the long hallway. He turned back and spoke over his shoulder to Lord Ashworth who watched their departure. "I'll take good care of your lady and her friends, my lord."

"Thank you, Mr. Crawford, for your concern," Gwyneth said.

Gabby appreciated their protection, but she also would be vigilant to keep her friends safe.

She had slept soundly for the first time since the news of Lucien's death. And she had awoken this morning refreshed with a new resolve. The loss of Lucien was a terrible shock, and she had needed time to absorb the pain. But many had lost loved ones in this time of unrest, and it was time to move forward. She didn't want to remain like a broken shell on the shore, swept back and forth with each change in the tide of men's greed and violence.

Aunt Euphemia had risked her life to save Gabby and her family. She owed Aunt Euphemia and her family a debt of honor. Like her grandmamma and Aunt Euphemia, she wouldn't allow Napoleon to wreak havoc on her friends or on herself.

Napoleon and his men would not intimidate Gabrielle de Valmont.

"Mr. Crawford, have you worked here for a long time?" Amelia asked innocently. "You must know everyone who works here. It must be a large group."

"I do, my lady."

Gabby caught on to Miss Amelia's purpose. "You guard the door against anyone who doesn't belong?"

"Of course, he does. It is why they have a gentleman of Mr. Crawford's bulk and strength at the door," Gwyneth added.

Mr. Crawford shrugged his shoulder, basking in the ladies' admiration. "I do what I must to keep the uninvited from wandering in. It's a little tricky with the young gents who have too much liquor... Oh, the stories I could tell ya." He stopped. "Excuse me, my ladies. I shouldn't be telling you fine ladies such tales."

"Oh, but Mr. Crawford, we would love to hear of the

gentlemen and their visits backstage, wouldn't we ladies?" Gwyneth snickered.

Unfortunately, they had reached the end of the hallway. Gabby's heart kicked into a rapid allegro rhythm with the sound of a familiar male voice coming from behind the door of Madame Abney's dressing room.

Mr. Crawford knocked on the door.

"I thought Madame Abney didn't allow gentlemen visitors before a performance." Gabby's tone came out strident with the realization that Michael was back in pursuit of the opera diva.

Crawford shook his head. "Depends on the gentleman."

The cad was back, pursuing Madame Abney after pledging his fidelity and planning a rendezvous with Gabby on the same very night. Gabby stewed in a mixture of disbelief and betrayal.

A young, plump woman, with round apple cheeks and a wide smile, opened the door.

"The ladies are here to see Madame Abney," Crawford said.

The woman blocked Gabby's view into the room. But she heard the singer's titter and then Michael's croaky laugh.

He'd asked her to trust him. Could she? Maybe he was innocent, but it didn't stop Gabby wanting to do something violent to his person.

"Bete, allow the ladies into the room," Madame Abney chimed.

Madame Abney's dresser fluttered her eyelashes and lowered her voice. "Thank you, Mr. Crawford."

Crawford grinned at the dresser before he stepped back to allow them into the room. Unlike the dark hallway, this was a bright and spacious room. An Oriental painted screen sat in the corner. A vivid red jewel-encrusted costume was hung partially over the screen.

Crawford bowed his head. "Have a good evening, ladies."

"Thank you, Mr. Crawford." The ladies all spoke at the same time, making them all laugh together.

"Ladies, what is so amusing?" Madame Abney sat in front of a large mirror, again in disarray, her ivory robe hanging over one shoulder, her dark hair hanging down her back. Unlike at her townhouse, she had blackened her eyes with kohl. The dramatic line made her small eyes appear large and intriguing. She pouted at herself in the mirror while she applied deep-red rouge to her lips.

Michael stood frozen like the marble statues at the Louvre, his mouth open in shock. The idea of the loquacious man shocked into silence would be amusing to Gabby if she weren't ready to combust in distrust and disappointment.

Part of her excitement for the evening was her secret rendezvous with Michael. She had been eager to share with him her resolve to be of assistance in finding the men, to not be seen as helpless in Michael's eyes. She wanted to be seen as a confident woman, like Aunt Euphemia, not someone who needed his protection.

Neither Gwyneth nor Amelia registered any surprise over finding Michael again in the presence of the singer. "Kendal, your face looks like…" Gwyneth pressed her fingers to her lips to stop the laughter.

"Were you going to say as if he has seen a ghost?" Amelia asked.

"Ladies, does Ashworth know of your appearance backstage?" Michael's voice was challenging, as was the way his eyes locked on Gabby.

Gabby stared right back at him. After this morning's decision, she wouldn't allow her feelings for one tempting man to rule her behavior. She was going to trust him and if he proved false, she would survive. Women survived heartbreak all the time.

"Tut, tut. Lord Kendal, didn't know you were so exacting on propriety. The ladies are here on my invitation. And Lady Gwyneth and Miss Amelia, do you believe in ghosts?"

Amelia said amusingly, "I'm not sure I do, but I do believe Lord Kendal does."

Gwyneth swept into the center of the room, her crimson gown matching the exotic hues of the paisley shawl draped across the settee. Two chairs were placed next to the sofa and gave all those seated a great view of Madame Abney's reflection in the mirror. Gabby didn't believe it was an accidental arrangement.

Amelia gasped on spotting a small anteroom overflowing with costumes and gowns. A long shelf above the rack of clothing held wigs, hair pieces, and hats. "Your costumes are magnificent. May I take a peek?" Amelia pleaded.

"Of course. I'm looking forward to your ideas on my new gowns and costumes."

Gwyneth sat on one of the chairs. "We've lost Amelia to any further conversation."

Thinking about what activities Michael and Madame might have been involved in before their arrival, Gabby refused to sit on the settee.

"Darling, would you be willing to serve the ladies champagne?" Madame asked Michael.

Gwyneth's eyebrows shot up with the endearment.

"Of course, Madame." Michael walked to a table, near the costume closet. He avoided eye contact with anyone.

Seated on the chair next to the settee, Gabby noticed the open music score for the Bach cantata on a side table. "May I look at your music?"

"Of course, mademoiselle. You must play this cantata for me. You have promised me. I have a feeling your interpretation will inspire me."

"When are you going to perform this wonderful piece?" Gabby asked.

"I'm preparing it…I'm not supposed to speak of it yet. But I've been asked to sing for His Royal Highness. He has requested this specific sacred cantata."

Amelia, unseen by Madame, whipped around and raised her eyebrows in question at Gwyneth and Gabby.

Gabby sat staring at the sheet. More handwritten notes, in the same scrawl as in Madame's townhouse, were made throughout the music. The scrawl suggested changes altering the timing of the trumpet, which musically made absolutely no sense.

"Your notes suggest rather radical changes to the music," Gabby commented.

"Those are my husband's notes. He still likes to fccl he is part of my music." She tossed her hair over her shoulder. "He resents my brother Jacques's involvement."

Michael walked toward Gabby. "May I see the music? I'm familiar with Bach's compositions."

"You're interested in sacred cantatas, Lord Kendal? With your reputation, I was led to believe your interests lay elsewhere," Madame flirted.

"Madame, please, there are ladies present." Michael voice sounded strained.

Madame gave her husky laugh. "And I'm not?"

Seeing the singer's eyes darken and her lips part, Gabby looked back at the music, unable to watch the obvious dalliance between the singer and Michael. Gabby felt unsophisticated and naive by the way Madame Abney licked her lips and gazed at Michael as if she could devour him.

Gwyneth interrupted. "You mentioned that your brother is a very skilled musician."

"Yes, Jacques is gifted and Francois is jealous of my brother's talent. My husband trained, but was never accomplished."

Michael leaned over Gabby. He smelled of the out-of-doors, fresh and clean, and of Michael. His hands wrapped around her fingers and lingered briefly before he took the music.

She glanced up and was captured in the longing and tenderness in his expressive eyes. This was the man she had fallen in love with, the open, caring man. But she didn't recognize or understand the posturing rake who dallied with experienced women.

She lowered her eyes, afraid to betray her insecure and hurt feelings. She wasn't sophisticated enough to play these flirty games.

But why was he playing this part with Madame when he had sworn he was innocent of any wrongdoing? Did he also think

Madame was a threat? He had promised Gabby that the situation wasn't as it appeared.

Madame rolled her head back and forth to loosen her neck, allowing her dressing gown to fall further down her shoulder. "How did we get on such a dreary conversation? Let's talk about new romance. I want Jacques to meet Mademoiselle Gabrielle." Madame turned her head and gestured with her hands. "Ooh, la la! What great music you'll make together."

Bete said in a quiet voice, "Please, Madame, you must not move."

Madame looked at Gabby in the reflection of the mirror. "I've arranged for us to have a late supper with my brother. He wanted to meet you before the performance, but he must warm up. I told him it must be fate that brought you two together."

Michael's face contorted by how tightly he clenched his jaw. Gabby had never seen such an aggrieved look on his face. "I'm sure Lord Ashworth plans for the ladies to return home after the opera."

Gwyneth tittered. "No, Ash is out at one of his clubs for dinner and then I believe he plans to go gambling. Miss Amelia, Mademoiselle Gabby, and I are unencumbered tonight. And I do believe mademoiselle was looking forward to sharing her experiences with the gentlemen about her beloved mentor."

Michael now gave Gwyneth the same black look, his eyes narrowed while his fingers drummed at his side.

"What a disappointment, Madame." He turned and looked at Madame in the mirror. He spoke in a silky smooth voice Gabby had never before heard. "I thought you and I were having dinner together."

Madame Abney's hands fluttered to her chest. Her voice became deep and sultry and made promises that Gabby didn't want to imagine. "After, *ma chère*...after we all dine together."

Gwyneth shot Michael a look that could cause unsuspecting people to wilt and then used her haughty, cold voice. "We wouldn't want to interfere with your plans with Lord Kendal, Madame."

"No, Lord Kendal will indulge me, won't you, *ma chère*? Can you blame me for wanting to matchmaker for my brother? Have you seen a lovelier French creature, and also a gifted musician who also studied with Monsieur la Toure? It is fate."

Michael shifted his weight back and forth while he pulled on his cravat. "As you wish, Madame. We will all dine together."

"Now, I must warm up. Bete will escort all of you to the wings."

Gabby and Gwyneth stood. "Thank you, Madame. We are looking forward to watching your performance."

Gwyneth walked to the closet. "Come along, Amelia. We must leave Madame to prepare."

Amelia stopped in front of Madame. "Seeing your costumes tonight has already made the evening extraordinary. I will look forward to your performance."

Gwyneth and Amelia followed Bete out the door.

Michael took hold of Gabby's elbow and held tightly. "Allow me to escort you, mademoiselle."

He walked slowly, allowing Gwyneth and Amelia to move out of earshot.

He whispered. "Are you insane? Do you know what you've stumbled into?"

Gabby took umbrage at his angry condescending tone. "Why do you have to treat me as if I'm an infant?"

She tried to free her arm, but his grip was tight. "I've never thought of you as an infant. Not since I discovered you weren't a boy in those breeches." His voice sounded different as if he were strangling.

"I can't be this near to you without…" His breathing accelerated, his words rushed. "My God, what am I doing?" His thumb rubbed along the sensitive skin above her glove. "Gabby, you and the ladies need to leave. It's not safe."

A shiver of apprehension skittered down her spine with his warning.

Bete waited in the middle of the stage, preventing any further discussion.

Amelia gasped at the first backdrop painted with the Greek Parthenon, and Greek columns. "They are wonderful. I feel as if I'm walking in ancient Athens."

Gwyneth groaned. "I feel another toga obsession blossoming."

Amelia took Gwyneth's arm. "You told me my togas were inspired. And Bete, is it permissible to examine the back drop more closely?" Amelia was already dragging Gwyneth toward the painted scenery.

"Of course, my ladies."

Gabby didn't follow the ladies, but remained close to Michael for a reason she didn't want to examine.

Bete spoke in a serious manner, aware of the honor to be presenting to the fine lady and gentleman. "The opera has artists who paint the backcloths and flats. The men change the scenery by a system of ropes and pulleys." Bete pointed to two workmen who stood ten feet above them on elaborate wood scaffolding.

"It is best if you stand close to the curtain, away from where the men are working during the performance or…"

Bete stopped midsentence when she noticed Crawford standing near the heavy forest-green velvet curtain. The man sauntered toward Bete.

"Excuse me for a moment, my lady and my lord." Bete curtsied.

A violent tremor went through Gabby when one of the stagehands, in cap pulled down over his eyes, stopped working to watch her.

She stood still, like a deer trapped in the hunter's stare.

She heard a voice shout and then a whirl of motion. It all unfolded slowly. Michael jumping toward her. The rush of cold air before Michael threw her to the ground. Shouts and screams bombarding her while she flew through the air. An explosion of stars and bright lights burst in front of her eyes when she hit the hard floor. And then nothing.

CHAPTER TWENTY-EIGHT

It was pure instinct.

One minute Michael was admiring the realistic painted scenery, the next he sensed imminent danger.

He had time for only one reaction.

He had looked up at the moment before the workmen released the heavy metal pulley aimed to swing down and fall dead center where Gabby stood.

Michael leapt through the air, unaware of the shouts and screams, tackling Gabby to move her out of the path of destruction.

He shoved her hard. Not judging his strength and speed, fear fueling his momentum, he pushed her right off her feet.

Shocked, she teetered back and forth, unable to regain her balance.

He reached for her, but was unable to grab her before she slammed onto the floor, hitting her head against a wooden prop box.

With the loud crash of the pulley splintering the wood floor inches away from them, Michael threw himself on top of Gabby to protect her.

His hands shook and his heart leapt, trying to escape his chest.

Gabby lay still beneath him.

He levered himself on his arms to look at her. "Gabby?" Icy fear consumed him. She was unresponsive. Her face and lips without color. "Gabby, darling, wake up."

The saucy feathers she wore in her hair were smashed and lying on the ground next to her. He gingerly lifted her head and felt the cold stickiness of her blood.

Gabby's blood. Gross and ugly terror coiled around his heart. He refused to think about the possibilities. She needed a doctor. He jumped to his feet to shout for help. Amelia was kneeling down beside Gabby. Seeing the blood on his hand, Amelia had taken out her handkerchief and carefully lifted Gabby's head, putting pressure on the wound.

Amelia spoke in a quiet, controlled voice. "She's going to be fine."

"There is so much blood."

"Head wounds always bleed profusely."

Michael finally became aware of the chaos around them. The workman had swung by a rope to drop to the ground. He now sprinted across the stage and jumped into the empty auditorium.

Ashworth and Chalmers and Fenton raced across the stage after him. Why were Chalmers and Fenton helping Ashworth? Was no one in London truly who they were supposed to be?

Ashworth shouted to someone in the wings. "Cut him off at the front door."

Michael bent down and lifted Gabby into his arms. "We need to get her away from here." She was a wee little thing, weighing practically nothing. Although he was careful, she moaned with the sudden movement. Grateful to hear a sound from her, Michael spoke soothingly. "Everything is going to be fine."

"The man..." she sucked in a painful breath. "A ghost."

"Hush, darling. He'll never hurt you again. Ashworth will get him." And Michael didn't add that if Ashworth didn't get the bastard, he would kill him with his own bare hands. Michael loosened his tight protective hold on her slight body when she whimpered.

Amelia handed him the handkerchief. "Keep the pressure on the wound. I'll summon a carriage and send a messenger for the doctor."

"Thank you." His voice was rusty and rough with emotion.

Michael walked slowly and carefully around the stage to the backstage exit. He gazed down at Gabby's fluttering flaxen eyelashes, the only color on her pale face. He shifted her in his arms to descend the steps down from the stage. She moaned in French and then opened her unfocused eyes, a fathomless pool of blue. "My head aches."

"I'm sure it does, darling. I knocked you into a prop box."

She winced in pain. "Not your fault."

It *was* his fault. All of the bloody mess. He had failed to protect her when she was standing right next to him. Despite being well-guarded, the bastard had gotten to her. How could he protect her when he didn't know why the French would want to harm her? Had Napoleon decided he didn't need her alive to get her fortune?

He spoke quietly. "Don't talk. Rest. We'll get you in bed soon."

"Don't want to rest. Want to hear the opera."

Michael squeezed her gently. "I'm not sure with your headache you want to listen to a lot of caterwauling."

Her lips curved into a faint smile before he lifted her into the waiting carriage.

CHAPTER TWENTY-NINE

"Lose them." Anatole jumped into the carriage, which had been waiting around the corner from the opera house. Tearing off his workman's disguise as they bounced along Floral Street, he donned the waistcoat and top hat of an English fop. He'd disappear into the bowels of London's East Side, among the gambling and prostitution holes, looking like any other indolent gentleman, seeking the next thrill.

He was getting too old for the game. He had almost been captured this time. Unprecedented.

He had missed his target, too, alerting the English to his presence in London. Fouché would not be pleased. Fouché's method of expressing his displeasure could be fatal. He chuckled at his little witticism and then reached for the brandy in his waistcoat pocket.

He gulped the French brandy, enjoying the smooth heat moving down his throat and warming his stomach. Fouché had only one precept. Kill or be killed. Since he was Fouché's assassin, who would Fouché hire to kill him?

Maybe it was time to disappear into Spain. In the moment when the workman on the scaffolding dove for him, he thought he had seen...a ghost. He shook his head. It wasn't possible.

He never failed and he wouldn't this time. He sank back into the leather seat to decide his next move. Desperate times required a novel solution. And despite his occupation, he had no desire to die. He would have to draw her out, since she was always guarded by at least two men. And not the usual dimwit thugs, but observant and skilled men.

Killing her brother had been so much easier.

CHAPTER THIRTY

Michael paced in Ashworth's library. The doctor and Amelia were upstairs with Gabby. What was taking this long? Primal, ugly fear knotted and twisted in his gut.

The library door opened. Finally. Michael rushed to the door.

Instead of Amelia or Morley, it was Rathbourne. Mighty hell. He didn't need his brother-in-law's pompous posturing right now. Of all the blasted times for him to appear.

"How is she?" Rathbourne's tone wasn't his usual—precise and businesslike. He actually sounded concerned.

"The doctor is with her now. But I don't know why it is taking so long."

Rathbourne walked to the side table and poured two generous brandies. "Drink this." He handed Michael the glass filled to the brim with the deep amber blend.

Michael sipped the whiskey. "If I hadn't pushed her... When I saw the pulley coming straight at her, I panicked and pushed her too hard."

Rathbourne stared at him. "Have you considered that if you hadn't pushed her what the consequences might be?"

Michael threw back the rest of his brandy. He winced with the hot burn of the alcohol down his throat and into his gut. "Of course, but the possibility of...the outcome. Someone wanted to kill her."

Rathbourne slumped into a chair near the fireplace. "Not a comfortable feeling when a man can't protect the woman he loves."

Michael looked over his glass at Rathbourne, who wasn't acting like his superior, but a friend. "Why are you here? Did my sister send you?"

Rathbourne ran his hands through his coarse, black hair. "No. I haven't told Henrietta yet. In her condition, I don't want her to hear the stressful news."

"But Henrietta barely knows Gabby."

"But she knows how you feel about Gabby. I will wait to hear what the doctor says and then I will reassure Henrietta that both Mademoiselle Gabby and you are fine."

"Oh, bloody hell! I don't want Hen to worry."

Rathbourne gave a rueful laugh. "My sentiments exactly."

"I was standing right next to Gabby and she almost…" The awful words caught in his throat.

"First of all, it wasn't your job to protect her, but Ashworth's, and thus mine, ultimately." Rathbourne shifted in the leather chair in front of the fireplace. "We miscalculated."

"Miscalculated?" Outrage flooded Michael. "That's what you're calling her near-death? A miscalculation?"

"We anticipated that they would try to kidnap her. Not kill her."

Michael took a slow breath and sat down next to his brother-in-law. Rathbourne looked dog-tired. He had prominent dark circles under his eyes, his skin was sallow, and his hair looked like he had run his fingers through it repeatedly.

Despite needing to vent his anger, Rathbourne didn't deserve to listen to Michael's frustration. Rathbourne carried incredible responsibility—keeping England safe from Napoleon. Michael wouldn't want his job for all the tea in China.

"Is it someone else who wants Gabby killed? And why?" Michael demanded.

"It makes no sense for Napoleon to have her killed. He wants to cement his bloodlines with Gabby's lineage and her fortune. It has to be her close association with Madame Abney. My sister has told me that Mademoiselle Gabby studied with the same mentor as Madame Abney in Paris. Mademoiselle Gabby must have rattled someone or gotten too close to their operation. It is the only reasonable deduction since she's barely been out in society except for the opera house. I need to talk with her."

"You think she has learned something that made the French spies want to kill her."

"Exactly."

Michael jumped to his feet. "She can't go back there!"

Rathbourne raised his eyebrow. And Michael lost all his feelings of comradery with his brother-in-law.

"You are not going to send Gabby back into that den of murderers."

"You know she must do this if she is ever going to be free. And we need her help to end the spy ring."

"It is unsafe. How could she have learned anything about the spies? She's a musician. She's only talked about music with Madame Abney."

Rathbourne raised both eyebrows. "Exactly."

Michael paced the room. Why hadn't he seen the possibility? Because he was too busy trying to fight off Madame Abney and explain himself to Gabby. "I can't believe she's learned anything critical." Then he remembered Gabby's comments about the notes on the side of the music in Madame's dressing room.

"You've remembered something. What is it?"

Michael hesitated. "Gabby made a comment to Madame about the notations on her music for her royal performance."

"Bugger to hell! No one is supposed to know about the performance. I'm trying to maintain secrecy around the whole event. But the king refuses to let the threats affect his behavior. It is commendable, but he's making my job a damn nightmare."

"You think the coded messages are specifically about harming the king at the concert?"

"It is the natural deduction. Madame Abney and her musicians will have the opportunity to be close to the king."

Michael stopped. "They're planning to kill the king? Why? I thought Napoleon was posturing to be friends with England."

Rathbourne ran his hand through his hair again. "He wants us to believe he doesn't have any designs on England, but trusting him would be like trusting a rabid dog. Our diplomats are pretending to accept the French's pretense of still seeking peace, while we prepare for war."

"But if the French kill the king, we'll seek revenge and attack France. Napoleon's strategy is to distract England while he builds his empire in the rest of Europe."

"You are quite knowledgeable. I didn't realize how much you've been helping Henrietta with the Abchurch work."

"Pursuing Madame Abney is mainly a nighttime activity. Besides, doing the code work with Hen is much simpler than fighting off an aggressive French opera singer."

Rathbourne chuckled. Michael was glad to entertain his brother-in-law.

"A plot to kill the king makes no sense according to our intelligence, unless it's a distraction."

"Either way these are serious killers. I don't want Gabby involved."

"You know it's too late for that sentiment. She *is* involved."

"But you don't need to tell her what you've just told me."

Rathbourne shrugged. "Do you really believe she won't be wondering who wanted to kill her and why? What would you have me do?"

"You plan to use her to try to stop French spies from killing the king. And last week you thought she was a French spy."

"I never said I thought she was a French spy. And I'm not asking her to take down the spies. Only to continue her relationship as an interested musician with Madame Abney. And, in case you haven't noticed, my sister, Ashworth's wife, and Amelia are all part of this mess. And none of those men are happy with their loved ones involved, but these are not easy times."

"But no one has tried to kill them despite the fact they were there when Gabby spoke about the music to Madame."

Rathbourne leaned forward in his chair, bridging the distance between them. "This work is not always logical and precise, like code breaking. We're always trying to stay ahead of our enemies, second-guessing their motives. What we know is that messages are being passed, most likely in the music, and Mademoiselle Gabby's life was threatened after she made Madame's acquaintance. Are they all related?" Rathbourne shrugged. "We will be vigilant and hope either you or Gabby makes headway with the music."

Michael wanted to rush Gabby to the countryside and out of harm's way. "I can't stand by and let this happen."

"I know this is difficult." Rathbourne stood.

Michael ignored his brother-in-law's sympathetic tone. "You've no idea."

"Your sister was almost killed trying to negotiate the code book for your life. Have you forgotten?"

"Bloody, bloody hell."

"I will ensure that Mademoiselle is safe."

"You can't guarantee her safety. Chalmers and Fenton guarding her couldn't stop a single man from trying to kill her."

"Actually, there were two men on the scaffolding, but Fenton thought the one man looked as if he was trying to stop the other from releasing the pulley."

"Who would be the other man?"

"No idea since he wasn't one of my men. And Chalmers and Fenton weren't guarding Mademoiselle Gabby."

"Then what were they doing backstage and then running after the murderer?"

"They were guarding you."

"Fenton and Chalmers are my bodyguards?" Michael was incredulous. How many bodyguards did he need? "I thought Denby was."

"Denby, as your valet, can't attend the opera and other gentlemen's pursuits. You are an important asset with your skills. Your safety is of national importance."

Michael raised his hands. "I'm not that bloody important."

"Maybe not." Rathbourne smirked. "But Henrietta would never recover if anything happened to you."

"My God, are you protecting everyone in England?"

"Some days it feels like it," Rathbourne straightened his cravat, his voice tinged with sardonic amusement. "You needn't worry about Mademoiselle's safety. I have the best man to guard her."

Michael bristled. "And who that might be?"

"The man who has the most to lose if anything happens to her." Rathbourne took one last swallow of his brandy and placed his glass on the table.

Michael wanted Gabby protected, but the idea of another man more capable to keep her safe was more than disconcerting and humiliating. "And pray, tell me who could that possibly be? The king?"

"No, old man. You. You saved Gabby tonight. And because of your association with Madame Abney, you'll be close by to guard Gabby."

Michael recognized the logic in Rathbourne's idea. That didn't mean he had to accept it.

"But I must tell Gabby the truth about my relationship with Madame Abney and my work."

"Of course, she must know all the details to protect herself and to help in the investigation. I'm still interested in what role Lord Weston and Lady Sauvage play. I don't want you to interfere with Weston's interest in Gabby."

Michael was bone-tired of all the intrigue around Gabby and the way his brother-in-law stayed in the wings, acting as a puppeteer, orchestrating everyone to act by his direction without full understanding. "You should have informed me about Lord Weston. How dare you keep information from me that could be dangerous to Gabby?"

Rathbourne stiffened. "And watch you run him through in a fit of jealousy?"

"You don't think I'm capable of acting logically?

"No. A man in love does not act logically. And it isn't singular to you. My policy is to not involve anyone in an operation when their personal attachments may influence their judgement. Their behavior and the outcome are too unpredictable. I can attest that my own concern for your sister clouded my judgement and could have gotten Henrietta killed."

Michael couldn't refute Rathbourne's reasoning. It didn't stop him for wanting to tear Weston apart. Weston had been close to Gabby at several events. Why would he want to harm Gabby unless he was hired by the French? Michael agreed with Rathbourne's approach in theory, but this was Gabby's life they were discussing. Michael bolted out of the chair and braced himself for the fight.

An unfazed Rathbourne looked up and spoke in a precise and unruffled manner. "Mademoiselle Gabby is the center of the intrigue. I'm trying to deduce who might be trying to kidnap or harm her. Because of your relationship with Mademoiselle Gabby, you're now involved up to your neck in a French intrigue. And because of your work and your sister's affections, I will not inform you of every decision I make to ensure your safety. You will have to trust me that I have your and Mademoiselle Gabby's welfare foremost in my plans."

"My God, and you expect me to protect her without knowing who you think might be a threat?"

"I am trying to unravel a spider's web. The work is meticulous and painstaking. It is possible Weston isn't a threat, only a gentleman pursuing a beautiful young woman. But after tonight, we must treat everyone who is interested in Gabby as a suspect. I am now informing you of the possibility, as I will Mademoiselle Gabby when I speak to her. You now know about Weston, but you must not interfere with his pursuit of Mademoiselle Gabby."

CHAPTER THIRTY-ONE

Michael sat in a stuffed armchair beside Gabby's bed, pouring over Madame Abney's arias. Every few minutes he would get up and check on a sleeping Gabby. The covers were pulled up to her neck, revealing only a mass of honeyed curls and her pale skin. Since the attempt on Gabby's life, no one cared about the rules of propriety. Lady Gwyneth and Amelia had retired after the eventful evening, leaving him in charge of Gabby's care.

He wanted to tend to every need for Gabby in the same gentle way she had cared for him. But since everyone had left, she slept deeply and restfully.

Gabby had sustained a nasty head wound and subsequently a very bad headache. According to the esteemed Dr. Oglethorpe, she would be right as rain after a few days of rest. Michael should have been relieved by the doctor's prognosis, but her rapid recovery would mean she would soon be returning to the opera and to danger.

He was exhausted, but he needed to study the music. The sooner he figured out the pattern, the sooner Gabby and the king would be safe.

He leaned back in the chair, resting his neck, and closed his eyes to visualize the possible variations of coded notes in the music.

Michael woke to Gabby's voice. He bounded out of the chair

abruptly, sheets of music scattering across the floor. Confused for a brief second, he looked around the blue lady's room.

"Michael? Why are you sleeping in a chair? Here, in my bedroom?" Gabby was wide awake, her eyes shining bright, and color had returned to her smooth skin. She was upright with the pillows behind her back and the covers pulled up to her neck.

He couldn't stop staring at her striking fresh countenance. Michael sat down gingerly, on the edge of her bed, careful not to jar her. He took her hand that rested on the top of the cover. "I was tending to your care and studying Madame Abney's arias, until I fell asleep."

"Does Lady Gwyneth know you're here?"

"Yes, I have everyone's blessing. And I've sworn to be here only in the role of nurse."

"You're my nurse?" An attractive pink color flushed across her face.

"After what happened last night, everyone is more concerned for your safety than the rules of propriety."

"Aunt Euphemia knows about your presence here…in my bedroom?"

"Yes, my dear. But their opinions wouldn't have mattered. I was not going to leave your side."

Gabby's eyes widened. "Oh."

"Do you still have a headache? The doctor left a powder for you if your head hurts." Michael squeezed her hand.

"I'm fine. Only a bit of a headache."

"I'm so sorry, Gabby. It was my fault, I shoved you too hard."

"No, you saved my life. If you hadn't seen those men, I don't know…"

"Don't think about it now. You need to rest."

"I don't feel tired. What time is it?"

Michael stood and moved to open the heavy drapes. He spread them apart and peered up at the dawning light.

"The sun is about to rise." He came back to stand next to her. He wanted to soothe the corkscrew curls from her forehead as he had done during the night. "Do you want a sip of water?"

She gave him an impish smile. "I had some while you were sleeping."

"What a nurse I've turned out to be. Not doing half as well as you did taking care of me."

"You were really very ill. I'm not sick. I injured myself and will be better in no time."

"Are you sure you don't want to try to fall back asleep? Everyone will be up soon and will want to check on you. For the short time you've been in England you've developed loyal friendships." Not that Michael was surprised, since how could anyone resist her gentle, loving nature. He wasn't sure when he'd lost his heart completely to the French minx, possibly when she had soothed his hurt feelings over the change in his household.

"Did they catch the men?"

Michael wasn't sure how much he should confide when she had just awakened. "Why don't I call your maid? And I'll come back this afternoon and we can talk about what's happened."

"No, I don't want my maid. I want you to tell me what you know."

Michael looked down at her serious face, her blue, blue eyes focused on him. She deserved to know. "The men escaped. No one knows who they were."

"But they have to be Napoleon's men."

"Gabby, I have a lot to tell you. Are you sure you don't want to wait? We can talk this afternoon."

"If someone tried to kill you..." Gabby shuddered involuntarily, "...would you want to wait?"

Michael took a deep breath. "Only because you insist. And if I see any signs of fatigue, those bright blue eyes getting droopy, I'm going to stop. Agreed?"

"Agreed." Gabby shifted in the bed and the covers dropped, revealing her thin muslin nightgown, and although it was buttoned up to her neck, Michael couldn't stop from staring at her rounded, full breasts and couldn't stop the heat of lust roaring through him.

"Michael, what's wrong? Your face is bright red."

"Because, my sweet innocent, I've sworn on my honor to be a gentleman, but you in bed, in an alluring nightgown, makes it hard for a man to honor his pledge."

"This nightgown isn't seductive. It's a plain muslin gown."

"It's not the nightgown, it's you, Gabby. You in a nightgown is too tempting for a man…"

Innocent as Gabby was, her lips turned into a knowing, womanly smile. "But my plain bedclothes pale in comparison to Madame Abney's dressing gown."

"I never had trouble breathing, feeling as if all the air has been sucked out of the room, in response to Madame Abney in her dressing gown. Only because of one pink-faced, seductive French siren in a white nightgown." He leaned over, placing both his hands next to her shoulders. "I wasn't pursuing Madame Abney. I am trying to find out whether French spies are sending messages in her music."

Gabby flinched. "Madame Abney is a spy?"

"Possibly."

She whispered, as if someone might hear her. "She's sending messages to spies in her music?"

"We know that messages are being sent to French spies from the opera house."

She leaned away from him. "Are you sure you should be telling me this information? Do you know that my brother was a French spy?"

"Yes, I've gotten approval to tell you about my work because of last night. We think you might have discovered something in Madame Abney's music and that was the reason that man tried to kill you."

Gabby clenched her hands on the bed covers. "It wasn't Napoleon's men?"

"Napoleon doesn't gain anything by having you killed."

Gabby chewed on her lower lip as she stared into space. "I was wondering the same thing. The only reason I could come up with was Napoleon is angry that I defied him, the First Consul, so he ordered me to be killed."

Michael hated seeing the bewildered look on Gabby's face when she explained the reason Napoleon wanted her dead. He took her hand and pressed it to his cheek. "I'm sorry. I wish I had the answers."

"But wouldn't I know if I discovered something in the music?"

"Most likely not since they're using codes in the music to hide messages."

"And because you're skilled in deciphering codes, you are supposed to find the message."

"How do you know about my skills?"

"You talked a lot when you had the fever."

"Holy..." Michael stopped himself. "Why didn't you tell me?"

"How would I tell you? Tell you I knew you were in France on a secret mission? I'm French. Our countries are at war. And then, when I found out my brother was a spy, I thought you'd never trust me."

Michael pressed his lips to the warm tender skin on her wrist. "I trusted you the minute I met you."

"But I was disguised as a boy."

"And you couldn't stop laughing when I fell off the settee. I think I fell in love with the impish smile then."

"Love?" Gabby eyes searched his face.

"You must know how I feel about you. I promised to court you, but I'm not sure I can wait. My promises are honorable."

"But you and Madame Abney on the settee?" Her lashes lifted, treating him to the sight of her vulnerable and questioning eyes.

"I swear, on my French mother's good name, I was trying to escape the lady's clutches." Michael watched Gabby's eyes warm.

She followed a thread on the counterpane with her finger, avoiding looking at him. "Courting one woman and having an affair with another is done all the time by French gentlemen. My father had a mistress. My mother pretended it didn't hurt her, but I never could be as complacent as my mother."

Michael lifted her hand. "You never have to worry about me. I will never hurt you, Gabby." He rubbed his finger in light circles on her soft wrist, enjoying the way Gabby's breath quickened and her lips parted.

He could seduce her right now. His sweet French musician wanted him as much as he wanted her. No one would be up for another hour. They could marry by special license. He lifted her hand to his lips and used his tongue to paint circles on her sensitive wrist.

Gabby gasped. Her sweet breasts moving under the virginal nightgown. He wanted to unbutton every one of the pearl buttons and then use his mouth and lips on her soft, flushed skin.

He started to reach for her, when he stopped suddenly. Someone had just tried to kill her and he was thinking about his own needs, not about what Gabby needed.

He jerked up from the side of the bed, walking toward the window. "My God, Gabby, you're a test of my control."

Her pupils were dilated, her breaths coming in little pants.

"Let's talk about what you saw in the music. Can you remember anything?" He was trying to get his mind onto another topic rather than on seducing his sweet Gabby, an injured and innocent woman. He was turning into a cad, but only around Gabby, only Gabby. "I'm sorry, you've had a horrible night. My questions can wait."

"No, I want to help. I need to see and hear the music."

Michael rushed back to her side, knelt by the bed, and took her hand. "My God, if there were any way not to involve you, I would do it."

"No, I want to help. I want to be of use. Don't shield me as if I'm still locked away to be kept ignorant in a convent. I wouldn't be able to stand it. Please, let me help."

Michael released her hand and stood. "You're like Hen. She needs to be involved, to use her mind."

"Thank you for understanding why this is important to me. I can't remain unware and uninvolved."

"I'm not agreeing that I won't do everything in my power to keep you away from the danger."

"Of course." With her sweet gentle manner, Michael knew he'd probably never be able to say no to this one woman who captured his heart.

He walked to the window and opened the curtains wide. "When we were in Madame Abney's dressing room before the opera, you were perusing her music and said something about the notes. Do you remember?"

"Yes, the notes by her husband made no musical sense. He had scrawled changes to the rhythm along the side of the sheet, next to the bars of music. He had changed the entire rhythm by altering the whole notes and rests into quarter notes and half notes. I need to see the notes again to look at the pattern."

"Was there only one page of his writing?"

"No, he made notations throughout the cantata."

"My God, the notes are the coded messages. I've gone through the opera repeatedly and found nothing. I need to see those notes. I need to see Madame Abney today."

"You're going to see her?" Gabby voice squeaked.

"Gabby, darling, I've got to find the code. These contain plots against the king's life. I must find their messages to prevent calamity."

Gabby chewed on her lower lip. "I'm not being a jealous woman...well a bit, since I did see the way Madame Abney looked at you as if you were her favorite dessert."

"Gabby, you're not supposed to know such things." Michael felt the tops of his ears burning.

"I've a better plan that doesn't involve the lady and you. What if I send a note telling the lady that, during my recovery, I would like to practice the music before I perform for Madame? It is a reasonable request."

Michael paced. "But if you ask for the music, it might alert Madame that you know about the messages or the person who tried to kill you. It means the person will come after you."

"Exactly. But I don't believe Madame is passing the

messages. It must be her husband. Madame is a musician, and she'll want to hear me play and want to share her passion. And I'm happy as long as she doesn't share any of her passion with you."

"It is too dangerous. I can't allow you."

"I'm not allowing you to see Madame Abney without me."

Michael recognized the same tilt of the head, the same pinched lips, that his mother called Hen's Gallic stubbornness.

"You know it's the best solution. If you rush over there, what chances do you have of actually analyzing the music instead of being chased around her room? And if you show too much interest in the music you'll alert Madame or her husband."

Michael hated to admit that Gabby was correct. Not that he didn't appreciate her canny ability to solve a problem, but it meant placing her right in the middle of an espionage plot of violent men.

"These men are dangerous. Have you forgotten last night?"

"No, but we all believed there would be attempts by Napoleon to kidnap me, not spies who want to murder me. Now that we know who our enemies are, we can be better protected. You can tell Lord Ashworth about our suspicions about the husband and someone can watch him, right?"

Michael snorted. "It's already been done." He leaned down to tweak her nose. "You do realize that you're an amazing woman."

Gabby pulled on his hand. "You will be here to protect me as will Lord Ashworth, and Aunt Euphemia."

Michael wished he had the same faith as Gabby. His analytical mind couldn't negate all the possibilities for errors and mistakes. And this was Gabby's safety and her life that they were gambling with.

CHAPTER THIRTY-TWO

Gabby rose from the desk when she heard Michael's voice in the hallway. He must have come immediately after receiving her message that Madame Abney's music had arrived.

She tugged at the bodice of the lavender day dress Amelia had chosen for her.

Morley announced Michael in his deep, sonorous voice.

Michael bowed and Gabby curtsied, but she didn't believe for a minute that their formal behavior fooled Morley, who was aware of everything that went on in the house, including Michael spending part of last night in her bedroom.

Michael gave her his deadly dimpled smile, and her heart danced in the romantic gavotte rhythm.

He was dashing in his blue waistcoat and buff breeches and his worn leather riding boots. His injury must be completely healed since he had returned to riding. His face was clean-shaven and Gabby was a bit disappointed. She had liked his night beard stubble and the rough feeling against the sensitive inside of her wrist. Remembering the prickly sensation and Michael's harsh breath bent over her sent her heart aflutter in triple time.

Gabby waited for Morley to close the door so she could throw herself into his arms. Their eyes met and Gabby couldn't look away from the hungry intensity of Michael's stare. Did he read her thoughts? Her need for him, only for him?

It seemed a century before Morley finally closed the door.

Michael walked toward her. "Darling, should you be up?"

Gabby didn't want to have his concern. After last night, she was a woman awakened to love. The feelings of being loved by Michael had been a startling awakening. Like on the first days of spring sunshine after the long winter rains, she felt renewed, alive and hopeful again. Michael loved her and she loved him.

She glanced up at him, her eyes and heart filled with yearning for this man. This man who made her laugh, who made her believe in love and hope after terrible times.

His rich laugh rumbled in his chest. "Gabby, you can't look at me like that and not expect a kiss."

"Am I that obvious?" She placed her arms around his neck and pressed against his solid, hard body.

"Gabby." Michael tightened his arms and pulled her closer. Gabby felt herself soften around his hard planes and unyielding ridges.

His warm lips tenderly touched hers. He rubbed his lips over hers and her melting body molded around him, wanting to take him in. He took little love bites on the corners of her lips, as if she were a delicious treat.

Gabby didn't know if she could remain standing by the sensations he elicited with the tip of his tongue, exploring and prodding her to open to him.

And when he pressed his tongue into her mouth searching, her knees wobbled and she tightened her hold on his neck.

Slowly his tongue did gentle forays into her mouth, filling her. Her breasts tightened against his chest, and she rubbed along his maleness.

His short, hot puffs of breath against her face drove her erratic heartbeat faster.

His arms locked her tight against him, and he angled his mouth to take control. His body and tongue moved against her in a demanding, possessive way. Gabby reveled in the sheer pleasure of his need.

She didn't know that a man's need could fuel a woman's need. That there was intense, driving pleasure in being desired, basking in the sensation of his heavy breaths, the burning heat radiating from his body, and his hardness forced against her.

She held onto him, her breath and her knees weak.

Suddenly Michael shuddered in a deep heave and stopped kissing her. "Gabby, we have to stop." He slowly loosened his hold. "This is not the time nor place." His sharp cheekbones were as flushed as they had been when he had the fever. The contrast made his shining eyes luminous.

Gabby couldn't catch her breath. She could barely hear over the roaring pulse in her ears. Michael unwound her hands from around his neck and pressed her palm hard to his mouth and jaws. He rubbed his hot, rough jaw against her tender skin.

His breathing was fast and jagged when he reluctantly released her hands. "Darling, please don't look at me like that or I won't be able to stop."

"But I don't want you to stop."

He brushed an errant curl behind her ear. "Sweet Gabby. If I don't stop now, I won't be able to. And I refuse to rush you or me in such an exposed setting and in a hurried way."

Gabby felt the thrill of anticipation fading, her skin cooling, and her heartbeat slowing. "But I wouldn't mind if we hurried. In fact, I think I would like it."

His voice was rueful and amused. "What am I going to do with you?"

She pressed against him, not willing to give up his heat and hardness. "I don't know and that is what I was hoping to learn today."

He rubbed his nose against hers. "You're incorrigible. And one of us has to be the responsible one."

Gabby traced his lips with her tongue as he had done to her. "After last night I feel free and alive."

She liked the sound of Michael's sudden heavy intake of breath, and the pounding of his heart against her breasts, when she slipped her tongue into his mouth. He took possession of her lips again, pushing his tongue into her moist mouth. He was demanding in his hunger and need. And for a minute they were lost together, their bodies melded, their tongues intertwined.

He stopped as abruptly as he had started. He lightened his hold and scattered kisses on the sides of her lips, on her cheeks, and on her nose. His voice reverberated close to her ear sending hot and cold chills dancing along her skin. "You're a very fast learner."

Gabby twisted the button on his waistcoat and looked up into his smiling eyes. "I'm learning from the master."

"I need you to sit down or I won't be the responsible one." Michael linked his fingers between hers and led her to a chair. "For someone who was injured, you've made quite an impressive recovery."

Gabby sat and stared up at him, her heart and feelings reeling. She was thunderstruck and in awe. "You're a very powerful medicine."

Michael bent over and gave her a small peck on the lips. "For that praise, you get one more kiss, Gabby. But only one. Once we know you're safe from this madness, we're going to spend days in bed together. And we aren't going to stop."

Gabby wanted to sing, dance, and play Bach's *Prelude in C*. She felt more vibrant than ever in her life.

Michael went to the side table, which held the decanters. "Do you want a sherry?"

Still breathless, she tried to gain control over the unruly and ungovernable emotions and sensations. "I had told Morley to bring a tea tray."

And as if by premonition before Gabby could finish, Morley knocked then entered. "Mademoiselle, shall we bring in the tea tray?"

Michael raised his eyebrows at the timely interruption.

"Thank you, Morley. If you'll place the tray on the table." Gabby kept her gaze down, away from Morley's astute scrutiny.

A footman carried the heavy silver tray. Morley followed to ensure the correctness of the ritual. "Mademoiselle, do you wish me to pour the tea?"

"No, thank you, Morley. I will do the honors." Gabby reached for the teapot to hide her rioting emotions.

Morley nodded and followed the footman out of the drawing room.

"Shall I pour you tea or are you happy with your brandy?" Gabby asked.

"I think I will forego the tea since I need to fortify myself after receiving your urgent message." Michael brought the glass to his lips. Gabby didn't miss the teasing smile.

"I did not summon you just to kiss you, if that is what you're thinking." Gabby poised on the end of the chair and poured tea into a china cup. "You make me sound like Madame Abney."

"Darling, there is no comparison between you and Madame. And if I had known how urgent your need was I would have rushed over, forsaking shaving." His voice was light and teasing.

"I've assumed you would want to immediately see the music."

Michael sat down across from Gabby and crossed his legs. "How did you acquire it so quickly?"

"Madame sent me flowers after last night's incident. She feels horrible since she arranged for me to be backstage. She believes it is her fault and she apologized profusely about the 'accident.'"

She had planned to also tell Michael about the note from Lady Sauvage when he arrived, before they looked at the music, but she had gotten distracted by her giddy rush of feelings. Her reactions were new and she was having trouble controlling them with Michael so near.

"I haven't forgotten that your presence backstage was because of Madame Abney's invitation." Michael's tone became forceful. "Not many people knew of your plans. For the time being, we must pretend that last night was an accident to not raise any suspicions."

"Yes, I understand."

"Asking for the music might have alerted your assailant."

A wave of fear crashed through Gabby. She shivered in response but forced herself to appear calm. "Yes, but we have no other choice."

Michael took a swig of the brandy. "I'll be damn glad when all of this is over."

"Madame Abney knows my interest in music is real. I sent a message back thanking Madame for her concern and described how playing the cantata would help my recovery."

"I would say you've found a much better way to help your recovery." Michael captured her in his demanding, hungry look.

Gabby felt the giddy feelings overtaking her. Unfamiliar feelings swelled within her to give whatever Michael wanted and needed from her. She wasn't embarrassed by his devouring stare, but instead reveled in his need of her.

He suddenly stood. "Where is the music?"

Michael was obviously more experienced in controlling his needs. She was a muddled mess whereas he was focused on solving the problem of the French spies and ending the danger. She needed to pull herself together.

"Doesn't this support that Madame Abney isn't the one sending messages, or why would she give me the music? Within the hour, the music arrived—her copy, with her husband's notes."

Michael paced in the center of the room. "This music is dangerous to have. I want to get started, but maybe I should move it to Kendal House, away from you."

Gabby wasn't surprised by his keenness to decipher the messages and desire to protect her. She pointed to the stack of papers on the desk in the corner. "I want to help you. I'm a musician. I already started looking for patterns in the first page of his notes."

Michael bent over the desk, his back to her. "Of course, I know you've been a great help. But the more you know, the greater danger you're in." He picked up the stack of papers.

"I'm already in danger. And working together will be an advantage."

He twisted back, his face searching hers. His voice grew quiet. "You're absolutely right, but it doesn't make this any easier for me. Having you involved."

"I want to share the work and the danger with you." Gabby tried not to sound pleading, but her need to be part of the work was important. Important to her, but also important for their future together. She wanted Michael to see her as capable and be willing to turn to her for support.

Michael turned back to the papers. "Do you want to continue to work on the first page or shall I? Or would you prefer playing the music he's written? Everyone has a different way of approaching the problem."

Gabby put her teacup down and stood. "You're the most amazing man. Do you know that?"

Michael turned sharply to look at her, his brows furrowed together. "I haven't deciphered the code yet."

"I'm sure you will. I'm impressed that you are willing to accept my help. Most men wouldn't consider women capable of thinking."

Michael shrugged. "Growing up with a sister who is smarter than me, I didn't have a chance to develop the typical male pig-headed thinking."

"Really? Henrietta must be brilliant."

"Thank you." Michael's head was bent over the pages he leafed through. "Hen is smart as a whip, but wasn't allow to attend university because she's a woman. When in society, she's had to pretend she has no brains, especially with clodhopper men. I'm glad she married Rathbourne; he appreciates her talents."

Gabby came up behind him and ran her fingers through his hair. She had gotten used to touching him during the days he was ill. "When you were ill, I would run a cold cloth on your face and scalp and then I would do this. It seemed to help you when you were thrashing." She massaged his head. "You have the most wonderful thick hair, the color of winter wheat."

Michael grabbed both her hands and squeezed them. "Darling, if I don't solve this, you won't be safe, nor will the king." He twisted in the chair and tugged her onto his lap. Shocked, she gasped and then laughed.

"I'm sorry. I didn't mean to distract you, but it has been hard not to touch you after our time in France." Gabby looked up into his eyes.

"Your plan to distract me isn't necessary. Everything about you is a wonderful and an astonishing distraction."

"Really?"

"Yes, really. And it does seem you had more fun in France than I did." Nuzzling her neck, he whispered into her ear. His warm breath sending chills along her skin. "Were you a naughty girl, Gabby? Did you do more than massage my neck?"

Outraged by his suggestion, Gabby pushed against his chest to jump off his lap. "Of all the crude things to say to me!"

Michael held her tightly, preventing her movement. "I have a feeling neither of us will get much work done..." She felt his erection pushing against her. His cheeks had a sun-kissed color and his green eyes gleamed. He took her lips in a hungry, demanding way, thrusting his tongue into her mouth while he rocked against her. Unlike the tender kisses before, this was about possession and primitive hunger.

Gabby felt heat slide down her throat, to her breasts, her stomach, and lower. She pushed back against his movement.

"Gabby, darling. I know what you need."

Gabby's eyes widened. "You do?" Her voice came out husky in wanting.

"Let me help you." He brushed his knuckles along the sensitive exposed skin above her bodice. "Do you want me to kiss you here?" His head descended and he trailed wet gentle kisses, along her neck and earlobe.

He toyed with the fabric of her bodice before he slowly pushed the fabric down to expose her breasts, covered only in the chemise.

Gabby squirmed, unable to control the sensations assaulting her body.

Her breasts seem to expand and tighten with his intense gaze. "Beautiful, like I knew they would be." His fingertip traced one of the erect nipples and Gabby gasped.

"Do you like that?" His low voice was wrapped in dark velvet.

Gabby could only nod. Her breath was coming in little bursts, anticipating every new touch by Michael.

He lightly pinched her nipples, rolling them between his fingers. Gabby shifted her weight, moving against his erection straining beneath her.

He lowered her chemise down, exposing her breasts to the cool air. "What do you think I should do next?" He lifted her breasts in his hands.

Gabby was speechless and agitated. Nothing could come out.

He rained kisses along her breasts at the same time he squeezed them gently. "Shall I taste these delights?"

Stunned by her own reaction, Gabby wanted Michael to put his lips on her breasts. He bent and put his tongue to her nipple and his intimate touch shot straight to her womb. Her body flooded with heat and moisture. She threw her head back offering him herself, wanting more.

Michael took her other breast into his mouth and tugged on her nipple, rolling the erect tip between his teeth. Gabby couldn't breathe, couldn't think. She was a jumble of heat and responsiveness.

Michael's breath was fast and hard and she wanted to touch him, feel his hot skin, suck on his neck, but she could only take in the sensations overtaking her body. She didn't know what the morning would bring. She wanted to experience what this one man she loved was offering.

"Darling, spread your legs." Michael's voice came out harsh and rough.

He cradled her back into his arms while his calloused fingers explored her calf, his fingers playing along the edge of her stocking. "I will spend time kissing you here." His finger moved higher until he touched her inner thigh. "And more time kissing you here on your pale, white skin."

Gabby stopped breathing and lay back in his arms, a molten mixture of burning need and desire. She couldn't imagine Michael's lips on her thighs when she could barely withstand the riot of overpowering emotions from his finger's light touch.

Reaching for more, her body arched toward the next feeling.

Michael stared at her, capturing her in his hungry gaze. "I'm going to kiss you right here, Gabby." And his finger glided over her opening. Heat flooded Gabby. His fingers played and explored her wetness, causing her body to tighten in anticipation.

"Do you think you'll be embarrassed?" He looked down at her with passion and tenderness.

Gabby could only nod, her body a riot of sensations.

Michael's lips curved and eyes blazed in mischievous delight while his fingers pressed into her, spreading her apart, readying her for the intrusion of his finger. "You won't be embarrassed; you'll beg me not to stop."

She already wanted to beg him to answer her growing need. She panted, unable to catch her breath or focus on anything but the feelings Michael elicited. She was coiled tight, ready to explode.

Michael took her breast and sucked hard at the same time he played with her like a violin string, flicking his finger to elicit nuances of the intimate music of her body.

"Fly, my darling." And Gabby did. She flew into space where white sparks danced before her eyes, and she floated into a warm sea of bliss, and a Beethoven sonata.

Michael kissed her, swallowing her joyful screams.

She floated on notes, the melody carrying her in sweet contentment. Gabby didn't know how long she laid boneless in Michael's arms.

"Darling." Michael pressed his lips to her forehead. "Can you wake up?"

Languid, Gabby drifted, moving with the gentle waves of a slowed and sluggish rhythm. "You are gifted."

Michael chuckled. She wanted to stay wrapped in his warmth, the safety of his heartbeat against her ear. "I should have known you were a woman of deep passions. I'm glad to help you express your passion in ways other than music."

She started to drift again in his warmth, a sea of pleasure. "He uses too many eighth notes... Code must be in the time signature." She wanted to tell Michael about the quarter notes, too, but couldn't gather her strength. Later...she would tell him later.

CHAPTER THIRTY-THREE

Michael kept looking back at Gabby, covered in her shawl, sleeping soundly on the settee. He was glad he could help her relax. What a joke! He had given her screaming pleasure. And he either deserved a medal or to be committed to an asylum for resisting her innocent and seductive overtures. His little musician was a passionate seductress without any effort or guile. He had been seduced by the best, and none could compare to his Gabby, who didn't even try.

She also was cracker-smart like his sister. He had broken the code while she slept. But it was her insight that led to his breakthrough, recognizing the correlation between the pitch and duration of the notes for the code. He would have eventually come to it on his own, but he liked that Gabby had readily seen the association. Their children were going to be gifted. And after today's encounter, they'd better wed quickly. He didn't know how much longer he could resist her.

He turned to the sound of the door opening. Instead of Lady Gwyneth as he expected, it was Lady Euphemia. He had only met her at dinner the night he had arrived from France and they hadn't really conversed.

He stood and bowed and whispered to not wake his sleeping beauty. "Lady Euphemia."

He should have woken Gabby to have her rest in her bedroom, but he didn't want to interrupt her deep sleep and he didn't want to be separated from her. Although she protested that she was fine from her injury, she had taken a hard fall and obviously needed sleep, as evidenced by her light snores.

He held his breath and waited for Lady Euphemia's outrage over finding him with a sleeping Gabby.

The lady swept into the room in a bright green and a pink turban with birds tucked into the folds. "Please call me Aunt Euphemia. We are now family." She also spoke in hushed tones.

"Poor gel. She's had a rough time of it. I'm glad to see she is resting. She feels safe in your presence. Her grandparents would have approved of you."

Michael must have shown the shock on his face. "Gabby hasn't told you that I knew her grandparents?"

"No, my lady."

"Call me Aunt Euphemia." She had moved to the desk and was looking at the papers spread across the surface. Michael couldn't rush over and cover up his work. But he could pretend to be helping Gabby with the music, if she questioned him.

"How are you doing deciphering the code? Found anything?"

"Excuse me, my lady…my…Aunt Euphemia."

The lady chortled. "Don't get choleric. I know of your work with the opera and the plot against our king."

"But…how, my lady. I haven't told anyone about my work."

"Of course not. My nephew informed me."

Michael must have left his mouth open since the lady brayed. "My boy, you know the first principle of espionage. 'The least expected is the most dangerous.'"

"You're a…?"

The older woman shrugged her shoulders, making the birds dance on her turban.

Michael appreciated how effective Aunt Euphemia would be in a covert mission. No one would expect this eccentric, old-fashioned woman to be carrying out espionage.

"Have you made any headway?"

"I have cracked the code with help from Gabby's musical insight."

"Of course you did. You're going to make a good team. I'm

sorry her grandmamma isn't here to see what a wonderful woman she has become."

Both Aunt Euphemia and Michael startled when Gabby spoke. "Aunt Euphemia?"

"I'm sorry, my dear, I never learned to whisper. Did you have a good lie down?" Aunt Euphemia sat across from Gabby, who rubbed her eyes like a young child waking from nap time.

"Shall I ring for hot water for the tea?" Aunt Euphemia asked. "It appears you and Kendal never got to have tea."

"Allow me, my lady," Michael said.

"Tut, tut, my boy," Aunt Euphemia chided.

Michael grinned. "Allow me, Aunt Euphemia." He pulled the bell next to the fireplace to summon Morley.

With his back turned he could hear the two ladies snicker.

"Are you going to tell her about the code?" Aunt Euphemia asked.

Gabby swung her legs around to the floor and patted her curls. He had planned to wake her up before he left with a sweet kiss and watch her come into slow awareness, to see her skin flush with remembering what they had shared. Impatient, he was ready to have this whole damn business settled so he could claim Gabby as his own in every way.

Aunt Euphemia reached for a strawberry and took a big bite. "She is going to be quite pleased."

Michael sat in the chair next to Aunt Euphemia. If the lady weren't here, he would swing Gabby in his arms to celebrate. But he really shouldn't be quick-tempered about the older woman's presence. She had Gabby's best interest at heart, and if Aunt Euphemia weren't present he might have difficulty resisting the sleep-tousled Gabby a second time.

"Michael, tell me. Did you figure out what you were working on?"

Michael couldn't hold back a wide grin. And he was about to tell Gabby but realized she didn't know about Aunt Euphemia's secret identity or did she?

"Gabby already knows that I do work in His Majesty's service. You can tell us both."

Michael jumped out of his chair. "Gabby, you were right. The values of the notes signal which part of the alphabet the message is written in. And the pitches match the letters."

"A two-step process. I knew it couldn't only be the pitches. But this is more time-consuming to decipher."

"I'm sorry but I'm a bit lost." Aunt Euphemia looked between them.

"Let me get an example for you to see." Michael retrieved the first sheet of the cantata.

He bent over Aunt Euphemia to show her the sheet of paper. "The scrawl on the side is the message."

"And who wrote these notes?" Aunt Euphemia asked.

"Madame Abney's husband," Gabby answered.

"He also has travelled with his wife to Germany and Italy and was in France with her. I wonder who in France made him an offer he couldn't resist. Money to pay for his paramours, perchance?" Aunt Euphemia rubbed her chin and stared at the ceiling.

Since her questions were rhetorical, Michael pointed to the music. "To understand the message, you have to read both lines. Let's use the first bar of music. The eighth note is on the G pitch. But the second note is a quarter note, which signals that you must switch the pitches to the second half of the alphabet, H to N, giving you an L on the pitch. Then a half note is for the alphabet O through U, and so on. This bar of music spells 'gloves.'"

Gabby sat straighter and tried to smooth her wrinkled gown. "How long have I been asleep that you could figure out the code and read the messages?"

"Not more than two hours. I haven't gotten through the entire cantata."

"Impressive, my boy. No wonder my brother-in-law considers you a national treasure."

Michael didn't know where to look when both ladies smiled

at him like a prized hog at the town fair. "It really is like a giant puzzle. Nothing that difficult."

He glanced back at Gabby whose eyes locked onto his with loving admiration.

"Well, don't keep us in suspense. What is their plan?" Aunt Euphemia piled cheese and a slice of beef on bread. "Where is Morley?"

And as before, Morley knocked and entered at the mention of his name. "May I be of service?"

"Morley, we need hot water. These children never got to their tea. I can't imagine why," Aunt Euphemia's gravelly voice teased.

Michael shifted in his chair. Aunt Euphemia was turning out to be more of a surprise than he had expected.

"I'll see to it right away, my lady." And Morley quietly closed the door.

Aunt Euphemia chewed around her bite. "You were saying?"

"The first message is 'A man on Mount Street in Mayfair who will deliver the gloves.'"

"But the king's gloves are from Gieves & Hawkes in Piccadilly." Aunt Euphemia put her bread down and turned to look at Michael.

"There is also a mention of cyanide."

"Interesting. Cyanide is deadly on the skin. I've used…" Aunt Euphemia reached for a lemon tart. "Never mind."

"Are they planning to use cyanide in the gloves?" Gabby asked.

"But cyanide has a definite odor. Wouldn't the king or his valet detect the odor?" Aunt Euphemia looked up at the ceiling pondering the problem. "Of course they would have to hide the scent."

"The king's gloves are scented to prevent the possibility of him ever smelling any foul or sour odors," Michael added.

Aunt Euphemia's rheumy eyes danced. "And Mount Street."

Michael interjected. "Is where the Royal Perfumery resides."

"You must get this information to Cord immediately."

"I had hoped to figure out the exact dates for their plan, but now that we have an idea of their plan, I will depart."

"Good job, Kendal. Rathbourne and his men will take over once you finish with the deciphering."

"Will Lord Rathbourne arrest Madame Abney's husband?" Gabby asked.

"It will be up to my nephew whether he'll stop the messages or possibly convince Madame Abney's husband to send a few of our own messages. It would be difficult not to exploit the potential of this situation. I will discuss this further with my nephew. I'd planned on visiting Charles and Edward this afternoon. I've been quite fond of both those rascals, and of course dear Gus and I share the same affection for tea trays."

"But those men tried to kill Gabby. Surely Rathbourne will take them into custody," Michael said.

Aunt Euphemia sat back in her chair and crossed one leg over the other. She spoke gravely. "Are you sure those are the men? I'm not as convinced as my nephew. Something doesn't feel right about this whole business with Gabby."

The fine hairs on Michael's neck prickled in portent. Tension tingled along his spine. Gabby needed to be protected.

Aunt Euphemia cleared her throat. "I'm in need of tea to contemplate all the possibilities. Where is Morley with the hot water?"

And magically, Morley entered with a teapot. "If I didn't know better, Morley, I'd believe you were listening at the door." Aunt Euphemia chuckled. "Lord Kendal is riding to Rathbourne House. I want two men to ride with him."

"Yes, my lady."

Michael stiffened. "Aunt Euphemia, I don't think it is necessary."

"My boy, you, with the help of Gabby, have just stopped a plot to kill our king and you are carrying the proof with you. You must trust me on this. You and Gabby are at risk. And you will be well-protected until this whole business is concluded."

By the way Aunt Euphemia's jowly chin jutted and her voice

grew severe, he believed she was capable of commanding anyone to do her bidding.

Michael stood, went to the desk, and packed up the music into a folder.

He wanted to kiss Gabby good-bye, but instead took her small hand into his and pressed a kiss. "You are to rest. Cancel whatever plans Lady Gwyneth has for you."

"Tonight is Lady Appleton's musical. And isn't it important that I act like last night was an accident? And continue the charade with Lord Weston?"

Of course Gabby was right, but it didn't help the cold dread and panic churning through him. The only way to stop the madness was for her to make herself a target again. His heart beat harder, faster just thinking of the possibilities.

He hadn't released Gabby's hand. He smiled down at her, giving her his best wide grin since he didn't want her to detect his concern. "Please, spare me. Not more music."

He didn't get the returning smile he had hoped. Her blue eyes were wide and teary.

"Please be careful." Gabby's hands were shaking. "If anything happened to you..."

"Nothing is going to happen to me. I've got Morley and his men guarding me. Isn't that so, Aunt Euphemia?"

"Don't make light of the danger."

"I will be fine and I will see you tonight at Lady Appleton's. But when this is finished I'm going to tear Weston apart."

"But we don't know if he has any part in the threats," Gabby said.

Michael knew he was being totally irrational. But his need to act, not wait for another threat against Gabby, was pushing him to violence. "I don't care. I'm still going to tear him apart. It will make me feel better."

Gabby giggled. "Men and their problem-solving."

Aunt Euphemia added, "It's exactly why our country is constantly at war. If women had a say in the running of governments..."

Michael made a hasty retreat. He had to deliver the messages to Rathbourne to get this whole damn business settled, to finish the threats against Gabby.

He nodded to Aunt Euphemia and left Gabby.

CHAPTER THIRTY-FOUR

Lady Sabine Sauvage, wearing only a black negligee cut to her navel and a jet beaded choker, served him a brandy. With each step she took toward him, the thigh-high slit of her silk nightgown revealed her slim leg. How twisted and desperate his world had become. A woman he had used sexually in the past for relief from his own darkness was now his strongest ally. When Sabine believed he was dead, she had tried to protect Gabrielle from the English by sending her a note and meeting with her. And now he had to trust Sabine with his well-guarded secrets.

"What has happened tonight to cause such a killing scowl?" She sat across from him on the sofa, knowing not to come close when he was in a rage.

"I almost had him." After months of waiting, he was moments and inches from choking the life out of the bastard. He clenched and unclenched his hands. The feel of revenge vibrated in every sinew of his being.

"The bastard swung from the ropes before I could get to him. He tried to kill her backstage at the opera."

After last night's attempt on Gabrielle's life, he didn't want a fast death for the bastard, he wanted to have him suffer for hours, days, weeks in pain the same way he had.

"Your murderous black looks don't put me off." She stretched her foot to his crotch and rubbed along his length. "In fact, I find them quite stimulating."

Sabine thought she was daring because she liked the lash of

the whip across her bare ass. The pampered aristocratic woman knew nothing of pain or suffering.

The constant pain from his injury had changed and etched him into a cruel bastard. He needed Gabrielle. She'd bring him back into the light.

He brushed her foot away and stood. He wasn't in the mood for sex games. "With all the English guarding her, I'm going to need your help to draw him out."

"You're being so vague, darling. Who is he? And how will I draw him out?"

"You won't draw him out. Gabrielle will draw him out. You will entice Weston to bring Gabrielle to the grotto at the Appleton's estate."

"But as you said, she is well-guarded. How will Weston draw her away from the guards?"

"I'm going to create a diversion enabling Weston to bring her to the grotto. It will give Anatole opportunity to try to kill her. And then I'll have him."

"Anatole?"

"Fouché's assassin. Fouché has sent him to kill Gabrielle to cover his tracks, his sins against Napoleon. If Napoleon ever found out about Fouché's perfidy, he'd be a dead man."

"I'm still confused. You want to kill Anatole, Fouché's assassin? I thought all this business was to remove Mademoiselle from London?"

"Trust me, you get Weston to bring Gabrielle to the grotto. And I will do the rest."

"But how will Weston induce her to leave the party?"

"He will tell her if she doesn't come, Lady Gwyneth will die."

"Lady Gwyneth. You're going to kill Lady Gwyneth? I refuse to be part of killing a lady."

He laughed. The sound was brittle and empty like his black soul. "I'm not going to kill Rathbourne's sister. It is a ruse. Weston will tell Gabrielle that she must come or Lady Gwyneth will die. Gabrielle is a loyal French woman. She'll risk her own life for a friend."

"And what do I get for all my trouble?" She leaned toward him to give him a full view of her mauve nipples on her pendulous breasts, erect in her excitement.

"What you deserve. A severe punishment." He'd play Sabine's games one last time before it was finished. Before he had Gabrielle.

CHAPTER THIRTY-FIVE

Sipping champagne, Gabby and Gwyneth stood together near the open windows to escape the hot and stuffy ballroom, avoiding the crowd gathered at the refreshment tables. Lord Weston, playing the part of the devoted suitor, had already brought them champagne. Gabby, needing to keep up the pretense of enjoying Lord Weston's company, was grateful when another man waylaid the villain. Anxiety played upon her nerves, heightening all her senses, making her jittery. Could she keep up the sham and play her part tonight?

"You look weary. Are you sure you're up for another night of intrigue?" Gwyneth asked, her midnight eyes alight.

"I am tired, tired of this entire business. I'm willing to do anything to end the danger to everyone I care about. Last night if you and Amelia hadn't moved to look at the backcloth..." An icy shudder wracked through her. "You, or possibly Michael, could have been hit. You're all in danger because of me."

"But we weren't injured. And I'm grateful for the diversion in an otherwise very boring round of social requirements. Ash is involved in intrigue and espionage, and I'm supposed to be thrilled to say the same things repeatedly, each night, to the same people." Tonight Gwyneth resembled a pagan goddess in her crimson silk dress, with her raven hair flowing around her shoulders, held only by a diamond clip at her temple. "I'm sorry I wasn't there to minister to your wounds. But once I saw that he had missed you, I chased him."

"You chased after the man who tried to kill me?"

"No, I ran after the other man who was on the scaffolding."

Gabby stepped back to look at her friend. "Michael told me there were two men. But why in heaven's name would you pursue him? He obviously was dangerous."

"Because he was getting away while everyone else chased your assailant. It was chaos and I spotted him jumping from the scaffolding and running toward the stage door. My gown slowed me down or I would have caught him. He ran out of the stage door and disappeared in the alley."

"But what if instead of running, he had turned and confronted you. He might have killed you." Gabby couldn't breathe around the fear knotting in her chest by the danger her dear friend courted.

"That is exactly what my husband said."

"Oh, my goodness." Gabby pressed her hand on her chest as if to stop the pounding. "Ash must have been livid about the risk you took."

"He was a little bit upset." Gwyneth rolled her roguish black eyes. "But, as I pointed out to him, I had my pistol ready to stop the crook. And I'm a deadly shot."

Gabby took Gwyneth's arm. "You shouldn't take such chances. I hate that I've involved you and Amelia in peril."

"I was made to take risks. My soul will shrivel up and die if I'm not involved in intrigue. It's in my blood. As you now know, my brother and my aunt have been doing this work for years, and I am no different. You have your music, Amelia has her art, and I have espionage."

Gabby stared at her friend, trying to take in Gwyneth's glib remark. "But I can't imagine Ash allowing you to put yourself in treacherous situations."

"It is the one down side of having a husband. They do put a damper on one's fun." Gwyneth threw back her head and laughed. "Oh, my goodness." She raised her hand to her head. All color drained from her face.

"Are you alright?"

"I'm not sure. The room is starting to spin." Gwyneth swooned backward.

Gabby wrapped her arm around Gwyneth's back. "Lean on me. I'll escort you to the ladies' retiring room."

Gwyneth's champagne glass fell out of her hand and crashed to the floor. There were gasps while everyone in the ballroom turned to the clatter.

"Everything is going black. It must be in the champagne." Gwyneth collapsed, folding into a heap. Gabby couldn't hold up the larger woman who was now limp against her. Gwyneth slid to the floor in a silken muddle.

Gabby bent over her when Ash appeared suddenly and knelt down next to his wife, feeling for her pulse. Gabby was shocked by his appearance since he wasn't supposed to be attending the ball.

Ash cradled his wife's head with his arm. "My God, Gwyneth. Wake up."

Gabby looked for Michael, who stood in a group of gentlemen. A man she didn't know grabbed Michael's arm, preventing him from coming to her. Michael shook his head but remained on the other side of the ballroom.

Aunt Euphemia rushed over to Gwyneth. "Thank God, she's breathing." Aunt Euphemia briskly rubbed Gwyneth's hands. "Let's get her away from this room."

Aunt Euphemia looked up at Gabby. "What happened?"

"We were talking and sipping the champagne when Gwyneth grabbed her head and said the room was spinning. I started to take her to the ladies' retiring room, and she collapsed." Gabby's knees wobbled at the awful sight of vibrant Gwyneth, pale and listless, lying in her husband's arms. Was her friend poisoned? Gabby looked at her half-drunk champagne glass.

"Who gave you the champagne?" Aunt Euphemia voice was sharp.

"Lord Weston."

"I'm going to take him apart piece by piece." Ash's quiet

threat was made more menacing by the fierce, violent look on his face.

"Not now. Gwyneth needs you. Cord will take care of him. We need to empty Gwyneth's stomach of the champagne."

Ash picked Gwyneth into his arms. She was so still, the pallor of her skin in sharp contrast to her black hair, dangling over Ash's arm.

"Gabby, are you feeling any symptoms?" Aunt Euphemia asked.

Jolts of fear crashed through her, making her unsteady. "No, I feel fine." The idea that Gwyneth had drunk the champagne that must have been meant for Gabby was too awful to consider. The tremors started in her hands and then moved to her legs before taking over her entire body. She shook uncontrollably.

Aunt Euphemia followed Ash. The crowd parted; the music had stopped and the hushed undertones echoed in Gabby's head. She started to follow them when Lord Weston took her elbow and whispered down close to her ear. "Come with me, if you want Lady Gwyneth to live."

He held her elbow tightly, leading her toward the French doors opening to the garden. "I will take you out for a breath of fresh air after the excitement. Fan yourself."

"Outside?" She couldn't stop the shaking and it took all her effort to prevent her teeth from chattering.

"There is someone who wants to see you."

"No, he wants to kill me. Please don't do this."

"He will not harm you." Lord Weston kept a tight grip on her elbow.

"Why would you do this? You don't even know me." Gabby started to feel the hysteria mounting and the overwhelming panic to run. Where was Michael? Why wasn't he stopping Lord Weston?

"Who hired you?" Gabby twisted to look at him.

He led her down the gravel path to the classic Greek grotto overlooking the extensive gardens of the estate.

His gentleman's façade gone, he spoke in a mocking tone

filled with amusement. "You're too innocent to understand men's appetites."

Gabby couldn't breathe. She couldn't get air into her lungs. She was alone in the dark garden with Weston, being led away from the party. Were the men following her? Was Michael behind her, waiting for the opportunity to grab the killer? She tried to reassure herself that this was the plan, was what she'd wanted. But her heart pounded against her chest so loudly that she could hear nothing else.

She pulled free of Lord Weston's arm, refusing to be forced into the role of a victim, and climbed the steps to the hidden grotto. The grotto was surrounded by shrubs and trees on three sides creating the illusion of being in the midst of a forest, with sweeping views of rolling green hills sloping down to a river.

A willowy, lean man with blond curls similar to her own stood at the back of the grotto waiting. The way he jutted his hip to one side in an arrogant fashion was familiar. With only lanterns illuminating the grotto, the light must be playing tricks on her vision. For a minute she thought... No, it couldn't be possible. She stopped and stared.

"Gabrielle, my dear."

No, this couldn't be. Her brother was dead. The killer was playing a trick on her, trying to confuse her. But that voice, with the same arrogant tone, was the voice of Lucien.

She stood frozen. "Lucien?" Her whisper resounded in the grotto. "Is it really you?"

"Come here, my dear." He opened his arms. "Oh, little one, it is good to see my sister."

And she ran to him as if in a dream of the past, when he was her laughing, happy older brother. He moved toward her, favoring his left leg, and wrapped her in his strong arms, squeezing her tightly. "This will all be over in a minute."

"What will be over? And why must we meet here in such a mysterious fashion?"

"Gabrielle, get behind me and don't move until I say you can," Lucien commanded in a sharp voice.

"You can come out, Anatole." Lucien pulled out a gun that was tucked into the back of his breeches.

Gabby peeked around Lucien's back. A heavyset man with rough, broad features, and with a pistol in his hand, stepped out from one side of the grotto. "You bastard, Valmont. I thought it was you on the scaffolding. You were supposed to die."

"I was left for dead after you shot me in the back, you coward."

This was the man who had tried to kill her last night. He had shot her brother? Nothing made sense. Someone wanted to wipe out the Valmonts.

"For trying to kill my sister, you will suffer death a hundred times over, just as I did, lying in a coma, wanting to die."

Anatole shrugged insolently as if the threat against him was of no consequence. "But before you shoot me, I'll get one shot off. And once you're gone…I will finish my mission."

Anatole was going to shoot Lucien and then kill her. Should she step out and prevent him from shooting Lucien? Where was Michael? And all the men guarding her?

Lucien stiffened and widened his stance, his pistol directly pointed at the man. "You assume you'll be able to hit your mark when you've already failed too many times to count. What an assassin you've turned out to be." Lucien laughed, a dark black laugh that sent chills down Gabby's spine. "If you survive today, Fouché will rid himself of his inept assassin."

Anatole stepped closer to Lucien. "You always were a cool bastard."

"Before I kill you, tell me what other subversive plots Fouché is behind against Talleyrand. This newest plot against the king smells of Fouché's treason."

"Go to hell."

"So that is a yes?"

Anatole started to raise his gun when Gabby heard Michael's voice.

"Gabby."

Oh no, Anatole would kill Michael. Gabby screamed, "He's got a gun."

Anatole turned halfway toward Michael. A blast rang out. Lucien had fired at Anatole, hitting the man in the back. Lucien muttered as the man fell forward to the ground. "A coward deserves to die a coward's death."

Gabby ran out from behind Lucien to go to Michael, but Lucien grabbed her by the arm and pulled her close to his side. "Wait. Anatole still has his gun."

Anatole lay on the floor of the grotto, writhing and moaning while his life blood poured out, saturating the cold, hard floor.

Michael stepped over to Anatole and kicked the gun out of his hand, keeping his gun pointed at Lucien.

"Release her or I'll shoot you," Michael commanded.

"Michael, stop. He's my brother."

"Your brother is dead," Michael instructed her as if she had forgotten.

Gabby tried to pry loose to go to Michael, but Lucien kept his arm tightly around her shoulder.

Gabby smiled at Michael. "It seems not. Michael, meet my brother Monsieur Lucien de Valmont."

Lucien tucked his sister next to his side. "I don't like him."

For some inexplicable reason, probably because it was exactly like her brother to make a quick and contrary judgement, Gabby started to laugh and couldn't stop. The overwhelming fears, the violence, and the relief combusted together into joyous, almost hysterical laughter.

Lucien looked down at her in a mixture of disbelief and shock. "This has been too much for you."

Gabby hugged her brother and broke free of his hold. "I'm so glad you're not dead."

And then she walked into Michael's waiting arms. She turned back toward Lucien. "You will have to like him. I love him. And plan to marry him."

Lucien said in his typical condescending voice, "But he's English."

In the meantime, men stormed the grotto, with Lord Rathbourne leading the way. "Valmont?"

Lucien tucked his gun into his breeches and sauntered nonchalantly toward Rathbourne.

"It took your men long enough to find us. I was waiting for you to distract Anatole so I could shoot him. But this impetuous fool came instead." Lucien nodded toward Michael.

"We had you covered and were waiting to see if he would give up any more useful information. But one gentleman, like his sister, rushes into situations against orders, obviously risking all for love." Rathbourne smiled at Gabby.

Bending over the fallen Anatole, Rathbourne asked Lucien. "Who is he?"

"Anatole."

"Anatole Roache? Fouché's assassin?" Rathbourne stared at the bleeding man. "Get the man a doctor." Like her brother, Rathbourne was in control of the situation and the men around him.

"Why did Fouché want you and your sister killed?" Rathbourne demanded.

"Anatole was to kill me to prevent Napoleon from discovering that Fouché was blackmailing me to do his dirty work in England. Fouché threated to kill Gabrielle if I didn't cooperate."

Gabby wanted to rush back to her brother when she heard that her brother had been shot protecting her. Michael tightened his hold, tucking her next to his side.

"I had her hidden in a convent. But I knew it wouldn't be long before Fouché found her. I asked Mother Therese to get her out of France."

"But you told me that I was there to be out of the reach of Napoleon," Gabby said.

"I did hide you from Napoleon, but Fouché was the more immediate and deadly threat."

"Lucien, it was Michael who got me out of France." Gabby smiled at her brother's scowl.

Lucien glared at Michael while speaking to Gabby. "We will discuss Kendal later."

Michael released Gabby and walked toward her brother. "I will call on you tomorrow to discuss Gabby and my wedding plans, Monsieur de Valmont."

"But, Michael." Gabby followed him.

"Your brother only cares about your happiness. And I will convince him that there is no one who will make you happier."

Gabby couldn't stop a wide grin of love spreading across her face. "That is the nicest thing anyone has ever said to me."

Michael winked at Gabby then turned to her brother. "Will they stop coming after Gabby?"

"When I make a deal with Talleyrand to spy for him in exchange for my sister's safety and marriage of my choice." Lucien glared back at Michael.

After seeing to the body of the assassin, Rathbourne came and stood with the group. "I will look forward to working with you, Valmont, instead of against you." Rathbourne shook Lucien's hand. "By surviving, you have made your sister very happy. And your skills as a double agent will help us immensely."

"But what about Gwyneth?" Gabby interrupted having forgot about her dear friend in the shocking appearance of her brother. "Is she all right? Did they get the poison out of her system?"

"She wasn't poisoned. And she is sleeping soundly. Weston put a sleeping draught in her champagne to divert our attention. We've got Weston. But I have a feeling Weston wasn't clever enough to come up with the classic spy trick of divert and distract." Rathbourne tilted his head toward Lucien.

Lucien shrugged his shoulders. "Please tell your sister she owes me after the chase she gave me with her drawn pistol at the opera house."

Rathbourne grimaced. "She is going to be mad as a hornet to have missed out on all the excitement."

"Maybe Ashworth should consider sedating his wife more often." Lucien chuckled.

Gabby was outraged at Lucien's cavalier attitude. "Lucien, what a terrible thing to say. She has been a wonderful friend to me, and you are going to like her a lot."

"Dearest sister, although Rathbourne and I've come to an agreement that is mutually beneficial, you and I will not be socializing with them." Lucien emphasized the "them" to make clear how distasteful he found the English.

"But dearest brother, Lord Rathbourne is married to my fiancée's sister. He and Lady Gwyneth will be family."

Lucien growled, "Another reason I'll never agree to this wedding."

Rathbourne laughed out loud. "I could never have the foresight to envision you as my relative."

"I want you to know that the Valmonts are one of the oldest and most esteemed aristocratic families in France." Lucien raised his strong chin, in the manner of one from a long lineage of French aristocrats and walked away.

CHAPTER THIRTY-SIX

Michael felt like an explosion had gone off inside his head. He saw double—double fury and double murderous rage. He gripped the heavy paper with white-knuckled fists and reread the message signed with a heavy "R." Of all the nerve! The outrageous gall of his brother-in-law.

Today of all days, Rathbourne wanted him to compose a coded message to the French spy ring operating out of the opera house. On his wedding night, he was to forego making Gabby his wife in every way a man considered making a woman his wife, to bait the French spies.

He stormed down the hall to his library, struggling to regain his composure, to find his logical, analytic side. But the male brain was not logical when clouded with white-hot lust. Like a typical male, his physical needs were divorced from his intellect. His reasonable side recognized that he was the only one in England who could bait the mastermind behind the plot to poison the king.

Only a few minutes ago, he had been happy and grateful that he and Gabby could finally escape the elaborate and endless wedding luncheon at Rathbourne House. Trying to dispel the images of Gabby preparing for bed, changing into her nightclothes, only made the images more graphic and made him more desperate.

Gabby had been the perfect, blushing bride in her ivory dress created by Amelia. The simple wedding gown clung to her magnificent soft curves, emphasizing her innocent sensuality.

After two weeks of waiting for the wedding night, his muscles clenched in anticipation, heat pooled and pulsated through his body. The images of a naked Gabby awaiting him was emblazoned on his brain. Frozen, he stood in the hallway, unable to act.

Should he go upstairs and explain the delay to Gabby? But if he saw Gabby in her nightclothes in their bedroom, he wasn't sure he'd be able to leave. He calculated that writing the coded message would take no more than forty minutes, an hour at the latest. It wasn't a difficult task, but took longer because of the tedious, two-step process.

Pushed beyond his limits, he envisioned his hands around his brother-in-law's throat. The idea of strangling Rathbourne, watching the authoritative man beg, gave him a moment of satisfaction.

Clinging to the vengeful thought of doing violence to the man who was both his brother-in-law and superior, Michael walked down the hallway. He finally reasoned that the sooner he finished the task, the sooner he be able to join Gabby. His already tightly clenched body clenched tighter with the idea of literally joining with Gabby. He took a shuddering breath and opened the door to his library.

Gabby, in a low-cut, clinging negligee, was seated at the grand piano, her fingers flying over the keys. She played the Mozart aria that Madame Abney had sung at the wedding. And all he could think about was how he wanted her slender fingers to play him in the same passionate way.

She looked up and gave him an impish grin. "Darling, what has you scowling on the happiest day of our lives?" She ran her hand along the front of the piano. "I still can't believe you convinced Madame Abney...I mean...Jeanne to sell her grand."

Michael tried to keep his eyes on his wife's face and not the tight-fitting nightgown that hugged her full breasts and opened so far down the front to her... But all he could do was stare hungrily at the white flesh framed by the flimsy material.

Gabby raised her perfectly arched eyebrows, her eyes dancing mischievously. The imp knew the wicked effect she was having on him. "You must have been very persuasive."

He jerked his head up. His voice sounded rusty. "It was a straight business interaction, nothing else—one grand piano for you to be her piano mentor. She also was grateful that I vouched she wasn't involved with her husband in the spy ring."

Gabby laughed, drawing Michael's eyes to her expanding chest. "I think she was relieved to have her husband taken away. What a despicable man to use his wife's position in such a vile way."

It took all of Michael's self-restraint to carry on a normal conversation and not fall on his wife. His words came out rushed. "He is somewhat redeeming himself by keeping the messages going between the spies."

Gabby stood and sauntered toward him in a way he had never seen her walk or imagined in his deepest fantasies—a siren, with her hips swaying and her lush lips parted. The delicate negligee hid nothing from his close inspection, rose-crested breasts, womanly curves and valleys, all her femininity veiled in a golden shadow.

His breathing deepened to hungry surges. The pulsating blood expanded and extended all the pulse points in his body. "Gabby, you look…"

Stalking him, she moved like a cat ready to pounce on a poor creature. And he was that poor creature, ready for whatever she wanted to do to him.

"Lord Rathbourne asked a favor of me before we left his house today," she confided in a hush tone.

His feet were stuck to the floor. His heart drove sharp blows against his chest.

Did she have any idea what fantasies were racing through his mind at this moment? If she did, she would be running out of the room.

He was transfixed by the sight of Gabby's long legs, outlined in the see-through material, and the way, with each step, the fabric clung to her round thighs. The candlelight gilded her skin like glistening honey.

His breath hitched. "A favor?"

Gabby stopped in front of him and lifted her long, sooty eyelashes to gaze up at him. Michael mustered all of his discipline to not grab her.

"He explained that he needed you to compose a message because the king refuses to cancel tomorrow night's concert. Lord Rathbourne must now close down the whole operation. He was quite frustrated that they can't maintain the ruse to see what other plots the mastermind is hatching."

Rathbourne was frustrated! What a bloody joke. And now, Michael couldn't even blame Rathbourne. He had to blame the king himself for ruining his wedding night.

"Rathbourne told you the message?" Michael was impressed he could follow the conversation with Gabby this closely, while all he could think about was how he wanted to tear back the fabric clinging to her burnished skin and unwrap her like a Christmas present. She was soon to be his. Only his.

"Lord Rathbourne warned me about his request. He was afraid you might try to kill him on the spot if he told you at the luncheon. And he didn't want Henrietta upset."

Gabby's scent of wild flowers filled his nostrils. She smelled of honeysuckle and wild flowers, and the scent of Gabby.

"He asked me to forgive him for imposing on us on our special day." She toyed with the button on his jacket. "He hoped that I'd find a way to make your problem not so onerous."

"Darling, you and your glorious body in that…is not helping my onerous problem." He traced the edge of the material cradling her breasts. "Your…nightclothes are a part of the problem."

"They are?" Her voice lowered and her skin flushed. "Amelia guaranteed you wouldn't be able to resist me in this nightgown. But what's the other part of your 'problem?'"

Michael hesitated. Could he tell his virgin wife about his rampant erection that was drawing all the blood and thought out of his brain to his body? She stood on her toes and reached up, putting her luscious breasts against him to run her fingers through his hair. "I can't believe I can do this, touch you whenever I want."

No sane man could resist such a temptation and at this moment he didn't feel sane. "Gabby, you're playing with fire here."

"I'm not sure what Lord Rathbourne was suggesting by assisting you with your 'problem,' but I've decided I'm going to take the 'problem' into my own hands." Her slender fingers tentatively touched his hard length.

Her full lower lip was caught between her teeth. Her lustrous wide eyes watched his face, gauging his reaction while her fingers explored, getting the feel of him.

His erection swelled at her touch. He was lost in the sensation, aroused to the point of pain. His heart pumped hard and fast.

"Do you like it like this?" And she wrapped both hands around him, inflaming him to the point that all he could do was nod. She squeezed him tight and pushed him out of control.

"That's it, Gabby."

He clamped his arms around her and crushed her mouth beneath his, showing her what he wanted to do to her. A moment later, they broke apart, stunned by the ferocity of the kiss. Her eyes were wildly dilated, her chest was heaving. They stared at each other then grabbed each other as though they were locked in a fight to the death.

He yanked her negligee apart to get to her breasts and lifted one to his mouth. He had to taste her. He had spent last night dreaming of her breasts just like this in his hands, in his mouth.

At the first touch of his lips and tongue, Gabby gasped and then clutched his hair and pulled him down to her breasts. She writhed and arched against him, offering more.

He lifted her high against his chest and walked to the door to lock it.

Her soft body was pressed against his hard, feverish body. He was aware of her every breath, the short wafts of her warm breath against his neck.

"You liked the way I touched you?"

His entire body and brain were clamped in arousal by her innocent touch. His only response was to laugh, a shout of joy. "Yes, I liked it way too much. I was ready to explode. And a man has his honor to take care of his wife first."

"Take care of his wife?" Gabby's licked along his neck and then nibbled on his ear. At the same time, her hands were busy unbuttoning his shirt. "That sounds ominous."

"Oh, I can guarantee you will like it." He lowered her to the settee. Frantic insanity was rampaging through his body when he looked down at his beautiful Gabby laid out like a feast before his eyes. She was magnificent and fearless, his wife.

He tried to remember he was the experienced partner, but Gabby, only Gabby was the most tempting seductress. He had enough self-control not to take her for the first time in the library, didn't he?

"Gabby, darling. Do you want me to carry you to the bedroom?" He panted between breaths, not wanting her to know how much it hurt to utter those words.

She pulled on his hand, bringing her closer. "Silly man. I came down here for you, my husband. I want you. I want all the promises you've been making these last few days with lingering kisses, soft touches, and the looks that set my body on fire."

His heart lurched against his chest. He had been starting to feel back in control until he was undone by Gabby's erotic words. He'd never had trouble curbing his carnal drives. He had refined his lovemaking into a choreographed act of seeking mutual pleasure. But now, with Gabby, he felt as if he were the untouched virgin. Did he have enough command of himself to bring her satisfaction?

Seeing Gabby's hesitancy helped him regain his equilibrium. He would do fine as long as his wife didn't touch him.

"Darling, are you sure you don't want to wait until we go upstairs?"

Gabby beamed and opened her arms—the invitation he had been hoping he would receive. He slipped off his drawers. His body trembled when he lowered himself. He moved slowly against her, savoring her soft, pliant flesh pressed against him.

Gabby gasped with their touching and fisted her hands into his hair, drawing down to kiss him.

She slipped her dainty tongue into his mouth and, like a flame to a bonfire, ignited his burning passion instantaneously. He plundered her mouth, his tongue thrusting in a wild intimate dance. Gabby pushed her hot body against him, imitating the rhythm of their thrusting tongues.

He kissed along her neck, sucking on the pale flesh, feeling her body quivering against his.

He slowly made his way down her delectably tender neck and chest, taking love bites until he got to her puckered nipples. He laved the rosy nipples while he lifted her nightgown. His fingers explored her, slowly touching her wet, hot heat. Gabby pulled on his hair, thrashing against him.

"Is your body on fire now, Gabby?"

Gabby groaned. "Yes, Michael, please."

He knelt between her legs and positioned himself to take her. "Forgive me, Gabby."

With the first thrust, Gabby whimpered in pain. He kissed her gently on her lips and whispered, "It will be better soon. I promise."

He held perfectly still, waiting for her body to adjust to him while he continued to rain tender kisses on her eyelids, her damp hairline, her flushed cheeks. He hated that he had given her pain when his every intention was to give her pleasure.

When Gabby moved sinuously against him, Michael couldn't wait any longer. With his eyes locked on hers, he moved in slow, easy lunges. "How does that feel, Gabby?"

She wrapped her arms and legs around him and followed the rhythm he set. He watched her increasing arousal. With her eyes closed and her lips parted, she panted and moaned in a low husky sound. He quickened the rhythm, pushing them both into the feverish bliss.

Michael couldn't take his eyes off Gabby's glowing face as the pleasure took her. A fierce possessiveness surged through him as he surrendered to the driving beat of his body. "I love you, Gabby."

He collapsed onto Gabby, feeling the last tremors of her pleasure as if they were his own.

Gabby shifted and then slowly opened her luminescent and shining eyes. Her body was soft and relaxed underneath him.

He traced his finger along her pink cheeks, her eyelids, and her delicate jaw. "Did it hurt badly, my darling?"

Gabby's lips turned up in a bashful smile. "Only at first, but you more than made up for the discomfort."

He kissed the tip of her pert nose before he rolled over and pressed her against his side. "Now you are my wife."

Gabby's warm lips were on his throat. "And now you are my husband. I still can't believe that Lucien finally agreed to our marriage and was even willing to escort me down the aisle."

Michael had spared Gabby from her brother's threat to disembowel him if he did anything to hurt Gabby. Michael also didn't mention that Lucien had come to the correct conclusion that Gabby was safest under Michael's protection from Fouché and Napoleon's threats while he was away in France.

Gabby's light touch meandered down his chest and he really didn't want this happy moment taken up with discussion of his mercurial brother-in-law.

"You'll like him once you get to know him."

Michael chose not to comment on his own view on his newest family member. If he had realized that he would be related to Rathbourne and Valmont, he might have remained in France. But then he wouldn't have Gabby, his sated and warm wife, lying next to him.

Gabby followed her gentle touches with wet kisses to his chest. "Lucien's a changed man. He's grown bitter. When he returns from France, we'll help him find a new life."

"Gabby, when he returns to England, we'll make him welcome to our family. But he has seen the violent destruction of his parents, his estate, and his heritage. It may take a long time for him to figure out his way." Michael didn't mention that Valmont was driven by his desire for revenge, not wanting a new life but destroying those who had taken from him.

With Gabby's sweet curves and her sweet kisses pressed against him, Michael felt his body already hardening. He couldn't take his wife again, could he? She'd be sore, and she was new to lovemaking. But he could find other ways to pleasure her.

"Gabby, you know your enticing touches are starting something you might not want to finish."

"I'd like to continue the lessons you've promised me. That is, if you're not too tired." Gabby kissed down his chest, her hand seeking him again. It seemed his wife liked to touch him. How lucky could a husband get?

EPILOGUE

Gabby, from her safe position behind a column, watched Michael's university friend Pudgy tune his violin, along with the three other string musicians. It was easy to identify Madame Abney's brother with his thick, dark hair and dark eyebrows, the same as his sister and their Roman ancestors who had invaded France centuries before.

The hefty trumpet player shifted his weight while he nervously adjusted his music on the stand. The harpsichord player sat erect on his bench and stared straight ahead, unaware of the babble of the sparse crowd in the vaulted ceiling room.

Gabby's stomach fluttered. She was unsure if her jitteriness was due to nerves or the excitement for the king's attendance.

Because of concerns for safety, no other woman was allowed to attend the concert. She was the exception because of Madame Abney's insistence. Lord Rathbourne didn't want to arouse Jeanne's suspicions since the singer knew nothing of the plot against the king.

The men were adamant that Gabby stand behind a column and near a door to enable Michael to whisk her away at the first sign of trouble. She had readily agreed to her position since it meant that Michael would also be out of the range of danger. She also wanted to protect Michael in case the spy had deduced that her husband was England's top code breaker. Of course, she would never have shared her fears with her husband who would have simply laughed them off.

Considering the possible danger, Gaby must have tightened

her grip on Michael's arm since he bent down and whispered close to her ear. "No need to worry. Nothing is going to happen except to hear more of Madame Abney's caterwauling."

Gabby looked up to glimpse Michael's bright eyes focused on her. His hungry look heated her body with sensations of the last night, the hours of their passionate and tender lovemaking. Michael's ravenous stare aroused a shocking and hungry need shooting through her body. She had to control herself not to touch him, lean into his hard body.

Whatever Michael saw in her face, she felt his breath hitch and his body tighten next to her. His hot breath against her ear sent shudders of longing through her. "Darling, you can't look at me like that. These antiquated court clothes hide nothing."

As a wife of experience, Gabby looked at the front of his breeches. "Gabby, don't stare. That will only make matters worse." His laugh rumbling in his chest ignited a sweltering desire in Gabby with the memory of how she felt his laughs and breaths upon her breasts when they were joined.

She fanned her face and tried to concentrate on looking at the few other people in the room to assess who appeared suspicious. The only men she recognized were Lord Rathbourne and Ashworth.

The side doors opened and everyone shifted to watch Jeanne sweep into the room. The swishing sound of her deep burgundy velvet gown brushed along the marble floor resonated in the well-designed royal music room. Jeanne smiled at Gabby when she walked past her to stand next to the musicians.

Her dignified and confident posture showed no signs of apprehension she might be experiencing for her royal command performance. There was complete silence with a sense of rising tension as the musicians readied themselves while everyone else waited for King George.

Lord Rathbourne stood by the door where Gabby assumed His Majesty would enter since there was one large chair with cushions placed directly in front of the door. Ash stood amongst several of the men who were stationed on the opposite of the room from Gabby and Michael.

Gabby wasn't privy to the plan, but she assumed that most of the men in the chamber were likely under Lord Rathbourne's direction.

Finally, the door was opened by two footmen in red and white livery. Everyone turned to the king's entrance. A dour-looking gentleman, accompanied by two more gentlemen, walked behind the king.

All the men in the room bowed. Jeanne and Gabby curtsied, not that the king would notice Gabby's curtsy from her barely-visible position behind the column.

Jeanne, with all her French panache and theatrical drama, bowed so deeply that Gabby worried that she might not be able to rise in her heavy, cumbersome gown.

Lord Rathbourne nodded to the king before His Majesty moved to greet Jeanne.

King George's formal and polite manner was nothing like his son who was known for his rude and oafish manners. "Madame Abney, after hearing your performance of *Merope*, I look forward to your performance today of my favorite Bach cantata. I hope you have also prepared Handel."

Jeanne rose from her low bow and gave a charming smile. "Thank you, your Majesty. It is an honor to perform for you today. And knowing of your enjoyment of Handel, I've prepared several selections for you."

Hidden away behind the column, Michael groaned. "Oh, no. How long do we have to stand and listen? These pointed shoes are damned uncomfortable."

Gabby wanted to giggle at Michael's irreverent remark. She knew he joked to help her relax, and how could she not fall more in love with her sensitive husband.

About to shush Michael for his cheeky remarks, Gabby's attention was drawn to the nervous trumpet player who had somehow knocked his music off the stand. His music fluttered to the ground, and he bent to pick up the scattered papers.

Gabby saw the glitter of steel caught in the candlelight reflection as he pulled a knife from his boot.

Pudgy threw himself on top of the king, who fell forward onto Jeanne, who stumbled and fell under both men.

With the quick action by Pudgy, Michael shoved Gabby behind the column, protecting her with his body. There was a loud commotion. And then silence.

Gabby turned back as Michael was dragging her out the door. She almost missed how Ash had wrestled the man to the ground and Lord Rathbourne had wrested the knife from his hands.

All the men were huddled around the king who now was back on his feet. Pudgy was helping Jeanne up who didn't seem flustered as she adjusted the feathers of her plume.

The king's loud sonorous voice echoed in the hall. "Rathbourne, is that your man?"

Michael was about to close the door when soldiers came racing down the hallway.

Michael pulled her out of the way of the running soldiers. "Who would have suspected the trumpet player?"

His droll comment precipitated hilarious laughter.

When they both had stopped laughing, their eyes met. Gabby couldn't look away from Michael's feverish stare. After only one night, Gabby understood her husband's look and knew he wanted her. Her body inclined toward him. "Shouldn't we go back in?"

"For what reason?" Michael ran his finger along the top of her bodice, sending shivers down her legs.

Michael's eyes were down, watching his exploring fingers. But Gabby saw the color in his cheeks and the way the timbre in his voice darkened. "Let me consider the decision. We can either go back where our presence is redundant or we could go home and continue exploring our newly wedded state. It is up to you, dear wife."

"Home, I say, home, and you. I've already heard the Bach cantata."

The End

Enjoy an excerpt from

A
Code
of the Heart

BY

JACKI DELECKI

PROLOGUE

Edworth House Party
Christmas Eve, 1802

Miss Amelia Bonnington braced herself as the crowd bumped and pushed, straining to get close to His Highness. The crème of society shoved and elbowed, politely-of-course, since one would never want to be accused of bad manners.

The Prince of Wales stood on a small platform elaborately decorated with heavy boughs of greenery and red velvet, matching the Christmas décor of the massive ballroom. Hundreds of beeswax candles burned. No expense had been spared for the house party celebrating his royal visit.

Amelia had no desire to be part of the prince's circle; they were a ghastly group interested only in themselves and their own pleasure.

She sucked in the little air left in the room and pushed, courteously-of-course, toward the door. The crowd and the heat were unbearable. She wasn't one to swoon, but with the thick mix of perfume and the hot bodies, she felt tonight might be her first. She, one of the steadiest women, felt unsteady and unsafe. The last days of upheaval must have had a greater effect on her than she wanted to believe.

Her whole world had been turned upside down and twisted sideways at this house party. In the last two days, her friends had been poisoned and held captive, and she had been ensnared in the French villain's trap. But the deadly crisis had to be kept secret. Nothing must look out of the ordinary. No one outside the intelligence world must ever know about the enemy's threat to the Prince of Wales's life. The ball must go on.

Amelia looked over her shoulder for the closest exit, but the throng pushed her forward. She needed to escape from the packed room.

A gentleman used the chaos in the crowded room to crash into her, to take liberties with her person. After spending the last four years in congested ballrooms, she fully recognized the scoundrel's ploy. His heavy eyelids didn't conceal his hungry eyes as he focused down her cleavage. As he remained fixated on her breasts, he grabbed her elbow, pretending to help her when in fact he intended to pull her close against his hefty, malodorous body.

His reek of stale alcohol and sour sweat constricted her stomach and burned her throat. She pulled her arm away from his grasp, repulsed by the wetness seeping through his gloves. "Sir, release me this instant." She was about to dig her heel into the supposed gentleman's fat toe when suddenly a space opened around her and a smell of fresh lime soap surrounded her.

The perspiring man stared behind her. His slack mouth and his blood-shot eyes widened in fear.

She recognized Lord Brinsley's scent without needing to turn; he was an impossibly difficult, yet irresistibly appealing man. His deep, velvety voice flitted down her skin like a caress. "Miss Amelia, may I escort you away from this mob?"

Relief, and something much more potent, buzzed all her nerve endings. She turned quickly and found herself pressed against the broad chest of the man she had been forced to conspire with to help her friends.

She hastily straightened herself. "I never thought I'd be happy to see you." She refused to be like all the other women who fawned for his slightest glance.

He lifted an eyebrow and the corner of his mouth in that sardonic way she always found irritating. He was too big, too handsome, and too confident for her to find him irresistible. She'd never let him have the satisfaction of knowing she found him…almost irresistible.

ABOUT THE AUTHOR

About the Author: Jacki Delecki is a Best-Selling, Romantic Suspense writer. Delecki's **Grayce Walters Series,** which chronicles the adventures of a Seattle animal acupuncturist, was an editor's selection by USA Today. Delecki's Romantic Regency **The Code Breaker Series** hit number one on Amazon. Both acclaimed series are available for purchase at http://www.JackiDelecki.com.

To learn more about Jacki and her books and to be the first to hear about contests and giveaways join her newsletter found on her website: www.JackiDelecki.com. Follow her on FB—Jacki Delecki; Twitter @jackidelecki.

Made in the USA
Columbia, SC
04 March 2021